A FAIR

A FAIR TO DIE FOR

The Seventh Something to Die For Mystery

by Radine Trees Nehring

Oak Tree Press   Taylorville, IL

Oak Tree Press

Oak Tree Press books may be purchased for educational, business or sales promotional purposes. Contact Publisher for quantity discounts.

First Edition, June 2012

Cover by Reese-Winslow Designs

Interior Pages by Linda W. Rigsbee

ISBN 978-1-61009-122-0
LCCN 2012934293

DEDICATION

To:

Elise Roenigk

who, like me, found her

home in the Arkansas Ozarks

ACKNOWLEDGMENTS

One of the many pleasures I value as an author is seeking out expert information about events and locations in the plot I am creating. In no instance has this been an unpleasant task. People who are knowledgeable about their fields have been eager to help me get the facts straight, and I always enjoy learning from them.

I am grateful to the following people for telling me the truth about many topics discussed in A FAIR TO DIE FOR. If in any detail I miss the mark, it's my fault, not theirs!

Thomas Flowers, Agent in Charge, Fayetteville Resident Office, Drug Enforcement Administration

Officer Travis Grant, Gravette Police Department

Detective Lee Lofland, Police Procedure and Crime Scene Investigations Expert

D.P. Lyle, MD

Trent Morrison, Chief of Police, Gravette, Arkansas

Detective Lonnie L. Nichols, CID, Washington County Sheriff's Office

Jack Phillips, Gravette, Arkansas. Former dairy farmer

Greg Steckler, VP, Log Rhythms, Inc., Log Homes on the Internet, Bend, Oregon

And, last, but far from least, for her continuing help:

Dana Sutton, Treasurer, War Eagle Fair Board

John Bohnert, who appears in this story as "Chef John Bohnert," is stolen from the pages of the DorothyL list for mystery fans. John is known there for telling us, not only what he is reading, but for the mention and sharing of his many intriguing recipes. Thanks to him for helping improve Carrie and Henry's cooking skills (and mine).

And, in honored memory of long-time friend, mystery fan, and book reviewer, Eden (Edie) Embler, I named Carrie's astonishing new cousin Edie Embler.

Chapter One

THE SECOND PHONE CALL

C arrie clicked "Play." Neil Diamond began singing to her about Sweet Caroline, and she increased the volume on her CD player to wall-shaking level. Henry King's taste in music listening ran to a volume that, he said, their neighbors a mile away couldn't hear, so she waited until her husband wasn't home to play her favorite CD's—whether Brahm's First Symphony or their Elvis Gold album—loud enough to be *felt*. Henry was joking about the neighbors hearing anything, but she still tried to keep the volume down when he was home.

She'd been to enough live concerts to know how loud the music could be there. At the last Elvis concert she'd attended . . . whoo-ee!

She moved toward the kitchen sink in dance steps. Oh yes, Neil would get her through potato peeling in style.

Carrie was only half way around the first potato when the phone rang.

Henry? Meeting running late again, I'd bet on it.

She put the potato down, rinsed her hands, and softened the music before she said "Hello."

"Hi, Little Love. Our board meeting is going to run about an hour over-time. A new rural area wants to join our water district, and there's a lot to discuss. Hope that doesn't complicate supper."

"Nope. I was just starting on potato peeling. I can put them in a bowl of water to wait for you."

"And then where are they going?"

"Oven. I thought we'd have oven-fried potatoes with sliced ham and cole slaw. There's left-over fruit gelatin, too."

"Ahhh, I'm in love with a cook."

They laughed, and, as she walked around the center island to move one of her prized Delft canisters back into line, she said, "Me too. Your turn to cook tomorrow night."

"Good. Got to go, we're only taking a short break before we start to unknot the problems for this new area. See you in about an hour and a half. Roger has already called Shirley, so you don't need to do that. I'll phone again when the meeting's over so you can put those potatoes in the oven."

"Okay. Big hug for you, and back to the kitchen sink for me."

She heard him laughing as the phone went dead.

"Cracklin' Rosie" was the woman of choice when she turned the sound back up and returned to potato peeling.

Neil had progressed into "Song Sung Blue" when the phone rang again.

Oh, for gosh sake.

"Hello."

"Carrie Culpeper?"

It was a female voice. Using her maiden name. "Yes, who . . .?"

"This is your cousin Edie. Remember me? It's been a long time. Edith Embler it was. Still is, actually. Took my name back after the divorce."

Edith Embler? Cousin? Carrie's thoughts went galloping back through the years. No, not possible. She had no living cousins. All she could think of to say was "Edie?"

"We moved away right after your fourth birthday, so maybe you don't remember me. Your father's sister Edith is my mother. I'm named after her."

"Sister? But I thought . . ." Carrie stopped. She knew her dad once had a younger sister, but all her life she'd understood that girl died as a baby. Revealing this right now probably wasn't the best idea.

Edie didn't seem to notice the interrupted sentence. "We lived in Tulsa until Dad got a job in D.C. He died years ago, or at least disappeared during a business trip to Mexico, and was reported dead. Mom's still perking at eighty-nine, and I promised her I'd look you up when I came this way. Your folks gone? Mom says they were middle-aged when you were born."

"Yes, they're both gone." Carrie's inner caution light was working overtime now, and she ran a hand through her grey curls. "Uh, did you say your father disappeared?'

"Yes."

"Well, I am sorry, it must have been a tough time for you and your mother."

Edie ignored the sympathy and said, "I remember coming to your house for Thanksgiving dinner when I was about seven. It was a pretty day, and our folks took us to the park after we ate. I pushed you in a swing, but pushed it crooked. The swing went sideways and you fell out. Bloodied your nose. Boy, I got in trouble for that."

Swing. She'd hit her nose on the swing seat when she fell. It bled. Had there been another girl there?

"I don't know if I remember falling off a swing," she said, unwilling to admit anything yet. "Do you know why our families didn't stay in touch, or travel for visits after you moved away?"

"I guess things just didn't work out. Dad had a top secret job with a government agency and was gone a lot. I suppose he had enough of travel through work. Besides, I don't think your dad and mine got along. Mom and Dad never mentioned family in Tulsa after we moved away. But now Mom has mentioned you, and here I am!"

Carrie managed only "Here you are," as she dropped into a chair at the kitchen table.

What, I wonder, is the real reason for this woman's call? Who is she?

Edie laughed and repeated, "Yes, here I am."

There was a pause filled with prickles, then Carrie said, "Well, where, exactly, are you? And how did you find me?"

"Oh, I'm in Tulsa now. Thought I might locate you here, though goodness knows why, since I knew you'd probably gotten married and changed your name. But, Mom insisted I try. Well, of course I didn't find you in the phone book, or anyone else named Culpeper. Mom doesn't remember your mother's maiden name, so there was no way to locate that side of your family. She did have the address where you used to live, so I drove there. The woman who answered the door said she didn't know of any Culpepers. She and her husband bought the house from people named Smith, and she never saw paperwork about previous owners. I tried houses on either side, but no one was home. A woman across the street remembered your family but all she could say was 'Those folks been gone for years.'"

"That would be Mrs. Murphy, and it has been several years. I sold the house to people named Smith, but it's obviously changed hands. So then, how did you track me down?"

"Went to the Tulsa County Courthouse. I found records in the county clerk's office that listed a Carrie McCrite who inherited the Culpeper house and sold it. But that was a dead end. Since the library was handy I walked across the mall to try a computer search."

"Ah." This woman was sure interested in finding her. But a cousin? How could that be? The only cousin she knew about, a boy, was on her mother's side of the family. Eric had died in Vietnam.

"I was just getting started on research when the computer did something peculiar and froze up. Frustrating."

"Computers can be very frustrating." Carrie was trying so hard to think back into the past it almost made her head hurt. If only she could remember anything at all about her father's sister, then maybe everything about this situation wouldn't feel so wrong. It would be nice to have a living cousin.

Be careful, be careful. "Looks like you found me anyway. So, what happened?"

She could almost guess. The library Edie had landed in was the one where Carrie had worked until her marriage to Amos McCrite.

Edie laughed. "The computer problem turned out to be a piece of good luck. I had to get help, and when I told the woman who came what I was looking for, she knew who you were because you'd worked at that library years ago. She called in another employee who worked with you back then. That woman knew you'd moved to Arkansas. She hesitated about giving me your current address, but finally did give me this phone number."

"My goodness, that must have been Irene. I haven't seen her for a while. It's time I planned a trip to Tulsa to have lunch with her."

"That's the name, Irene. Now then, if you'll tell me how to find you, I can come for a visit."

"Yes, well it's so nice of you to have taken this trouble to look me up. My first husband, Amos, was killed several years ago. I'm re-married now, almost a year. Henry and I will both be glad to meet you. We can come to Tulsa tomorrow."

"I'd rather come there, if you don't mind. I've never been to Arkansas. Could I come see you tomorrow?"

What in the heck am I supposed to do about that? I sure wish Henry was here. Could this be someone from his work in the Kansas City Police Department? Could it be someone dangerous?

"We'd love to have you visit us, Edie. Give me your phone number. Henry is away at a meeting right now and I'd want him to be here to meet you too. He'll be home in a couple of hours. Let me check with him on his schedule and call you back."

"Instead I'll call you around six-thirty if that's okay."

"All right. Talk to you then.

"Whew," Carrie said to no one, and, giving up on Neal, went back to peeling potatoes.

While she and Henry ate supper, Carrie told him about the phone call. "So," she finished, "what should I do about this supposed cousin I didn't know existed? It's all so strange. I have wondered if she might even be a danger to you."

"Anyone coming after me could find me easily without going to all the trouble of pretending to be your cousin. And it is strange indeed, if she says she's the daughter of your father's sister, and that sister died as a baby. Why, I wonder, did that part of your family vanish?"

"She says it's because her father had some kind of job my Dad didn't approve of. Top secret, she called it."

"The plot thickens." He smiled. "You've got to admit it's intriguing."

"Well, maybe, but not in a good way. Henry, it was almost like Dad's sister never existed." She thought for a minute. "It is possible no one actually said she was dead, but all my years at home I don't remember anyone mentioning her, except somehow I knew he'd once had a sister. After supper I'll go through the box of photos my folks left, and see if anything there jogs my memory. As a young child I wouldn't have been all that interested in a missing aunt if anyone did talk about her. But now Edie says they ate Thanksgiving dinner at our house before they moved away. That's kind of a major activity, but I guess I was too young to remember it. Anyway, all this makes me feel squinchy."

"Interesting word choice."

"Squinchy? That's something I do remember from childhood. It was a family word."

"It describes the feeling well, and no wonder you feel squinchy. After all these years of silence, the daughter of a woman who supposedly died as a child, and certainly couldn't have if her story is true, has appeared. Would you be glad if she turned out to really be a cousin?"

"I . . . guess so. I have almost no family left."

"Then I think we should go ahead and invite the woman here tomorrow. We won't find out more unless we do that, and maybe the mystery surrounding your dad's sister will finally be explained."

Carrie brought a box of black and white photos to the kitchen table after they finished supper clean up. Most of the people were known to her, and as she laid each picture on the blue and white checked tablecloth, she identified them for Henry, pointing out with special pride a faded photo of her great-great grandfather in his Civil War uniform. "That blotch on his pants leg came from a bullet wound in the leg," she said. "I guess uniforms were hard to come by, and they didn't worry about a few holes or bloodstains. Grandpa had a later picture of the man leaning on a cane. He was tall for the times, and distinguished looking."

"He's distinguished looking here, too," Henry said, tapping a fingernail on the photo, "but it's obvious the height didn't pass down to your part of the family."

"Hey . . . "

"Don't 'hey' at me." He began singing, "Five foot two, eyes of teal blue. . ."

"Good grief," she said, as she continued laying out the box's contents.

There were photographs of her grandparents and parents through the years, and two aunts on her mother's side. She smiled when Henry exclaimed over her baby pictures and a progression of photos marked on the back with captions like "Carrie, 3rd birthday," and "Carrie's first day at school." She figured his comments about how cute she was were either prejudice or diplomacy, but, nevertheless, they were nice to hear. "You looked cuddly and soft, even then," he said, reaching over to squeeze her hand.

There was one worn manila envelope tied up with yellowed seam-binding tape that obviously hadn't been disturbed in years. "Gosh," she said, "this was in the stuff I packed up after Mom died, and I obviously never got around to looking inside."

She untied the tape and spread the envelope's contents out on the table. After studying the assortment, Henry pointed with a finger, and said, "Your grandparents, right? I assume this must be your dad. He looks about eight. Then, who's this little girl? Could she be the missing sister?"

Carrie said nothing as she studied the photo, then scanned the remaining pictures. "Here's a photo of my dad with his parents. Maybe he's late teens here?"

"Um hmm, and this picture seems to be the latest one in the bunch. No girl, but that really isn't definitive."

"No. We still have no concrete answers, though if that girl in the one picture is his sister, she couldn't have died before she was, what? Four or five?"

The phone rang and Carrie looked at the clock. Six-thirty. At least the woman was punctual. "Good timing," she said to Henry. "Lunch tomorrow?"

He nodded.

"Hello."

Chapter Two

A SHOCKING STORY

"Tomorrow would be fine, Edie, Henry can be home all day. How about lunch? Noon? Most of the highway here from Tulsa is four lane. Should take you two and a half hours, tops. Got a pencil and paper? If you have a GPS, that will help, or you can call us if you get lost. I assume you have a cell phone."

"Yes."

"Then here are the directions."

As Carrie hung up, the fact they would need to prepare the meal she had offered this woman sunk in. "Ohmygosh. She's coming. Tomorrow. Noon. For lunch. What on earth are we going to fix?"

"How about soup and sandwiches?"

"That's way too ordinary."

"I don't see why. It is a lunch. If you like we can cut the crusts off the bread and make fancy triangle-shaped sandwiches. Put them on your big glass plate and there you are—a gourmet lunch."

"I don't know . . . "

"Carrie, my love, we aren't serving the Queen of England here. A woman who claims to be your long-lost cousin is dropping in on us without much notice." He began chuckling. "If she expects caviar and all kinds of stuff with French names at our house we are about to educate her."

"There's nothing funny about this."

"Oh yes, there is. We'll just explain that both your former husband and my former wife were wealthy enough to hire cooks, and neither of us learned Meal Prep 101 until we were out on our own at very ripe ages. Then, for both of us, the basics sufficed. So, Cousin Edie will have to make do with basics."

Her unhappy look stopped him.

"Cara, will you feel better if I e-mail Chef Bohnert and ask what he suggests?"

"*Chef*? You know a real chef?"

"Yep, Chef John Bohnert. He has a cooking show on television in California."

"Henry, not only are you the handsomest man alive, you are the most surprising."

"Handsome, huh? Are you saying that just because I'm offering to find recipes to wow a maybe cousin?"

"Not at all". She got up to stand behind his chair, and began stroking the grey hair at his temples.

"Ummm. You don't do that often enough."

"You know I can't reach you like this when we're standing. I'd need a step stool. But, enough. How on earth did you meet a chef?"

"Facebook. I was commenting about growing heirloom tomatoes a few months ago and John picked up on it. We've stayed in touch. I didn't realize I hadn't told you."

"Never mind. By all means, ask him for ideas. Maybe you should phone. We only have a few hours."

"Don't know his phone number."

"Well then, get on the computer in a hurry and let's pray he answers right away."

He stood, saluted, and headed for his computer.

An hour later he had an answer. "John gives several choices. Here, I printed them out. I think the tuna salad recipe sounds best."

She took the papers from him. "Oh, Henry, tuna salad is so *ordinary*. I can make tuna salad, just stir in pickle relish and mayonnaise. What else does he suggest?"

She read down the list, feeling more discouraged with each turn of the page. "Some of these have long preparation times, and some call for ingredients we don't have on hand. Most are complicated. Oh," she wailed, "What am I going to do?"

"Carrie, calm down and look at that tuna salad recipe again. It has ingredients you've never put in tuna salad. Do we have celery seed and onion powder here?"

"Yes, but . . ."

"Okay. It's a little late in the day for sandwiches, but why don't we mix up a tiny amount of this with just one small can of tuna, and see what we think?"

Fifteen minutes later, Carrie said, "YUM! Thank you, Chef John Bohnert!"

"Whew, I'm glad that's settled. And I promise to create a super-terrific King of a gourmet tomato soup tomorrow. We already have fruit gelatin, ice cream, and brownies. So now we can brush the tuna off our teeth and go to bed."

Carrie was up early the next morning, her mind full of "to-do's."

Be sure the house is neat and dusted, I wonder what she looks like, sweep leaves off the porch, set the table with the good dishes, I wonder if she has children or siblings, make tea and lemonade, make Chef John's tuna salad, decide what to wear, should I use cloth or paper napkins?

While she was hurrying through her to-do list, Henry began creating his soup. She stopped in the kitchen, duster in hand, to find him with his head in their pantry. He was holding a can in each hand—tomato soup in one and chopped tomatoes in the other. "Where are the cans of tomatoes and green chilies?" he asked.

She pointed with the duster. "Down there, behind the salsa and spaghetti sauce. Don't make it too hot."

"I won't. You want crackers or corn bread?"

"Do we need either? We'll have sandwiches."

"Oh, sure, that'll be enough. We might put some chips out, though." He hesitated at the pantry door, studying her. "How are you doing? Eager anticipation?"

"Well, anticipation at least. Lots of trepidation mixed in. But it would be nice to have a cousin as a friend."

"You don't have any other cousins?"

"My mom and dad's generation wasn't much on producing offspring. Mom had two sisters, but one of them never married. The other had a son, an only child like me, but he was killed in Vietnam. So, unless she has younger brothers and sisters, Edie is it."

She looked at the kitchen clock and hurried to put away the duster. She still hadn't decided what to wear.

A small, tan Ford bumped down the lane at twelve noon exactly, and Carrie and Henry were already on the porch when it parked and the driver stepped out.

She's very tailored, Carrie thought. *No frills, straight hair, but she is short like me. Kind of skinny, though. Everything about her is beige, even her hair, though I suppose it's meant to be ash blond, and maybe you call those slacks taupe. Is there such a thing as beige lipstick? Probably. Goodness, I wonder what she'll think of my turquoise and green outfit? Too gaudy? Maybe I should have worn the dark blue . . . oh, never mind, I like this outfit, but I am tempted to give her one of my bright-colored scarves before she leaves.*

Everything about the woman matches, Henry thought. *All the same color. Even her hair matches, but I'd bet that hair color is fake. Carrie's grey curls are so much prettier. In Kansas City, Sgt. Creekmore dressed like this when she was keeping a watch on someone. It helped her fade into the background. As far as I can see, there is no family resemblance here, no softness like Carrie. The woman is all angles. I wonder if she'll turn out to be as dull as she looks. If so, poor Carrie.*

"Welcome to Blackberry Hollow," his wife was saying.

A smile of such obvious pleasure spread across the woman's face that Henry felt a twinge of regret about his earlier assessment. Edie spread her arms, inviting a hug, and, and after a short hesitation, Carrie responded.

When the women separated, Edie turned to him and, before Carrie could introduce them, said, "Hello, Henry. Carrie, you sure snagged one heck of a big, good-lookin' man. Looks like he could crush rocks with one hand. I'd best be good." She winked at Henry, and reached out to shake his hand. "Glad to meet you, cousin-in-law."

"Come on in," Carrie said, and opened the door, asking, "Shall we talk for a while, or eat first?"

"Eat, if that's okay," Edie said. "I'm starved. I was too excited to eat much breakfast this morning. We'll have all afternoon to talk."

During the meal Carrie learned little about Edie other than that she had no children and had been divorced for many years. Most of the talk was about food.

"Carrie, this tuna salad is magnificent. Did I detect celery seed? What a brilliant idea. And the soup was just right to go with it. You are obviously a marvelous cook."

"Thank you, but Henry created the soup, and the tuna salad recipe came from a . . . a friend, though I did change a few things." Carrie couldn't manage an admission that the recipe came from a friend of Henry's. She wanted to hold onto some credit for the meal, though Edie was spreading praise on a bit thick. And, after all, she had added more celery seed than the recipe called for.

"My goodness, a man that cooks. Carrie, he is a gem. Compliments to the chefs."

Carrie said "Thank you" again, and suppressed an urge to giggle. Nerves?

Henry rose from the table and picked up his plate. "You two begin catching up on all your news. I'll take care of lunch dishes and join you in a few minutes."

Carrie smiled at him gratefully, then waited a couple of heartbeats for Edie to begin raving once more about the wonderful attributes of her husband but, unexpectedly, nothing came. The woman remained silent, put down her napkin, and followed Carrie into the home's main room. She didn't speak until they were seated across from each other.

"So, Carrie, where shall we start? We can't possibly cover nearly sixty years in one afternoon, but I am eager to hear about your life. Begin at the beginning."

Carrie ignored the request. She wanted to learn more about this self-proclaimed cousin before she talked about herself, so she said, "Something besides looking me up must have brought you to this part of the country. Blackberry Hollow is a long way from the East Coast, and we're certainly off the beaten path. Are you on vacation?"

"Not really. I'm retired now, and I did come here mainly to see you, but I also hope to accomplish a bit of business in this area, perhaps with your help."

"You know, Edie, I haven't a clue what your profession was."

"Oh, here and there. Staff assistant, which is just a fancy name for secretary as I'm sure you know. Some of my working life in DC was spent as a general research assistant for various people in government, and, now and then, I helped write speeches for a couple of them. Sounds dull, but I've always enjoyed doing detail work and I like research. There's such a sense of accomplishment when you find a gem of usable information. With the Internet, the ability to access information has exploded."

Thinking of Henry's quick access to Chef John's tuna salad recipe, Carrie said, "It sure has, and your job doesn't sound dull at all. I wonder if, over the years, I've heard speeches you wrote."

Edie laughed. "They weren't necessarily memorable. Nothing of the 'Ask not what your country can do for you,' or 'I have a dream' class.

"Anyway, Mom was most insistent that I look you up, but I'd have attempted to find you even if she hadn't asked me to. There are so few family connections left for either of us." She paused, looked at her hands for a minute, then said, "If you don't mind, tell me about your life now. I'm wondering if you might be able to help me with a bit of research, but I need to understand you better before I ask."

"That's intriguing."

"Don't make too much of it. Dull stuff. But I really would like to know more about your life, what you enjoy doing, all that. Please tell me about you."

So Carrie did, talking briefly about her time at the university, her work at the library, and living at home with her folks until she was nearly thirty. She told Edie about meeting Amos McCrite, a successful and respected criminal lawyer, when she was assigned to help him with research in old microfiche files at the library.

"He invited me out to dinner a couple of times, which was a huge surprise. Then he asked me to marry him."

"Oh my, how romantic."

"Not at all. He made it clear it was really a business arrangement. Having a presentable wife with a friendly personality would be a good career move. He didn't promise romance—simply friendship, a nice home, and security."

Edie started to say something, stopped, gave her a pitying look and finally managed another "Oh, my."

"It suited me. I wanted a home of my own. I wanted children. I said 'yes.'"

"I hate to pry, but how did it work out? Were you happy?"

"Yes, especially after our son Rob was born."

"Son? So you did, uh, connect?"

Carrie laughed in spite of what she considered the personal nature of the question. "Interesting way to put it, but yes, we connected enough for Rob to appear."

"You said on the phone that Amos had been killed. How did that happen, or is it too painful to talk about?"

"It's not painful now. We thought it was a hunting accident, but, some time after I moved here, we discovered it was murder. Amos was about to expose a business associate's criminal activities.

"Henry and I had already met through a neighborhood organization formed to fight the siting of a stone quarry in the lovely valley below here. Then the woman who'd begun the organization was killed. Henry had known her years earlier when both of them lived in Kansas City, and he and I joined efforts to figure out what had really happened to her, and why. Evidence I understood, and the sheriff's deputies didn't, told the two of us her death had been no accident. Things kind of developed from there. We were able to prove that both her death and Amos's were murder."

"What a fascinating story! But couldn't you have been in danger?"

Carrie shrugged. "There was some danger involved, but it all worked out okay. Henry and I became good friends after that, and, under rather unusual circumstances, we've worked together to figure out background facts surrounding three or four other murders here in Arkansas. The crimes had nothing to do with us, but happened near places we were visiting. Henry is retired from the Kansas City Police Department, so he's pretty good at that sort of investigation, and as for me, well, I can sometimes help because I understand people." She laughed. "That's one advantage of a long life, isn't it?"

Edie was studying her thoughtfully. She remained quiet for so long that Carrie was about to ask if she wanted something more to drink simply to break the awkward silence. Then her cousin said, slowly, "This is all very interesting. I'd like to hear more about your experiences since you met Henry. It sounds as if the two of you have very special skills."

"Well, maybe so. We do enjoy solving puzzles. But tell me more about yourself now. I admit I haven't been able to remember anything about the time when you and your parents lived in Tulsa. I guess you're right, I was too young. Later, my folks never talked about a sister or her family. Lots of missing pages. Since you called, one thing I've wondered is if I had additional cousins. Do you have younger brothers or sisters?"

"No, I ended up being an only. And you and I never saw each other after the move because there was a serious break between our families."

"Why? Do you know?"

"I know more than I admitted when I called you. They never discussed it with me back then, but Mother says now that your folks considered my father a criminal. They didn't want his activities to contaminate or endanger their family, especially their precious little daughter."

Carrie said, "Oh, Edie, surely . . . "

Edie uttered a sharp "Shhh" and, startled by this, Carrie stopped talking.

She watched her cousin look around the room, then back at her before she continued in a monotone, "My father may have been involved in some kind of illegal drug business. Suspecting that has brought years of grief to my mother."

Carrie was unable to stop her quick intake of breath. She put her hand over her mouth and said nothing, mostly because she couldn't think what to say.

"I guess you're aware of the huge problems illegal drugs cause in this country?"

"Of course. One can't avoid knowing. The news is full of it almost every evening. Columbia, Mexico, poppy fields in Afghanistan, meth labs in our neighborhoods, all the ruined lives. Henry and I were even involved in a small way in stopping a very large marijuana growing and distributing business a couple of years ago."

"Either of you ever use recreational drugs? Maybe in the sixties?"

When Carrie just stared at her, Edie said hurriedly, "Sorry. That's an impertinent question. Forget it."

"Well, the answer is no, speaking personally. I really don't know about Henry, but as a man in a job that wouldn't tolerate drug use—a cop who was tested for drugs periodically—I doubt it, though I have never asked him."

"Implying I shouldn't have asked you. Well, you're right, I shouldn't have."

Edie wasn't aware that Henry had finished in the kitchen and was standing in the doorway behind her, but now he came to join them. "Did I hear my name?"

Neither of them said anything. The only sound was the soft swish of the dishwasher and an occasional bird call from the forest outside.

Finally, after a brief nod to Henry, Edie continued. "I've never really understood which side of the law my father was on. I suspect it might have been both sides, and that could be the reason he disappeared. Somebody found out. Somebody took exception. Somebody killed him."

"Do you really want to tell us this? I think . . ."

Edie held up her hand, silencing Carrie again. "No! I don't want to hear any pious protests. I came here wondering how much of my father's story I would be able to tell you. I feel okay sharing it now. Learning more about what happened to Dad is important to me, especially for my mother's sake, and I can use your help, if you're willing. But first you need to hear some history—some perspective.

"Addictive drugs have been a problem in this country for much longer than you probably suspect. During many of the years when various drugs were openly available, they were thought of as more benefit than problem. That, in itself, caused problems, though I think it justifies—or at least explains—people's interest in those drugs and their eventual addiction. I'm not excusing criminal activity, but many of the victims shouldn't be thought of as criminals, then or now.

"Marijuana was actually grown in Jamestown Colony as early as 1600. It was called hemp, and mostly grown for fiber, but smoking hashish, a version of marijuana, became popular to some degree, and had spread far and wide by the 19th century. It was thought to relieve all kinds of troubles—medical and mental."

Carrie, concealing her surprise with difficulty, said, "It sounds like you've done a lot of research."

Edie snorted. "You might say I have a family interest. My mother . . . well, I would like to find out what my father's business really was in the hope it will bring her peace. She's had to bear the sadness and uncertainty for so long."

Edie shut her eyes for a moment before she continued. "Opium was originally prescribed for female complaints and much more. Started out good, ended up bad. Coca Cola syrup really did have cocaine in it at the beginning. And, why not? In 1886, the Surgeon-General of the United States Army endorsed the medical use of cocaine.

"Then there's morphine. It was used as an injectable pain reliever during the Civil War. As a result, heroin was being marketed as a so-called cure, or at least a substitute, for morphine addiction by 1898.

"And, what about meth? I'd bet you think of it as a relatively new drug, but amphetamine was first synthesized in 1887, and widely distributed to soldiers during and after World War II to counteract fatigue and fight depression. Addictive drugs, most of them first used medicinally, have been part of our country's history, beginning in Jamestown a hundred and seventy-five years before we even were a country. I can't help but wonder what miracle drug today will become a public nightmare tomorrow."

Henry said, "Excellent point, and some doctors and pharmacists openly agree with you. The problem is made worse today because misuse of prescription drugs by teens is causing addiction, even deaths. But Edie, terrible problems with drugs once thought beneficial are far from being the only drug problem in the United States."

"I know. But I have wondered if my father wasn't in pharmaceuticals. That doesn't sound so bad."

"Well," Carrie said, "if he was, then why any need for secrecy?" She immediately wished she'd kept her mouth shut, and looked at Henry in dismay. His returning look was bland, but it included the tiniest hint of a smile.

"We may never know," he said. "So, Edie, tell us more about your work, and what growing up in Washington, DC was like."

That was that. It was obvious Henry didn't want to be involved in this cousin-or-not's quest for the truth about her father, and Carrie wondered whether she did . . . or not.

Chapter Three

HERE AND WHERE

T he remainder of the afternoon was spent talking about family news, looking at Carrie's box of pictures, then moving to the deck so they could enjoy the warm afternoon and hint of fall color. While they were outside, Edie often seemed to fade into her own private world, sitting silently and looking out into the forest.

Carrie thought she understood that. Visitors from a city were usually enchanted by this close contact with nature. During Edie's silent periods both Carrie and Henry were also quiet, though Carrie's mind was busy, wondering what the woman might be thinking. Guests at Blackberry Hollow often commented on their location in the middle of a forest, appreciating the peace they felt, and asking questions about this bird or that tree. Edie, however, kept her thoughts and any questions to herself.

I kind of like her, Carrie decided. *But she never laughs. Smiles only rarely. Does her quest to learn more about her father cause that, or is there some other burden weighing on her? I wish I could cheer her up. I hope she's enjoying her time here, and our company. At least we're providing a change of pace for her.*

When the afternoon sun began tingeing everything with gold, Carrie wondered briefly if she should invite Edie to spend the night, then immediately discarded that idea. Instead, she asked "Do you plan to drive back to Tulsa this evening?"

"No, I have a motel reservation in town," Edie said, "but I would like to take you two to dinner. Any suggestions?

Henry asked Edie the name of her motel, then suggested a restaurant near there.

"Before we go," Carrie said, "let me bring some of my scarves to show you. I think a scarf would look very nice with your outfit, and they're so easy to pack. I'd love to give you one of mine to remember me by."

As they left the restaurant, Carrie said, "Edie, would you enjoy seeing more of this area? We can pick you up at your motel in the morning and give you a tour if you like."

"Yes, I would like that. I'm in no rush to move on."

"Great. Shall we pick you up at nine?"

"Make it ten, if you don't mind," Edie said. "I wake up slowly, and I need to take care of some e-mail and a phone call to Mom in the morning. I do look forward to seeing the sights in your area, though. Isn't War Eagle an attraction in this part of Arkansas? I've heard of it. Can we go there, or is it too far?"

"I bet you mean War Eagle Mill, though there are several attractions in the area named War Eagle, including a lovely river and a cave. Nice to learn their reputation has reached the East Coast. They deserve it. We'll plan on visiting the mill tomorrow. It's not terribly far from here, thirty miles or so, and we go there several times a year. They sell stone ground flours and grains, and quite a few flour-based mixes. It's a working mill, begun around 1830's, and you can watch them at work while you're there. It's fun. When the mill is grinding, the whole building rumbles.

"I'm out of their biscuit mix, so a visit tomorrow would suit me fine. We can have lunch in the Bean Palace Restaurant on the top floor of the mill. Henry and I always enjoy that."

"I heard they have an extensive crafts display. Hundreds of crafters there?"

"No, not unless you mean the War Eagle Craft Fair. It's held on grounds across the river from the mill in October. War Eagle Mill has its own fair next to the mill at the same time. If it's crafts you want, you're lucky. Fall Craft Fair weekend begins next Thursday."

"Oh. So we won't see crafts tomorrow?"

"They do sell some in the mill's gift shop, but you'll have to wait a few more days to see hundreds of crafts around the mill; at the main fair area across the river and, in fact, all over Northwest Arkansas. The War Eagle Fair itself has been increasing in importance every year since it began around sixty years ago. Now it, plus many of the other fairs in Northwest Arkansas, are absolutely huge. Fair weekend here has become a Mecca for crafters, and Henry says the Arkansas Ozarks must sink several inches during craft fair weekends since so many people come to the state. Matter of fact, we have a friend displaying at the War Eagle Fair this year, and I'll be working there with her." Carrie paused, glanced at Henry, and said, "Edie, if you plan to be here awhile, would you like to move to our guest bedroom?"

"Thanks, but no. I'm a pretty independent person."

"Okay, I can understand that. So, we'll pick you up at the motel tomorrow morning."

"Good. Ten o'clock. And thank you again for the lovely scarf. I think the rusty fall leaf print goes well with my suit."

"Yes, it does, and you are most welcome." The two women hugged, and, with a wave at Henry, Edie headed toward her rental car.

"What do you think?" Carrie asked as they drove out of the restaurant parking lot. "I'm in a muddle over all this. What was her main reason for coming here? Was it really to find us, or, more accurately, find me? I'd sure like to think finding me was at least part of her reason, but what's the rest of the story? Why the great interest in crafts and War Eagle? My usual ability to read people has failed me. She hinted at wanting to ask for our help with something, probably research concerning her father's business activities and disappearance. Otherwise, why take the time to give us all the background history on drug use?"

Henry said, "It's quite possible she did it to soften a negative impact if she eventually told us about whatever her father's illegal dealings might have been—assuming they were illegal."

"Well, it fits. When she learned about you, and our adventures together, I think it fed an interest in asking for our help in some way. Henry, what on earth does she believe we could contribute? All we know about Mexico and drugs comes from the horrible stories we read in the newspapers. Things have undoubtedly changed a lot there since her father disappeared. Surely she must be aware of that."

Henry started the car and backed out of their parking place before he said, "Your ability to read people hasn't failed at all. I'd assess things, if that doesn't sound too cold, just as you say. Let's assume this Cousin Edie, maybe mostly because of a request from her mother, really did come here to find you. And, when she succeeded, somehow the story of our activities fed into her quest to learn the story behind her father's disappearance, and possibly other things beyond that. Maybe I stopped our learning more by shutting off the discussion about her father and drugs, but the whole issue makes me feel squinchy, as you would put it. Cara, I don't want us involved in this at all. We can keep Edie as a pleasant acquaintance and maybe a real cousin, but we'll stay out of the problems she is, unfortunately, involving herself in."

Remembering what Edie had said about her mother caused Carrie to hesitate. "I do like her, though, and maybe it's not as bad as we suspect. She said she wants to provide closure for her mother. Maybe there's some fairly simple way to find out where and how her father died. After all, he was an American citizen."

"Okay, Carrie, I like her too, she's an intelligent, pleasant woman, though perhaps a bit too serious, which is probably understandable, given her circumstances. I sympathize with your compassion for her. It's admirable. However, if she asks for help related to her father's disappearance, we must say no.

"Here's a question. If finding out what happened to her father is going to be simple, why wasn't it done years ago?"

She was silent for a couple of minutes, then said, "You're right, and I realize whatever is behind her story could be scary. It undoubtedly goes way beyond one man's business activities."

"Yes, exactly, and that's another good reason to avoid involvement. I don't want you to worry about it, or feel you're letting her down, but the fact you may be related to this woman shouldn't change the need to act wisely. We could so easily get in way over our heads.

"There's something else I've been wondering," he said. "Why now? What really brought Edie here *now*? She's been retired for several years, and her father has been missing much longer than that. Why come to look you up now?"

"I hadn't thought of that, but I see what you mean, though I really wish it had only been to find me, a long-lost cousin." She sighed. "Of course you're right about staying out of Edie's problems. We can be sympathetic, but cautious. Maybe nothing more about her quest will come up. She has to be aware you discouraged any approach to us for whatever help she imagines we might give. And, so far, she hasn't really proved she's my cousin, has she? I suppose she could have learned some of the family information she shared elsewhere?"

"Yes. With the Internet, exposure of too much personal information is often possible."

"I know, I know, but I wish . . ." She sighed. "Oh well, maybe tomorrow will bring more certainty." She took out her cell phone. "Speaking of information, I'm going to call Irene and thank her for guiding Edie to us. I know her well enough to guess she's probably agonizing about whether or not she did the right thing by giving Edie our number."

Henry, paying attention to driving, only half listened to what was obviously pleasant female chit-chat for a few minutes. Then Carrie's sharp question grabbed his interest.

"You *didn't*? Not at all? Well, that is interesting. Must be some mix-up on her part.

"Oh, yes, that's probably what happened. I know you can get a surprising amount of information from the Internet.

"Yes, okay. It might be interesting to learn that. Call me if you find out anything, but don't go to any special bother.

"Now, tell me more about your new granddaughter."

Sounds like, however she got Carrie's contact information, Cousin Edie didn't get it from Irene at the library. Hmm. Then, why did she tell us that? Surely she was aware Carrie might talk to her friend eventually, and find out. Whatever— it adds up to one more reason for staying away from this whole situation. I sure hope Carrie is being honest with me and feels all right about avoiding involvement. If they'd been in touch over the years it might be different, but, after all, they barely know each other. Blood relationship doesn't matter.

I hope.

As soon as her conversation was over, Carrie told Henry just what he'd already suspected.

"Irene says she hasn't helped anyone learn my location or phone number. Not a cousin of mine, not anyone, not ever. Besides that, yesterday was her day off.

"She says Edie must have talked to someone else in the library who knows I used to work there. That someone probably helped with the Internet search. She's going to ask around tomorrow to see if another library assistant remembers talking to Edie."

"Interesting."

"Sure is."

First thing the following morning Carrie did a computer search for information about herself. After some fumbling she discovered multiple listings, many of them connected to her work for several high-profile volunteer organizations. She learned, not only her address and phone number, but her birth date and age. *Oh, for heaven's sake, what's happened to privacy?*

Bother!

"I still haven't been able to figure out why Edie would lie about talking to my friend at the library," she said to Henry as they got in the car for the drive to Edie's motel. I can't see any reason for her to make up a story like that, can you?"

"Nope. Maybe she's an habitual liar. Some people lie almost without thinking."

"Ahh, maybe so, but why this particular lie? I don't see any need for it."

"Because she didn't want to reveal how she really found information about you."

'Oh gosh. I'm feeling squinchy again. Henry, this gets curiouser and curiouser."

"Uh-huh. Well, we know enough to be cautious, but that doesn't mean we won't have a good time today. We always enjoy going to War Eagle Mill, and we both love that bowl of beans with cornbread in their restaurant. Let's stop at Hobbs State Park first, since it's just down the road. If Cousin Edie is game, we can do a bit of hiking there. That ought to work up a good appetite for lunch."

"Great idea. Now I really am looking forward to today. Oh, slow down, I see the motel sign over there." She pointed. "Just pull up at the door; Edie's probably waiting in the lobby. I'll run in and get her."

In a minute she was back. "Better park. She isn't down yet. I'll sit in the lobby and wait. If she doesn't show up in a few minutes I'll ask them to phone her room. That'll give her a little hurry-up shove." She smiled at him, blew a kiss, and disappeared through the automatic doors.

It was several minutes before she appeared again, frowning this time. She slid in the car beside him and sat silently for so long he asked, "What?"

"She didn't stay there."

He stared at her. "Are you sure? This is the name and location she gave us. You wrote it down."

"They say she cancelled her reservation late last evening, so it's the right place—or was. I decided to call her room at 10:15 because I considered that too late for politeness. That's when they told me at the desk she hadn't stayed in this motel, though the clerk admitted she'd had a reservation here.

When I questioned him a bit too strenuously, he called the manager, and she confirmed what he'd said. Henry, what is going on? Should I go back in, show them the picture of Edie on my phone, and make sure they know what they're talking about?"

"It will be a different clerk on duty this morning. Besides, if you took the phone in to show a photo, it could cause more stir than we want. For some reason the woman decided to change motels or leave altogether. There's nothing we can do about it."

"Henry, what's up with her? We were home last night, and I told her we were early risers. Why didn't she call to explain, or to say goodbye?"

"I'm sorry, Little Love. It's hard not to be angry that she did this to you."

"I'm not angry, I'm worried. Just to go away without any . . . any goodbye, well, I'd *never* do that."

"I know."

"Henry, do you think she left because she figured we weren't going to be any help in finding out what happened to her father? Is that the only reason she came to see me?"

"She didn't seem to know you'd re-married. I assume she didn't know about our adventures before you told her about them."

"Maybe, maybe not. There's the Internet, remember? So, now what? I guess we should drive around the parking area to be sure her car isn't here."

"Okay." He said nothing more as they drove around all four sides of the motel and pulled up in front again.

"No tan Ford."

"Nope."

After a long silence, Carrie said, "Then that's that. Goodbye, Cousin Edie, it was nice knowing you."

He put his hand on her knee briefly and said, "Well, we're half-way there, so let's head for War Eagle Mill to get our biscuit mix and whatever else we need. Then, since it's a beautiful day, shall we go on to Hobbs Park and walk the Ozarks Plateau trail, maybe sit on one of the benches a while and enjoy the fall scenery?"

Her smile wavered as she said, "I'd like that. Hobbs is such a beautiful place. Too bad we couldn't show it to Edie, but it's just what I need right now."

Chapter Four

PREPARING FOR THE FAIR

On the following Monday morning, Carrie said, "You'll have a good time."

Henry turned away from the door to the garage, pursed his lips for a minute, then said, "Doubtful. A whole day in grade school classes? Dozens of kids staring at me? I haven't a clue what they expect."

"They expect a big, strong, handsome man who's going to tell them what it's like to be a cop—the good parts, at least. What you're going to say sounds great. They'll love it, especially the first-person experiences you'll be telling them. You've got your notes. You've practiced. Once you get started you'll forget about being anxious and really will have a good time."

"I don't know . . . I want it to be right, and things have changed some since I was a working law officer."

As he reached for the door handle again she said, "Phooey. Remember how you said you loved hearing your grandpa's stories from years past?" She swatted him on the rear and continued, "Go be Grandpa."

They both laughed. Then he was gone, and Carrie went to get the gift he had just given her, *The Grass Valley Bistro Cookbook*, by John Bohnert. She wanted to fix a really special supper for his return, and was counting on a recipe from the chef's book to help her out. Lunch in a grade school cafeteria probably wasn't designed for large males who were spending all that energy telling young kids about police work. Henry would be ready for a super-terrific supper. She was depending on Chef John to provide that.

After thirty minutes of studying recipes she decided on Crock Pot Beef Stew. Since she'd be helping Shirley get ready for her set-up at the War Eagle

Craft Fair all afternoon, and a meal prepared in a slow cooker pretty much took care of itself, the stew recipe was perfect.

She made a list of the ingredients she'd need, grabbed her purse, and left for the grocery store.

Carrie was putting the makings for beef stew out on the kitchen counter when a dark blue car bumped down their lane and pulled up in front of the garage doors.

Who?

Not a car belonging to any of their friends. Couldn't be the assessor, their cars were white, and clearly marked. Jehovah's Witnesses? Doubtful, they were here last week. Someone searching for a lost pet? Could be, but it looked like the two men in the car had on suits and ties. Law enforcement? Police officers and sheriff's deputies in this area wore uniforms.

"Oh my gosh, was it about Rob? No! Couldn't be. Her son had called from his apartment near the university not more than an hour ago. He had no classes or student appointments scheduled until afternoon, so planned to spend the morning at home grading exams from his American Indian History class.

Nevertheless . . .

When the man on the passenger side got out, his jacket swung back and she saw part of a shoulder holster. A gun? Well, not inside her house. She stepped back from the kitchen window and watched to see if the man with the concealed gun was coming to the door by himself. He was. The driver stayed in the car.

She would open the door to one man, just to make sure about Rob.

After the doorbell rang she continued to wait until she was sure the man in the car was staying put. Then she went to the hall, fastened the security chain, and cracked the door open.

"Yes?"

"Ms. Edith Embler?"

Is that a question? Does he know I'm not Edie? What should I say?

She studied the man, thinking she might need to remember him. *About Henry's size. Full head of dark hair with a bit of grey mixed in, tan skin like Henry's. Looks strong. Hulking stance is a bit threatening, but he's smiling, trying to be pleasant. I guess he's not sure whether I'm Edie or not.*

It took her only a flash of seconds to think this, and, if he even noticed she was hesitating, the man didn't seem to be bothered.

"No," she said, and waited.

"Is she here?"

"Who's asking?"

"I apologize." He took out a wallet and flipped it open, holding it next to the small gap in the door. "Agent Arnold—Arnie—Frost. FBI." The wallet flipped shut.

"I see." Carrie's defenses went up. "No one by that name here."

"Are you Ms. Embler's cousin, Carrie McCrite?"

Oh-Oh, be careful. "If I have a living cousin, I haven't been aware of that" (*not until last week*). " I assure you there is no one by that name here, nor do I have any idea where someone by that name might be. Is that all? I'm busy in the kitchen."

The man studied her face for a moment, then said, "Thank you for your time. We may call back later," and walked off her porch.

She shut the door and locked it. *Whew. Probably should have tried to find out more from good old Arnie. Henry would have known what questions to ask, and whether or not I should have told the man about Edie. But, these days wouldn't it startle anyone—a strange man coming to the door unannounced? Wouldn't anyone hesitate about answering his questions?*

Well, she hadn't said a word that wasn't true. There was only that tiny little deception, skirting around any admission she had ever heard of Edith Embler.

For the hundredth time Carrie wondered, *Is Edie really my cousin?*

Shoving that thought aside, she went back to finish assembling ingredients for her beef stew.

You might know, Carrie thought several minutes later when the phone rang. *I'm cooking, the phone rings.* She put a lid on the sputtering skillet, turned down the heat, and went to say "Hello."

"You still plannin' to come?" Shirley asked.

"You bet. I'm just preparing ingredients for Crock Pot Beef Stew, and I'll be down as soon as I get everything into the pot. That way I can leave the stew to cook by itself."

"Well now, I never heard of making stew in a crock pot. Good idea. Where'd you find that recipe?"

"Cookbook."

"Cookbook? Didn't know you owned one."

"Well, yes, this was a gift from Henry. He has a friend who . . ."

Shirley's hoot of laughter stopped her. "Who-eee, so it took Henry to do it. I wondered when you'd break down and get yourself a real cookbook. Helpful things, sometimes."

"I have my notebook, and a file box full of recipes," Carrie said, miffed. Then she remembered the time over a year ago when she'd had to call the county extension office to find out how to make meatloaf. Later, when she'd confessed that to Shirley, she'd endured a scolding and, in between laughs, the information that what Carrie should have done was call her friend, who'd been making meatloaf from memory for almost half a century.

"How many cookbooks do *you* have?" Carrie asked, and knew she sounded peeved.

"Mmmm, I guess six or so. They're on a shelf back in our office."

"See there? You can cook without looking at a cookbook. Well, I can, too!"

"Okay, but I've got *experience*." Another laugh. "Never mind, I also know from experience both you and Henry can fix good enough meals. So, where did this cookbook come from?"

Henry ordered it from a friend of his out in California. The guy is a real chef, the big deal kind. He has his own cooking show on TV, and a restaurant too, *The Grass Valley Bistro*. Henry met the man on the Internet several months ago, and, last week, got the recipe for tuna salad I told you about from him." Carrie put her finger in the page with the recipe she'd been following and closed the book to look at the cover. "It's called *The Grass Valley Bistro Cookbook,* by Chef John Bohnert. I can bring it to show you."

"No need. And calling yourself a chef doesn't make you a good cook."

"Well, maybe not, but it's pretty interesting, seeing how a chef puts things together. Most of his recipes have more ingredients than mine, though. My tuna salad has three ingredients. Chef John's has six. I made it when Cousin Edie came, and it was really good."

"Hmmmm. You ever hear any more from your cousin since she vanished last week?"

"No, not yet."

"Mighty peculiar, her disappearing like that."

"Yes, I know." Carrie hurried to change the subject. "The book has just a few slow cooker recipes and, since I wanted to make something for supper that could take care of itself all afternoon, I picked out the beef stew. Henry's in town talking about police work at the grade school today, so I knew he wouldn't be available to help get supper preparation under way. I'm almost done now. Be there in a bit."

"Good. Roger and I cleared space in the workshop and set up my booth there. The three walls are hinged so we can fold it all and load it into his truck. I'm just now starting to figure out where to put everything. When Jason goes out with the shop's deliveries, Eleanor's having him come by here with a few display stands she thinks I can use."

"I saw the stands when I was in town yesterday, and she said then she was sending Jason with the van to help carry your things when we go to set up at the fairgrounds on Wednesday. She'll stay behind and keep her flower shop open, but will be with us during the fair. Jason, and probably Henry, are working in the shop for the rest of the week while we're at the fair, and . . . ."

"Ummm," Shirley interrupted.

"Well, I guess she would have told you all that."

"Um-hmmm. You do know I've been plannin' on this fair thing for quite a while?"

"Yes, well . . . sorry. I wasn't trying to horn in." After an awkward pause, Carrie said, "I'm getting really excited, and so proud of you! It's a big honor to be chosen as an exhibitor at the War Eagle Fair."

"Well, I am a mite proud, but woman, if we keep talking you'll never get that pot filled. Finish your recipe and come on down."

"Yes-um."

Carrie had seen many of Shirley's sewing creations and admired them, but she stopped and gasped a squawky "Oh," when she walked into their dairy farm's workshop thirty minutes later. The shop floor looked like it had been scrubbed, and Shirley's display booth mock-up stood in the middle. Chalk lines on the floor marked the size booth she would have at the craft fair, and three walls made of white-painted hog wire stapled to wooden frames outlined that area. A few of Shirley's baby quilts were already fastened on the wire with wooden clothes pins painted in bright colors. Carrie's favorite quilt, the cow munching grass, was there, along with a sheep and a red Mack truck. A few small squishy-soft blankets made from polyester fleece were clipped on the wrought iron Christmas card tree Carrie had brought down a few days earlier. A sign near the top of the tree said, "Baby Cuddlys, $35.00."

"Wow, these are fabulous," Carrie said, stroking the fabric.

Ignoring her comment, Shirley said, "Okay, let's go to work." She pointed to a stack of quilts laid on a sheet on the floor. "How can we show off all these different kinds? I've got ten of the cows here, shall we start with them?"

Carrie was still fingering a Baby Cuddly. "This is impossibly soft, but it looks like it will wear longer than Rob's blankie did. I think every little kid needs one of these. *Baby Cuddly*. I love the name."

"They're made to last, I don't do junk. I think most little ones like a blanket to cuddle up to. When I felt of that polyester fleece in the store, I thought how good it would be for babies. I favor the name, too. I registered it in Arkansas. It belongs to me now."

"Smart idea. Shirley, what are these loops at the corners for? Look like fat belt loops."

"For the baby to chew on or hold to."

"You think of everything. Oh, how I wish I had a grandchild."

Shirley sighed. "If Junior marries the Tummelton gal I'll get a ready-made grandson, but her boy is too old for my Cuddlys."

"Who says they can't have more children?"

"Not me," Shirley said. "Now, about those quilts. How am I going to show them all off?"

Three hours later Carrie and Shirley were eating chocolate chip cookies and admiring their work. Carrie had made one trip home to check on her stew, which was filling the house with a marvelous smell, and to dig out the box of curtain rings she had tucked away. They were designed to turn flat fabric into curtains, and each ring had a clip attached. Looping the rings through the hog wire and clipping a baby quilt on each one made it possible to layer quilts so people could look through the selection and decide whether they wanted a brown flowered cow, a tan cow with polka-dots, or one with a black and white pattern, much like Roger and Shirley's real dairy cows. A parade of other animals marched across the back and sides of the hog wire frame, led by red trucks, green trucks, and blue trucks.

"When Jason brings the wrought-iron plant stands," Carrie said, "We can use your colored yarn to fasten Baby Cuddlys to the iron scallops that surround the pot platforms. I think I remember a dozen or so of those around each platform, so we can put quite a few Cuddlys there. What are you going to put where the flower pots are supposed to sit, though?"

"Got a surprise for that," Shirley said, going to a box in the corner. She pulled out a Teddy bear made from the same polyester fleece as the Cuddlys. I'll sit a bear in each pot holder."

Carrie smiled as she stroked the bear's soft head. "Can I buy a bear today?" she asked.

"Shoot," Shirley said, let me make you one later, or, if we have any left over after the fair, you can have one of those."

"There won't be any left," Carrie said, "and, until the stands come, it looks like we're about ready. Now might be a good time for you to teach me about the procedure we'll follow at the fair, how to do credit cards, and all. Oh Shirley, it will be such fun working together on a big project again. The three of us haven't done that since my wedding."

"Hard work is what it will be," Shirley said. "Not so much fun. But I couldn't do it by myself, so I am most grateful for the help. You'll have earned more than a free bear at the end of the four days."

"After all you've done for me, Shirley Booth, I . . . " Carrie stopped as images of past events rolled out from the corners of her mind. Shirley had been a calm, motherly, and caring friend more times than could be counted. Even when Carrie was in danger, Shirley had been there, miraculously, to hold out a saving hand. Without any visible hesitation, she'd even clobbered a couple of people who threatened Carrie.

Carrie looked up at the gaunt woman who's very plainness seemed so comforting and strong. "I . . . " she began again.

"Oh shoot," Shirley said, and she turned away to straighten a bunny quilt.

Chapter Five

LOOK WHO CAME TO THE FAIR

C arrie was stirring stew when Henry walked in the kitchen at 4:00. "Smells terrific in this house. What's cooking?"

"Beef stew, a recipe from Chef John's cookbook. But tell me about your day. Was it fun?"

"Sure was. The kids asked good questions, some of them funny. One question I got was 'How many things do you have hanging on those cop belts and what are they for?' I had to stop and count them off on my fingers, adding that the belt was like a police officer's tool box. They loved that. I'll tell you more while we eat. Is it going to be ready soon? I barely had time for lunch, with half the kids in the cafeteria crowded around me, jabbering. Give me time to wash up and I'll be back to help you."

"As soon as these rolls heat, it's all ready."

Carrie waited until Henry had finished his recital of the day's events before she mentioned her morning visitors.

"FBI, huh? Well, everything surrounding your mysterious Cousin Edie gets more peculiar by the minute, doesn't it? I can't figure out why the FBI. What the dickens is she involved in?"

"Isn't there someone you could call? Ask questions? Find out more?"

"We don't want to open that can of worms. I'm sorry things aren't working out well for your relationship with a family member, but . . ."

"If she is a family member."

"She probably is. Otherwise, why would the FBI identify her as such?"

"Oh. Well, yes. But what do we do if the FBI guy comes back?"

"Let's not cross that bridge unless we have to. Now, how are plans for fair set-up going? What's on our schedule?"

"All of us but Eleanor are meeting in Jason and Eleanor's driveway at 6:00 Wednesday morning. Jason is driving the van. He and Roger will take most of Shirley's stuff, but I have a few left-overs in my car. That's it. We find Shirley's assigned location in one of the tents, unload, set up."

On Wednesday morning there were so many crafters and helpers getting ready for Thursday's fair opening that the four long white tents and adjoining craft barn quickly took on the atmosphere of one huge party. Exhibitors who knew each other from past years gossiped back and forth, sometimes in shouts, while they worked on their displays.

Roger, Jason, Carrie, Henry, and Shirley were quickly absorbed into the hubbub as questions, advice, and shouts of "welcome to the mad house" greeted them.

At first, Carrie felt overwhelmed by sights, sounds, and hurrying people carrying all sorts of bulky equipment and merchandise. She, along with the men, spent a few minutes watching other vendors. But, seeing what was distracting her crew, Shirley hollered instructions, reminding them why they were there.

As soon as the three men had the booth's hog wire framework in place, Shirley sent Roger and Jason to carry boxes in from the van and truck, while Henry stacked, opened, and sorted. Carrie, assisted by Henry, was put in charge of hanging baby quilts, while Jason and Roger set up the sales counter and placed Eleanor's wrought-iron plant stands to suit Shirley. Then she handed the two men balls of colored yarn and instructed them to tie on Baby Cuddlys. When Jason tried making yarn knots rather than bows, Shirley said, in her best dialect, "Ye kin tie a shoelace? Then ye kin tie yarn bows. How do ye 'spect folks to get at the Cuddly they want if they hafta undo a knot?

"Um, bossy," Henry murmured. "Sergeant Shirley."

"Well, someone has to take charge." Carrie said, "And she's right about the bows."

Henry grinned and said, "Point taken, apology offered," as he handed a brown cow quilt and a curtain hook to her.

There were picnic tables across from the tents, and, when they stopped to eat the lunch Shirley and Roger had somehow found time to pack, Carrie didn't say much. She was having fun listening to conversations around them. Several minutes later she told Henry, "Folks come here to sell merchandise from as far away as California and Florida, and it sounds like craft fairs are a business for some of them. When they aren't making what they sell, they're traveling from fair to fair around the country. Amazing."

Jason, Roger and Shirley overheard her last sentence and Jason said, in a stage whisper, "See that couple at the end of our table? They're glass blowers, and they actually make a living traveling what they call the 'fair circuit.' Their home and studio are in Iowa, and all during the winter and in between shows they make flowers and other stuff from glass. In spring, summer, and fall they hit fairs all over the United States. It's their only business! I thought crafting was just a hobby."

"Watch it Jason," Roger said, grinning, "you're liable to hurt someone's feelings. I think what these people do is kinda like small-business manufacturing and sales, and, as you can see, they're mighty serious about it."

"Oh yes, yes," Jason said in a hurry, "and Eleanor would kill me if she'd heard me call people here hobbyists. I wouldn't dare call her flower shop a hobby—even though she *was* old enough to get Social Security when she opened it."

"Time to go back to work," Shirley said, gathering wrappers and brushing crumbs away. "But we're about done. Carrie and I will have time to rest up for the big day tomorrow. The fair opens to the public at eight o'clock, and I'm told there will be crowds waiting to get in by then.

There were. Carrie was glad she'd practiced writing tickets and taking payment, because customers surged around Shirley's quilts and Baby Cuddlys, and by 9:00, she had to begin filling empty spaces in the display while Shirley and Eleanor continued helping customers.

At 10:00 Shirley insisted it was Carrie's turn to take a break, and she decided to join the crowds walking aisles in their tent, wanting to see what other exhibitors were selling. When she rounded a corner and looked up the next aisle she stopped cold, then apologized when two women cannoned into her backside. But, but . . . .

Edie? Dark, curly hair, yes, but that could be a wig. She hadn't worn glasses at their house, but glasses could also be fake. The scarf tied casually over her beige sweater, however, couldn't be mistaken. It was the one Carrie had given her, tied just as Carrie had shown.

It has to be Edie—or whatever her name really is. Well, I have a question or two to ask that woman.

But just then "that woman" glanced away from the exhibitor she was talking to, saw Carrie, and rushed down the aisle, blending quickly into the crowd. Carrie shoved through behind her, gathering several annoyed glances, but Edie had already disappeared.

Pretty easy to do, when there are hundreds of people to hide among. But that proves I did really see the so-called cousin who came to my house! Well, RATS!

Carrie turned around and went back to the man Edie had been talking with. His booth featured beautifully made wooden toys and, once more, Carrie wished she had a grandchild to buy these treasures for. Still, Henry might get a kick out of that little police car. She took out her billfold, and when the craftsman approached, handed him the car and her cash. "I thought I recognized the woman you were just talking to," she said, as he wrapped her purchase in newspaper. "The one with the rust-colored scarf? Wasn't that Edith Embler?"

He stared at her, and, for a moment she thought the look on his face was fear. *Surely I am mistaken about that.*

After too much hesitation for a normal conversation, he said, "She paid cash, I don't know what her name was, and that would be private knowledge anyway." He handed Carrie her change and her package, then turned away to help his next customer.

Hmmm. Well, what now? Should I try to question him later? That conversation they were holding did not look like sales talk. Too intense by far.

Carrie hurried out into the open space in front of the tents and took out her cell phone to call Henry.

"Eleanor's Flower Garden," he said, "Henry speaking."

"Henry, I just saw Edie."

"Edie? Where? There?"

"Yes, talking to a guy with a booth in our tent. But she hurried away when she saw me, and I can't find her among all these people. Are you very busy? Could you come and look for her while I go back to work?

"Carrie, love, would that really be sensible? It will take me at least an hour to get there, especially with all the fair-going traffic. If Cousin Edie really wants to hide from you, all she has to do is get in her car and drive off."

"Oh gosh, of course you're right. But I'm so frustrated. I just . . . well, drat, drat, *drat!* Of all the confusing, messy . . . I wish I'd never *heard* of Edith Embler!"

"Cara, just forget about her now, and go back to work. Are things selling well?"

"You bet. I don't know if we'll have enough quilts to last the four days. It's going to be slim pickins by Sunday. Same with the Teddy bears. Shirley is a whirlwind, and mighty happy. I've never seen her so excited."

"Then you'd best go back and help keep her tied to the ground." He stopped talking for a moment, then continued, "I'm sorry to disappoint you, but I really don't think me being there would accomplish anything, and we are fairly busy here in the shop. People coming to the area for the fairs spread out into related businesses all over the place. We're selling a lot of artificial plants in those antique containers Eleanor bought when we were in Van Buren. You might tell her that."

"I will, and me wanting you to come here was silly. See you around 6:30—Oh, WAIT, Henry. The man Edie was talking to just left our tent. He's hurrying, almost running, going toward the field where exhibitors park their cars, trucks, and RV's. Hold on, I'm following him."

"Carrie, NO," the phone shouted at her.

"It's okay, I'm far behind him, and the parking lot is sort of on a hillside, so I can see pretty easily from a distance."

"Carrie, this is not your concern! Shirley needs you. Go back to her booth."

"Come to think of it, that vendor was alone when I saw him. I wonder if anyone is watching *his* booth."

"Carrie!" The phone was beginning to sound alarmed. "Oh, okay, I'm standing still. He's just gone into an RV. Don't you think I should watch to see if he comes out soon, or maybe Edie shows up there?"

"No, I do not think that. *Please* listen to me."

"Okay, okay. I'm going back to Shirley and Eleanor right this minute. I'll see you around 6:30."

"Cara, remember, this is not your concern. Cousin Edie is not *our* concern."

"Yes, I know. I'm walking back to Shirley's booth." She hesitated, then said, "I love you. Thanks for caring about me."

"You know I really do, and I've got to hang up. Two women just came in the shop and Jason's busy with people already here. See you at home." The phone went dead.

After one more glance at the RV, Carrie headed back toward Critter Quilts and Baby Cuddlys. But she changed course long enough to learn that no one was minding the wooden toys.

Chapter Six

MILTON SALES

D uring her mid-afternoon break Carrie walked around to check on the wooden toy booth. No one was working there. She turned to the man next door, admired his bird feeders and houses, then asked, "Has the guy who makes these wooden toys come back?"

"Yeah, he's been in and out. I watch his things best I can when he's gone, but he takes his money box with him so I can't sell anything. You know Milton?"

"Uh, he's a friend of my cousin's but I don't know him myself. I did see him go to one of the RV's in the parking lot mid-morning."

"It's his RV. I don't think he's feeling too good. We've known each other, let's see, twelve years now, because we've had booths next to each other that long. He knows he can trust me to keep an eye on things if he steps out for a while, and Betty on the other side does too. The three of us have been working this fair side-by-side for a dozen years, and Betty's been an exhibitor here for twenty-five. It's too bad he isn't here all the time, though. Lots of folks like those wooden toys and he's missing sales."

"You think he goes out to smoke?"

"Nah, doesn't smoke. Milton's kind of a queer duck, though. Other years he's left his booth for a time, and I never knew why. I think he's pretty restless."

"Milton?"

"Milton Sales." The man laughed, turned away to take money for a bird feeder and wrap it, then continued, "Milton Sales. Nice name for a sales-man, right? He doesn't seem to need the money he makes here, though. Close-mouthed about it, but I get the idea he retired early from some pretty high-flying job. That's not to take away from the quality of what he shows here, as you can tell. I saw you earlier, buying one of his cars."

The man stopped talking long enough to sell a birdhouse, then he asked her, "So, is your cousin at the fair? Milton's not married, and . . ."

"She was here earlier—maybe you remember a lady wearing a rust-colored scarf talking to him."

"Oh yes, I think I remember. Well, tell her maybe she should go to the RV and check on Milton, if she knows him well enough to do that."

"I'll tell her when I see her. If he comes back, you might ask him to come say hello to me—to ease my mind, you know. I'm helping out in the booth selling baby quilts, fourth from the front in the next row."

"Okay. Take care now." He went back to helping customers.

Milton Sales hadn't shown up to say hello by 5:00, so Carrie hurried around to his booth while Eleanor and Shirley were starting to close down. "Milton ever come back?" she asked the birdhouse man.

"Yeah, he was here for a couple of hours, but left a few minutes before 5:00. Said he didn't have time to go see you."

"I just wanted to be sure he was okay," Carrie said. "Thanks." She walked back to the quilt booth and helped Eleanor cover the displays while Shirley put lids on boxes of extra merchandise. Time to forget about Milton Sales. He was okay, that was enough.

And, after all, Henry had insisted none of this was their concern.

The three women left everything except money and receipts for sales under the watchful eyes of night guards and pulled out of the parking lot at 5:40. Since Eleanor was driving, Carrie phoned Henry as soon as they reached the highway. "Have any ideas for supper?" she said, "With rush hour traffic, I won't be home until at least 6:45."

"Already got the left-over stew on the stove."

"Ah, Good. There's a corn bread mix in the pantry. You might bake that. And I made a new bowl of fruit gelatin last night, strawberry this time.

"Great! When I hear Eleanor's car, I'll put it all on the table. We can talk about your Edie-sighting and the rest of the day while we eat."

"Looks like you've got company," Eleanor said as soon as she turned down the lane to Carrie and Henry's house.

"What? Good heavens!" Carrie peered out the van window.

"Wouldn't have seen it so soon if the car wasn't white and your post light wasn't on. Know who it is?"

"I haven't a clue." Carrie said. *But—oh, surely not.*

As soon as she opened the door, Henry called to her. "Cara? Guess who's come to dinner? Our cousin Edie."

He sounded relaxed, not a worry in the world.

She headed for the kitchen and stared in astonishment at Edie, who was sitting at the kitchen table in her own regular place across from Henry. The wig and glasses were gone, as was the scarf. *Well!*

"Hello Carrie. I've apologized to Henry for running out on you guys last week. It couldn't be helped, as I've explained to him. He's been kind enough to invite me to have supper and stay the night, I hope that's okay. I've told him why I disappeared, and I'll tell you both what I might call 'the rest of my story' after we eat."

Carrie only nodded, and Edie went on. "I mixed up the corn bread, by the way, and promised to clear away the dishes."

After glancing at his silent wife, Henry went to slice cornbread and fill bowls with stew. Carrie stood absolutely still, staring out the window while she repeated to herself, *She's not our concern. She's not our concern. And she's sitting in my chair.*

Edie said, "I'm sitting in your place, aren't I? I'll move around right now." She shifted to a chair between Carrie and Henry's usual locations as Henry put a bowl of stew in front of her. "Thanks, Henry, smells great. Hang up your coat, Carrie, and join us. You look dog tired, and, unless you've been snacking on fair goodies, I'd bet you're starved."

Still saying nothing, and fuming inwardly, Carrie went to wash her hands.

Supper, beyond polite conversation, was eaten quietly. At first Henry, chuckling frequently, talked about some of his amusing gardening experiences. He got little response from Carrie, and Edie, perhaps taking a clue from that, didn't say much either, only nodding from time-to-time. He finally lapsed into silence.

Edie did indeed take over kitchen clean-up while Carrie went to check the guestroom and learned that Henry—maybe with Edie's help—had already put fresh linens in the bathroom and on the bed.

When Henry didn't follow her to their bedroom for a conversation, Carrie decided she would take a shower and get into her pajamas, while he did . . . whatever he was doing. Helping Cousin Edie clean up in the kitchen?

When she went down the hall a few minutes later, Edie was unpacking in the guestroom, and she found Henry sitting in his favorite chair, reading the paper. He looked up and, when she sat on the couch, moved over to sit beside her.

"When did *she* get here?" Carrie whispered.

"Came in just after you called. She's explained her disappearance. Two men who sound like Agent Frost and his companion were at the motel when she arrived. For yet unknown reasons your cousin is aware someone, perhaps FBI, might be trying to find her.

"When she looked through the glass entry area of the motel and saw two men in dark suits at the desk, one of them holding out a leather pocket folder, she decided to go back to her car and wait. Eventually they came out and got back in their car. When they didn't drive away, she used her cell phone to call the motel, saying she had an emergency and needed to cancel her reservation. They allowed that, and even sounded relieved, she thought, so that made her certain the men had been asking about her and they were glad to avoid potential trouble. Pretty soon someone came out of the motel lobby and went to the car to talk with the men. After that they drove off.

"Edie went to another motel and registered under a similar, but false name, paying cash. She figured, probably correctly, that the men had the ability to check motel registrations. When the desk clerk asked for identification, she flashed her driver's license, and they glanced at her photo, but didn't catch the different name. After I told her two men from the FBI had been here asking for her, she agreed the best thing, at least for tonight, was for her to stay here."

"Why didn't she let us know she'd had to change motels?"

"Not sure of our loyalties. Came here this evening as a last resort."

"Oh, for gosh sake. And what if those men come back? Are we now *hiding* her?"

"I hope we don't have to deal with that before tomorrow morning, if at all."

"None of us will be here tomorrow."

"Exactly. I thought Edie could go to the shop with me, if nothing else works out."

"Go where?" Edie said, as she walked into the room.

After Henry explained, Carrie asked, "How do you know Milton Sales?"

"Ah."

"I suggest you bring us fully into the picture right now," Henry said. "We are sheltering you, and have a right to know what's really behind your visit here."

Since she hadn't told him about the afternoon's events, and he hadn't yet heard the name Milton Sales, Carrie was surprised and pleased when Henry picked up on her train of thought immediately. His manner remained friendly, but there was steel behind the request for information. She wondered if Edie understood that steel. Henry, when he took on his cop manner, could be intimidating. He wasn't quite there yet, but might be very quickly.

Did anything intimidate Cousin Edie? Carrie hoped so, because this whole situation was unsettling, if not scary, and Edie had involved them more deeply the minute she returned to their home this evening.

Probably all this evening's friendly behavior from Henry was by intent, getting Edie to let her guard down. Is she frightened of those two men? Of Milton Sales? Of something or someone else?

Carrie settled comfortably against Henry's side and awaited Edie's response.

Chapter Seven

LEARNING MORE

E die sat in Henry's favorite chair and, head down, she was silent for a long minute before she said, "Milton Sales was a much younger colleague of my father's."

When she said no more, Carrie prodded. "So you knew him years ago?"

"No. I didn't know him. But, back when Daddy disappeared and Mother and I were asking a lot of questions at his office about what might have happened, a woman there mentioned the name, and said she thought he had been working with Daddy at the time he disappeared. The three of us were alone when she said that, and after someone walked in the room, she quit talking. No one else acknowledged knowing anything about Daddy's colleagues, and we never located Milton Sales. But I didn't forget his name."

Henry asked, "Where did your father work?"

"It was called 'Torrance Export-Import,' but I have always thought the name was a cover for something else."

"What made you think that?"

"Doesn't export-import indicate the business is dealing with products; something coming and going? Toys, art, antiques, machine parts, whatever? Surely there would be some evidence of things to be sold. The office had a warehouse attached, and the warehouse had boxes. I managed to trip over one once, and I'm sure it was empty. Daddy never, ever, mentioned any kind of merchandise, and never brought samples home. He had no sales books or catalogues. After he died we were given all the stuff from his desk, or at least all they wanted us to have. Nothing there about exporting or importing. "

Carrie said, "You obviously learned more about Milton Sales later."

Edie nodded. "I did. Last winter, when I realized how badly Mother wanted closure for Daddy's disappearance, I tried to find that office. Not even the building was still there, and I didn't find the business name in the phone book or online. Then I phoned every export-import company I could locate." She snorted an attempt at a laugh. "Believe me, there were a lot of them. No one had ever heard of the Torrance Company. A woman in one company, however, did recognize the name Milton Sales. She said he was a sales manager with their firm for around twenty years, but had taken early retirement at least a dozen years earlier. He told her he was moving to Arkansas because he'd found a place he could sell the wooden toys and other products he had enjoyed creating as a hobby.

"That's when I remembered a wooden book rack Daddy had on his desk at home. It's beautifully made from three colors of wood. I wondered if Milton made it for him. He did. It was signed on the bottom."

So, Carrie thought, finding Milton Sales, not finding a cousin, is the reason Edie came here. She bit her lip to keep from saying anything she might regret, and hoped Henry would fill the conversation gap.

He did. "You've known much more about this area than you admitted." The steel was in evidence now.

Again there was silence before Edie responded. "Yes."

Carrie stopped biting her lip. "You used me, used us. You lied to us," she said, not sure whether disappointment or anger was causing tears to spill down her cheeks.

I never used to cry when I was married to Amos. I didn't cry when I lived alone. Now, people would probably say I had PMS or was headed into menopause. But, no excuses there. All that stuff was finished long ago.

Then, why the tears now? Why?

Could being in a loving partnership with Henry have something to do with this? She stared at the ceiling, distracted, not by her cousin's duplicity, but by an awakening realization. *For the first time, someone loves me fully, just as me. Not as a mom, not as a daughter, he loves me just because I'm me.*

Did my parents love me? Yes, I know they did, but they weren't demonstrative. And I think, as teachers, they sometimes saw me as an experiment in child rearing.

Amos? Well, of course, our marriage was a business arrangement. He needed a presentable, intelligent wife and hostess, and I wanted my own home and a child. We each got what we bargained for.

But now? Her tears began flowing more freely, if still silently.

Now there is Henry, and our beautiful, incredible, shared love.

Satisfied, and a bit overwhelmed by her thoughts, she sat in silence, and when Edie finally said "Yes, I did," it took her a minute to remember what her cousin was responding to.

Henry said, "No one likes being used. You're smart enough to understand that. I suppose you knew more about War Eagle than you let on. A simple Internet search?

"Yes"

And finding out about Carrie? The same? You lied about the library?"

"Yes." When Carrie finally looked up at her cousin, tears were streaming down her cheeks, too.

Edie pulled a tissue from her pocket and blew her nose, covering Carrie's own mop and blow. The two women stared at each other, then, suddenly, both of them began laughing.

"What a mess, huh?" Carrie said, when she could get the words out, and Edie nodded, retrieving another tissue to wipe her eyes.

Henry stared from one to the other, then said, "I don't see what's funny about any of this."

Carrie said, "Nothing, but our duplicate reaction is. Never mind, love, it isn't something that needs to be understood. Put it down to one of those mysterious female things. Please continue."

Henry shook his head, and, briefly, smiled at her. But in a second the steel re-appeared, and he asked "What about Carrie? May I assume you really are her cousin?"

"That part is true."

"So—you came to Arkansas to find Milton Sales."

"The woman who remembered he was moving to Arkansas also remembered the name War Eagle, and you're right. A simple Internet search, and I had the information I needed. Mother truly was eager to have me look you up, Carrie, but in a sense, I did use you. The fact you live so close to War Eagle Mill was fortuitous. But, don't you see, I didn't have to look you up to locate Milton Sales? I ended up finding the mill and War Eagle Craft Fair on my own. Of course I didn't know if Sales would be at the fair, but you couldn't have helped me with that anyway."

"Okay," Henry said. "Now, what about those two men who're looking for you? What's that all about?"

"I haven't a clue, but they frighten me. If my father really was doing something illegal, maybe they think I know about it and can give them information. Well, so far, I can't. Or maybe they know all about Daddy's activities and want it kept quiet, or . . . well, I don't know. Like I say, it's frightening. And I certainly want to know more about them before I meet them face-to-face." She paused for a moment before she said, "I'm wondering if they really are from the FBI."

Carrie said, "The one who called himself Arnie Frost flashed a badge, but that's exactly what he did, flashed it. I couldn't tell you now if it was really from the FBI. I should have looked more closely."

"People don't," Edie said. "I was pretty sure I could get away with using a false name, even if motel clerks asked to see photo identification. E. D. Fingler was one name I used. I hoped it was enough change, and anyone searching for me wouldn't notice. If it sounded like a man, so much the better. I only stayed at each motel one night, just in case. I also changed rental cars, as you saw."

Henry said, "And Milton Sales? What about him?"

"Of course it was a gamble that he was still using that name, and that he'd be at the fair. When you get there they give you a book that includes the names of exhibitors, what they make, and their booth location. He was listed. After that it was easy."

"Did he talk to you?" Carrie asked.

"I think he would have, but that's where my luck ran out. I told him who I was, and said I hoped to learn more about my father's disappearance so my mother could find peace in her old age. I did kind of dramatize that part. I asked if we could talk after the close of the fair that day, or at some other time convenient to him. He said he had his RV parked on the grounds and would meet me there around 1:00 when he went to get his lunch. He had just begun to describe the RV when I saw you. I didn't want you to complicate things or scare Sales off, so I got away as quickly as I could. When I went to the RV at 1:00 no one answered my knocks. I went back several times, but he never answered the door. I only checked his booth once after that. He wasn't there, but I didn't return. I didn't want to risk being seen there again."

Carrie nodded, and said, "I talked to the man briefly after you disappeared, Edie, but he didn't acknowledge knowing who you were when I asked. I guess it's possible my question spooked him, though I thought I mentioned you quite casually while I was buying something from his display. I saw him leave for the RV not long after. I did check at his display a couple of times this afternoon, but he wasn't there. According to his neighbor, he came and went the rest of the day, but that was standard procedure. The man said he was always restless."

She turned to her husband. "Henry, is there any way we can verify that those guys looking for Edie were really from the FBI? I know you don't want to rock any boats, but it would sure be helpful if we knew."

"I'll call Ray in the morning, but I won't press him to do an extensive search."

Carrie explained, "That's a friend of his, a deputy police chief in Kansas City."

Edie nodded, then yawned. "Excuse me. I haven't been sleeping too well these last few nights."

"You go on to bed. We'll make plans in the morning. I'm heading for bed myself. It was a long day at the fair."

Henry got up too. "One more thing, Edie. I think we should put your car in the garage and leave my truck in the driveway. That's in case anyone gets curious about a strange car here."

When he came in the bedroom, Carrie went to the hall and locked the door separating their area from the rest of the house. That also blocked Edie's access to the garage, but, with Henry's truck parked behind her car, if she ran away this time, it would be on foot.

Henry noticed what she was doing, but said nothing as he took her in his arms for a very comforting hug. Relaxing into his warmth reminded her of the first hug they'd shared.

They'd barely known each other back then. He'd come to her door, knowing that, minutes earlier, she'd discovered her best friend's body in the woods. He said only "You found her," and held out his arms. She'd gone to him, and—for the first time in adult memory—Carrie Culpeper McCrite had cried, making big wet spots on the front of Henry's jacket.

But now, nearly two years later, she didn't cry. She shut her eyes and smiled.

The bedroom phone rang at 4:15.

It was on Carrie's side of the bed, and she'd never lost the concerned mother's ability to respond quickly to nighttime phone calls, so she said a clear and wide-awake sounding "Hello."

"Carrie," Jason said, "I'm sorry to bother you so early, but Patricia phoned us awhile ago and told us Randy had been in a car crash when he was driving home from work."

"Oh, Jason! How is he?"

"He's in intensive care and, at last report, things were looking better. Broken bones and head injuries, but air bags undoubtedly saved his life. They weren't yet sure about internal damage when Patricia called again about an hour ago." Jason's voice broke, as he said, "A van full of sixteen-year-old kids was speeding, ran a stop sign on a blind side street, and smashed into the driver's side of Randy's car. The driver of the van was killed right there. All the other kids ended up in the hospital with various injuries from being thrown around inside the van, since no one was wearing a seat belt. The boy driving went through the windshield and clear over Randy's car. The girl who was sitting next to him is . . . well, we don't know." Jason's voice broke again, and he stopped talking.

In the silence Carrie said, "My prayers for all of you have already begun, Jason. Remember, God's love and care are with you right this minute—your daughter and son-in-law, you and Eleanor—those kids, everyone. You are not bearing this alone."

"Yes . . . yes. Thanks for reminding me."

"Now then, what practical help do you need? We're here to take care of it. I assume you're going to Ohio to be with Patricia and Randy and their twins?"

"Yes, we're getting ready to leave for the airport now. If you . . . well, there's the craft fair and all. We'll need to close the shop. Could you put a 'family emergency' sign on the shop door, and maybe Henry will take Eleanor's place at the fair?"

Carrie's mind was hurrying through options. *Edie? Well, why not? She couldn't cause Shirley any problems, and she would probably welcome a chance to put on her disguise and work anonymously at the fair.*

"Jason, you needn't worry. We have a houseguest right now who'll be able to take Eleanor's place. We'll get it all worked out, and only close 'Eleanor's Flower Garden' if we have to. You can forget about things here and give all your support to Patricia and Randy."

Jason sighed and took a shaky breath. "We're trying to think of everything, but I'm sure we won't succeed. We will be in touch to let you know how Randy is doing.

"Oh. Eleanor says she has no big events scheduled until next month, but you'll probably need to give live plants in the flower shop some care, and throw away any cut flowers that don't make it. We don't know how long we'll be gone, but, well, just keep praying."

"I will, and we'll take care of whatever needs doing at the shop and your house. Henry or I will check the house daily, and pick up your mail and newspaper."

"No need. I'm taking contact numbers with me. I'll phone from the airport to stop the newspaper. As for the mail, I can access USPS on line or call the post office."

"For now, Jason, let us pick up the mail. We drive by your house almost every day anyway. Easy to check the mailbox. That way, if something looks like it needs attention, we can tell you or forward it to you."

"Oh, Carrie, thank you, thank you both."

"Don't worry about anything here. And please call us when you can."

"I will. Yes. Well now, thank you again. We'll be in touch."

Her soft words, "Love to all of you" were swallowed up in a dial tone.

Chapter Eight

TOO MANY CHALLENGES

A s soon as Jason hung up, Carrie's thoughts turned to a favorite Bible passage that often carried her into productive prayer. The 91st Psalm—solace for soldiers in battle and people in any difficulty—guided her now.

He shall give his angels charge over thee, to keep thee in all thy ways. They shall bear thee up in their hands . . .

Henry cleared his throat.

Carrie turned to see that he was sitting up in bed and, from the worried look on his face, had heard enough to understand there was bad news. He reached his hand out to take hers, and said, "What's happened?"

She told him. After a contemplative silence, he said, "All right, we'll carry on as you promised, of course we will. But what do you really think about taking Edie with you to fill in at the craft fair? I could still take her to the flower shop and keep an eye on her. Can you not get along without her?"

"I suppose we could, but, in truth, Shirley's work takes some explaining, and people want to talk about it anyway." She mimicked various voices, "'Will this stand up in the washing machine? Can you put it in the dryer? Will it wrinkle? Do you have it in yellow? Can I order three trucks, one each in red, white, and blue? Is there a discount if I buy more than one?' That sort of thing goes on all day, as well as making sales, wrapping, straightening, and re-stocking. The three of us were kept hopping and, of course, each of us has to eat and take a break now and then."

"Ah, I see. But, I admit I'm still uneasy about her motives—her reasons for being here. I even wonder if she brings some kind of danger to you."

"I don't see how."

"Simply the association, if nothing else. We still don't know what we're dealing with. These days a lot of innocent people are put in danger simply because a single person is the intended target. What if her father's business had some connection to Mexican drug cartels?"

"Henry, he died around forty years ago."

"Yes, as far as we know, he did. Carrie, my love, if he was involved in the drug business . . . well, the drug business all over Central and South America was dangerous back then, too."

She bowed her head, and thought, *Please, I need help sorting all this out and knowing the right thing to do.*

He continued, "There's always a chance the two dark suits will look for her at the fair."

"But, how would they know to look there?"

"That's just it. We don't know why they're looking for her, what they know, or how they learned it. I can't call Ray this early, but will as soon as he's at the station. My hope is that he can at least tell us if Agent Arnie and his companion are really from the FBI."

"We have to be in Shirley's booth at the fair before 8:00."

"I know."

They were silent for a couple of minutes, then Henry said, "I'll shave and get dressed while you call Shirley. It's already five o'clock. They'll be up."

Shirley received Jason and Eleanor's news with practically laced sympathy. "Well, we were all mighty sad for them when Gertrude passed, but it's good they haven't adopted a new dog yet. We'd have to bring the animal down here, and, if it didn't get along with our dogs and know how to behave around cows, it would have to go to a kennel."

"Oh, yes, I hadn't thought of that."

They were both quiet for a moment, as if showing respect to the Stack's long-time pet. Then Carrie said, "You know, Henry and I still miss FatCat."

"Uh-huh. You gonna get a new cat?"

"Not unless we can find one just like FatCat."

Shirley said "You think so?" then changed the subject. "I'm glad your cousin's showed up, but it seems to me if she doesn't want to come to the fair, we can get along without either her or Henry today. It'll keep us hoppin' but we can do it. Henry needs to stay behind and mind Eleanor's shop. Besides he's got to be available so he can pass news from up north along to us. Saturday will probably be the biggest day for crowds and, need be, I can ask Junior if he thinks it would be okay for me to invite the Tummelton gal to help us out then. The boy will be with his daddy's parents this weekend, so she'll not be tied down beyond house chores and mebee grading papers or some other teacher job."

"Okay then. I'll pick you up at 6:30, with or without Cousin Edie."

Stuffed with oatmeal, bacon, and toast, Edie readily agreed to work at the fair. Carrie noticed she didn't show any particular emotion when the plan was proposed to her, even though it would obviously give her a second opportunity to connect with Milton Sales under the guise of an exhibitor's assistant.

She's a peculiar person, Carrie thought. *I'd sure like to know what she's really thinking.*

Before he headed for town, Henry said, "I'll phone you as soon as I get any information from Ray, or from Jason and Eleanor." As he kissed her goodbye, he murmured, "Stay in touch. I'll expect a call every couple of hours."

He really is concerned about danger associated with Cousin Edie, Carrie thought, as she headed down into Walden Valley to pick up Shirley.

Aloud, she said to Edie, "It's going to be another beautiful fall day in the Ozarks. We probably won't need our sweaters this afternoon."

"It is beautiful here," Edie agreed. "I had no idea!"

Shirley spent the hour's drive to the fair schooling Edie in what she'd face during the day. By the time they parked among the exhibitor's vehicles, Edie was able to repeat most of Shirley's instructions back to her verbatim, and therefore the morning went smoothly. There was no time for casual chit-chat. Except for Carrie's promised calls to Henry, talk was all business-related. During one brief phone conversation at noon she learned Ray hoped to get back with any information available about Agent Arnold Frost by late afternoon, and that Henry hadn't heard from either of the Stacks. "I wouldn't expect news until at least this evening," he said. "After all, they've barely gotten there."

During the morning Edie didn't mention Sales, and Carrie didn't know if she'd walked around to talk to him during her lunch break. On her own break Carrie hurried around to the next aisle. Milton Sales wasn't in his booth, and someone had put sheets over his merchandise. Carrie was itching to ask if the birdhouse builder had seen him, but there was a line at his counter, and the woman on the other side was also busy with customers, so Carrie couldn't ask if they had seen Sales or who had put out the sheets.

"Except for being busy selling, it's been an uneventful day," she told Henry during her afternoon break. "Edie is doing great, she hasn't mentioned Milton Sales once, and has agreed to help out here tomorrow. I imagine she's hoping to be able to question him at some time while she's here.

"Maybe I'm inclined to negative suspicion, but I wonder, could something have happened to the man? So far as I know, no one has checked his trailer, but someone has thrown sheets over the stuff in his booth."

"Does Edie know about the sheets?"

"I suppose so, but she hasn't said anything, and I haven't mentioned it either."

"I still don't like the feeling of all this. Please try to avoid getting involved any more than we already are."

"I promise. Don't worry, Henry. Except for the huge crowds of craft fair fans, things are actually pretty calm here. I know you're concerned, and I understand why, but really, we're okay.

"Now, you haven't told me if anyone has called yet—Ray, or Jason and Eleanor?"

"No calls from either. I have been busy, though. Thank goodness no one has asked for a corsage—or a spur-of-the-moment bridal bouquet! Jason taught me enough that I can construct a passable vase of flowers for a gift, or for someone to take to the hospital. Only problems are requests for delivery. I have to turn most of those down."

"Surely they understand when you explain the emergency."

"Yep. In fact, one guy came to pick up his flowers after I told him about Randy's accident. I am going to deliver a potted plant to a woman here in town after I close. It's her birthday."

She said absently, "That's nice," then went back to her concerns. "I do wish Ray would call back. I guess the Stacks will call as soon as they can get to the hospital and have seen Randy."

"Ray won't call until he has some information."

"I know, but waiting is hard."

"It often is, Cara. It often is."

After a pause, he asked, "Any ideas about supper?"

"Maybe we could eat out this evening? With all that's going on, I'm having an awful time trying to figure out how to feed a guest."

"Why don't I get a pizza for our supper? We can have carrot and celery sticks with it, and I'll put that frozen apple pie in the oven as soon as I get home. I checked in at Jason and Eleanor's this morning to be sure they didn't leave anything turned on or unlocked in their hurry to get away, so all I have to do there is grab the mail."

"Oh, that's great. See you around 6:30."

There had been no phone call from Ray by the time Carrie and Edie got home, but Jason had called to report Randy's injuries were not considered life-threatening, though he looked awful, with bandages covering the left side of his face and head. He had a concussion, but there was no discernable brain damage.

After supper, none of the three was in the mood for conversation. They dozed through the BBC News and "Washington Week," then Edie and Carrie gave up and headed for bed while Henry finished reading the paper.

Back at the fair on Saturday morning, Edie finally exposed her continuing interest in Milton Sales when she returned from her morning break to announce, with obvious distress, "It's all gone! His booth is empty!"

"Oh Edie," Carrie said. "Really all gone, everything?"

"Yes. Cleared out! Now what? What am I going to do next? *What?*"

Shirley turned to look at them, and said, "Somethin' wrong?" but was interrupted by a group of three chattering teens who wanted teddy bears. Carrie had just put her hand on Edie's arm when she was pulled away by a woman who'd finally decided which Baby Cuddly she liked best and said, "I'm next." Edie responded just as quickly to a couple asking questions about a bunny quilt, but her voice cracked as she began to explain hand tying.

The interruptions were welcome. Carrie had no idea how to answer Edie's question.

As soon as the indecisive woman had paid for her Baby Cuddly, Carrie hurried around to ask the birdhouse man if he had seen Milton Sales today.

"Nope. His stuff was gone when I got here, and Betty's sheets were tossed on the ground. We were both a bit late coming in, so probably just missed him. Thing is, he didn't take his shelves or selling counter. As you see, they're still here, and a few of his pieces are still on the shelf under the countertop."

"Have you reported his absence?" Carrie asked.

"No, and things are so odd now that I think we should. Both Betty and I are working alone today, so do you mind telling people in the office he's gone? Here's a sack. Why don't you wrap those pull-toy animals he left on the shelf and take them to the fair office when you go there? They're some of his nicest things. Expensive. I don't want the responsibility for them."

Reluctantly, Carrie agreed, wrapped the animals in scraps of newsprint, and headed for Shirley's booth. People were lined up there, waiting to be helped, so she put the toys in an empty cardboard box and went back to selling.

When there was a break in customers she told Shirley a vendor in the aisle behind them had gone missing and, since the exhibitors next to him were working alone, they wanted her to report his absence. Shirley started to ask a question, but stopped, and nodded. Edie said, "Let me . . ." but Carrie walked away and didn't hear the rest of her request.

Once outside, she headed down the row of tents toward a deputy sheriff who was directing traffic to and from parking lots. She asked if he had seen anyone coming in before the fair's opening to remove merchandise from a booth.

"Well, one guy was putting boxes in the back of his truck when I took over from night security. The guard said he had exhibitor ID so it was okay. The truck was blocking traffic though, so I told him he had to get out of the way, and that was that. He jumped in his truck and pulled out in the direction of Highway 12."

"Thanks." Carrie glanced at her watch. *Oh, dear.* She thanked the man and headed toward the fair office as fast as she could walk without knocking people down or tripping on tufts of grass. Then she stopped cold for a second, thinking she should at least have taken time to ask the deputy for a description of the truck and its driver. But, surely it had been Milton Sales. As she started her forward jog again, her eyes lifted past the tents to the exhibitor parking lot.

Milton Sales's RV was still parked there.

She was almost running when she got to the office, which was—thank goodness—next to the restrooms.

She hadn't been back at work long when a flurry of activity stirred the crowd in the open area outside the tents, and people shopping inside hurried out to have a look. Edie went to the entrance and came back in a hurry. "Looks like a couple of those sheriff's deputies from the parking lot are at Sales's RV," she said. "They're stringing crime scene tape. I'm going to see what's happening."

"No," Carrie said, "you are not. Stay here where you'll be safe and unrecognized."

"I can't! What if he's . . ."

"No! You have to stay here, Edie. I'll go check. Tell Shirley as much of your story as you can while people are outside gawking. It's safe to tell her, and, so far, all she knows is that you're my visiting cousin. You need to explain everything to her right now, and if you don't, I will when I come back. She's seen enough that she must be suspecting there's more to your reason for being here than just a family visit."

"I can't do that."

"Edie, she's my best friend and I know her very well. It's completely safe to confide in her, and she might even be able to help us in some way. As for going to Sales's RV, that's natural for me since I was the one who told them all the merchandise had been removed from his booth while the fair was closed, and suggested they check his trailer. No one knows you, or that you might have a connection to him. Be sensible. You must not appear to be involved."

Edie finally nodded and went back to Shirley while Carrie pushed her way through the crowds and headed toward the exhibitor parking lot.

Oh, surely he can't be dead, he just can't be! I need to talk with that man.

Then, hearing Henry's cautions inside her head, she amended this to: *Edie and I need to talk with that man.*

She took several more steps before she thought, *Well, at least Edie needs to talk to him. And I can stand by, of course.*

There is so much we don't know.

Chapter Nine

CARRIE IN TROUBLE

I ntent on finding out what had happened to Milton Sales, Carrie forgot common sense and caution. She lifted the crime scene tape already strung at some distance from the RV, ducked under it, and took a couple of steps toward the door. Then she stopped cold, imagining Henry's voice reminding her this was an uninvited intrusion on a possible crime scene, and she might be getting in deep trouble.

People in the gathering crowd behind her shouted questions: "What's going on?" "Is this your trailer?" "Is someone hurt—sick—dead?" Except for a single shake of her head, she ignored them.

On her left she could see a woman in a deputy sheriff's uniform hurrying toward her, but the male deputy she'd spoken with in the parking lot that morning came out of the RV just then. He stopped and looked her over, probably either trying to remember where he'd seen her, or wondering why she had the nerve to come inside the perimeter.

"Hello, Deputy Rainwater," she said, remembering the name on his badge. "Is Milton Sales inside? Is he okay?"

He waited a moment, still studying her, then asked, "This your trailer?"

"No, I . . ."

"You know who it belongs to?"

"I think it belongs to Milton Sales, one of the exhibitors in the tent where I'm working. He's probably the man you talked with this morning when he was loading his truck. His booth is empty now."

Ooops, she hadn't remembered to take those pull toys Sales left behind to the fair office. Okay, she could do it later, maybe even give them to him, on the chance he showed up again. A few toys made no difference here.

"Can you describe Sales?"

"Yes. Caucasian. Not very tall, probably five foot ten. Slight build, around 140 pounds. A full head of hair, light brown hair with a bit of grey. Clean shaven. Can't be sure about eye color, but I'd guess green or brown. I don't know what he was wearing today. Yesterday he had on a black pullover sweater over a blue dress shirt. Faded jeans."

"You're very observant."

"I've been told I am. Is someone of that description inside?"

"No. No one inside, but the place is wrecked. Somebody did a thorough search. Nothing broken, though. In these close quarters, the searcher probably didn't want to smash stuff, since the noise might be heard outside. But it's a good thing we got here when we did. Someone unscrewed the lines to the propane heater and cookstove. A close enough flame, a cigarette, and ka-blooey!"

"I do smell something."

"Unburned propane. We have everything open to disperse the gas, but that's why we're keeping people at a distance. Your name is . . . ?"

"Carrie McCrite."

"So, Ms. McCrite, what more do you know about Sales?"

"Not much, but his neighbors in our exhibitors' tent seem to know him pretty well. They're working without help today and asked me to report his absence at the fair office. First I came to you to find out if you'd seen any exhibitors leave."

"Uh huh. Well, the description you gave sounds pretty much like the man who was loading his truck when I arrived, so I think we should talk to those exhibitors. Give Deputy Rosten your name, phone number, and address, then would you please take her to where they are?"

She nodded, then waited while Rainwater murmured a few words to Deputy Rosten. Were they about her?

As the two women made their way through the crowds, Carrie wished the deputy had on something other than her official uniform. It would be better if she wasn't attracting so much attention. Made it harder to talk to people with all that notice.

"How did the intruder get in to the RV?" she asked. "Was the door broken?"

After a hesitation, the deputy said, "The lock on these things is flimsy. It wouldn't have been hard to force it."

"Oh. Well, are more deputies coming to help you? This is going to be a challenge if there are only two of you to control crowds and ask questions."

"We have asked for help, but, since no one has been hurt—well, it depends on what's going on in the rest of the county whether they can send anyone now."

"What about the gas?"

"Of course that does put a more sinister angle on it."

After a pause, Carrie asked, "Do you suppose someone in the RV could have smelled the gas and got out safely during the night or early this morning?"

The deputy looked at her. "You said you don't know the owner?"

"I don't, or, more accurately, I don't know Milton Sales if he's the owner. I did talk with him briefly on Thursday when I bought one of the wooden toys he makes. I also saw him going into that same RV not long after I left his booth." As an afterthought she added, "It was lunch time."

They were at the entrance to the tent, and Carrie noticed Shirley and Edie were both busy helping customers, and several people had crowded around them. With a twinge of guilt, she stayed with Deputy Rosten, leading her to the empty booth that had been occupied by Sales.

"People on either side of here have exhibited next to him for several years, so they probably know him pretty well. Sorry I can't introduce you. I don't know their names, other than that the woman is Betty."

The guilt about leaving Edie and Shirley to cope without her help was more than a twinge now, so, in spite of the fact she wanted to stay and learn what Sales's neighbors told the deputy, she made herself say, "I've got to go back to work. It's probably best if you don't interrupt these people in the middle of a sale, though your uniform may well cause customers to back off. But the whole point of any of us being here is to sell." At that, she hurried back to Critter Quilts and Baby Cuddlys.

Edie finished helping a woman put her new quilt in the large tote she carried, and then turned to hiss at Carrie, "What happened?"

"Milton Sales is missing. Unknown person or persons tore apart the inside of his RV looking for who knows what, then loosened hose connections to the propane tank, who knows why, since it looks like Sales wasn't there. If he was there, well, he isn't now. There could have been a nasty explosion and fire if anyone had come too close to that trailer with a cigarette. A deputy is on guard at the RV now, another is talking to the people on either side of Sales's booth space. He evidently packed up and left in his truck early this morning before many exhibitors were here. If we have a break, I'll go back and see what the deputy might be learning."

"I can go. I'll just hang around like I was interested in a bird feeder or the soaps and scents the other vendor there sells."

"No, you can't. For one thing, the guy selling the birdhouses would recognize you in that wig. And I don't think you want to take it off here. Right?"

"The deputy at the trailer doesn't know me. Besides, there'll be a crowd there."

"They were already dispersing when I came back this way. The excitement was over. Now, we'd both better get busy helping customers before Shirley has to ask us to. Did you tell her why you came to Arkansas?"

Edie nodded and said, "I wonder if someone wanted to blow up the RV to destroy evidence of . . . whatever?" Obviously not expecting an answer, she turned to help the next customer. After an apology and brief explanation to Shirley, Carrie did, too.

An hour later Deputy Rosten—Olinda Rosten, her badge said—appeared in front of Critter Quilts and Baby Cuddlys. Carrie noticed with relief that Edie stayed busy hanging up the remaining quilt stock, which kept her facing away from the deputy. Shirley, however, stared at Rosten with open curiosity. "May I help you?" she said, though Carrie was sure she knew this woman was no customer.

"I apologize, but I need for Ms. McCrite to come with me. We want to ask her some questions."

"Why now?" Shirley said. "We're mighty busy. I expect her to be here helping me until 5:00. I'm sure you can wait until then."

In spite of her sudden twinge of fear at the turn things were taking, Shirley's bold comment made it difficult for Carrie not to smile in the deputy's face.

Rosten blinked, said, "Well, we're investigating . . ." then stopped talking as she was shouldered aside by a woman reaching for a pink Baby Cuddly. Obviously the deputy's uniform didn't intimidate some people as much as Carrie had supposed.

"Excuse me," the woman said, handing the Cuddly to Carrie, "I'll take this one, and another in pink. My daughter just had twins, two little girls."

Ignoring Olinda Rosten, Carrie took the Cuddly and said, "Oh, congratulations. I suggest getting the second Cuddly in either lavender or yellow so, as they grow older, each girl can identify her own. They're so long-wearing that the twins will still be enjoying them as toddlers and beyond."

"Goodness, I didn't think of that. Perfect. In fact, give me four, two pink and two lavender. That way, if either of them loses one, or they need extras for day care, Marian will be prepared."

"Good idea," Carrie said, writing up a ticket, "and you're lucky. Those are the last two pink Cuddlys."

As soon as the twins' grandmother left the sales counter, a pregnant woman took her place. "We're doing the baby's room in lively colors. It's a boy, but I don't go for the blue-pink stereotype. I'd like that red truck quilt and a red Cuddly, please."

Carrie completed the sale, then glanced at Deputy Rosten, who was now being buffeted on every side by people surging along the aisle. The deputy looked at Shirley before shoving closer to Carrie. "Ms. McCrite, don't leave this area until a deputy questions you further." She pushed back out into the human tide and disappeared.

"Whew," Edie said in Carrie's ear. "I wondered if she was going to arrest you."

"The thought occurred to me," Carrie replied, "and now, come drought or high water, I'm phoning Henry. I could sure use his support. Eleanor often closes by noon on Saturdays anyway, so I hope he's not covered over with customers."

She paused for only a few seconds before she continued, " I'm afraid I've gotten myself involved too deeply in this mess," and wondered if she should have looked Edie in the eye and said, ". . . involved too deeply in *your* mess."

After a long and urgent conversation with Carrie, Henry, murmuring expletives he would no longer have said aloud, took rapid steps to close the shop. He made sure Eleanor's potted plants and the cut flowers in the cooler had plenty of water, pulled down the door blinds, locked the credit card receipts and cash in the safe, turned on the alarm system, and hurried to his truck.

Why couldn't Carrie have stayed out of Edie's business? Why had she gone to that RV? Her curiosity and interest in helping people had trumped wisdom and caution again. And this time it landed her in a ticklish or even dangerous situation. She might be considered an important witness, might end up in court, might even need a lawyer. *Blast, blast, blast!*

Trouble was, he could see the whole story from the deputies' point of view. Years of police work had made it easy to fit in their shoes. Carrie had gone to Sales's booth several times. She'd shown unusual curiosity about the man. Witnesses on either side had seen her, one of them had talked with her, and she'd asked him questions about Milton Sales. What's more, she'd made a special trip to the visitor parking entrance to ask the deputy on duty about a man—who turned out to be Sales—moving out of his booth two days early. And, finally, she'd hurried to Sales's RV as soon as trouble loomed there.

Once out on the highway, Henry made an effort to calm down, even to pray as Carrie did. At least that ought to have a calming effect, and he needed to be calm so he could think more clearly.

Cara, Little Love, stay safe, stay with Shirley. And, please, please, don't talk to anyone but Shirley and your customers until I get there.

As for Cousin Edie? This whole mess was her fault. If only she hadn't come to find Carrie. This time he swore aloud, but stopped in the middle of an especially spicy adjective. *No, stop it, Henry King.*

Reacting like this wasn't going to get him anywhere. Hang Cousin Edie, but it was too late to get her out of their lives. They'd just have to work through whatever problem she'd dropped on them. Still, why on earth couldn't Carrie have ignored anything to do with Milton Sales? Edie was the only one who had a reason to be interested in him.

While he paused for a traffic light, Henry began to calm down. It wasn't really fair to blame Carrie for Cousin Edie being here, and, after all, he was the one who invited the blasted woman to stay at their house.

Carrie would say we are given problems only because we're expected to solve them. Well, maybe. But now she's the one in trouble. That may change her tune.

Should he throw Cousin Edie to the wolves? Tell her story to the deputies to get Carrie off the hook? If it came down to the wire, he'd do it, even if it broke with his own idea of honor. But if Edith Embler was half a man , or, well, half a woman, she'd explain it all to the deputies herself.

He took in a huge breath, blew it out. *I need the wisdom of a judge and the patience of angels, so help me God.*

Were angels supposed to be patient? He'd have to ask Carrie.

He turned onto the road leading toward War Eagle Mill and the fair grounds, and noticed most of the traffic was on the other side, heading out. It was 4:45. A deputy was supposed to be back to question Carrie at five.

When he got to the parking area he noticed three deputy sheriff's cars. One man in uniform was directing traffic, another was just getting out of his car. Looked like the county sheriff's office had been able to send extra help, and traffic would certainly be a tangle without someone to keep things organized.

He parked in the just-vacated space he was directed to, and started across the parking lot through crowds of package-laden people swarming in his direction.

Chapter Ten

THE INVESTIGATOR

C arrie shifted in the car seat and looked away from her inquisitor. How the dickens was she going to get out of this new phase of what she'd begun to think of as "The Edie Mess?" She stared out the car window, not focusing on anything—until she realized the blue truck turning into the parking lot was Henry's. For a moment she wondered if it would be best to ignore him. After all, this criminal investigation guy wouldn't know who her husband was, and, even if they were introduced later, she could pretend she hadn't seen him arrive. Maybe, just maybe, the investigator would finish his questions and leave before Henry found out she wasn't in the exhibitors' tent and came back this way to look for her.

Her audible sigh stopped the man's next question. "Yes, Ms. McCrite?"

No. No getting out of it. She had to warn Henry off now, before he found Shirley and Edie waiting for her in the tent. She was sure he'd be tempted to expose Edie, thinking it would avoid trouble for her. She couldn't risk that, not yet at least.

They knew so little. Sure, it was possible she and Henry were sheltering a criminal, or maybe someone knowing secrets bad people wanted, but everything was still fuzzy in her thinking. She couldn't take steps for or against anyone, especially Edie, until she understood more.

She hoped Ray had called, and that his information would help them understand what was really going on here. Edie a victim? Edie, a woman doing exactly what she said, searching for the truth about her father? Or Edie involved in dark things neither she nor Henry wanted any part of?

"Ms. McCrite?"

She ignored the man, opened the car door, and shouted, "Henry" as the investigator said, quite loudly, "Stop. We're not through here yet."

"That's my husband," she told him, and added, "Retired Kansas City Police Major, Henry King."

The investigator said nothing while she stood beside the car to greet Henry, but at least he got out of the car too.

"Henry, this is Sheriff's Department Investigator Burke. He's asking me about a man named Milton Sales who's an exhibitor here and, it seems, has disappeared. Investigator Burke just arrived. Deputies Rainwater and Rosten were here earlier, and discovered someone had loosened hose connections to the propane tank at Sales's RV. Gas fumes could have killed someone, or there could have been a nasty explosion and fire. Fortunately there was no explosion, and no evidence that anyone was overcome by the gas, but they can't find Mr. Sales. They're asking me about him, though I sure don't know much to tell them. "

Henry came around to shake hands with Burke, then said slowly, "So, this Sales is an exhibitor here?"

"Yes," she said. "I met him, more or less, when I was taking a break and stopped at his exhibitor's booth. He makes wonderful things from wood, mostly toys. I'm spoiling the surprise, but I bought a toy police car from him to put in your Christmas stocking, thinking it would make a unique paperweight for your desk. I decided later he might have something Patricia and Randy's twins would enjoy, but when I went back to look over his selection again, the man was gone."

"I see." He turned to Burke. "Why question her, then?"

"Your wife has shown what we think is more than an average interest in Milton Sales. According to John Harley, one of the exhibitors next to the vacated space, she asked a bunch of questions about him during several visits there. She was the one who reported him missing, and she showed up at his RV when deputies went there to investigate her report."

Carrie started to say something, but Henry interrupted, "My wife is curious about many things, and, it seems to me, her curiosity about this Sales fellow is natural."

The detective was saying "Yes, Major, it may be," when Carrie broke in.

"Of course I was curious, anyone would be. And that man next to Sales's booth *asked* me to report him missing. It wasn't my idea at all. I was simply doing him a favor because he and the lady on the other side were both working by themselves. And, after I reported the absence, *as requested*, I was naturally curious when someone told me sheriff's deputies were at Milton Sales's RV."

"How did you know it was his RV?" the investigator asked.

"Saw him go in it during my lunch break. It was either his, or he knew who it belonged to. And later, the man in the booth next to him—John Harley, did you say?—told me it was his."

"I see."

Carrie took a key ring out of her purse and handed it to Henry. "Dear, would you mind taking these to Shirley? She's waiting for me to be finished here, and now that you've come, she might as well go on home in my car. We can pick the car up at her house later. Tell her I'd be glad if she'd stop at our place and drop off what she's carrying for us. House key is on that ring."

Henry looked at her only a minute before he asked, "Leave it at the house? Can't we get it later?"

"No, I need it this evening."

"Are you sure?"

"Yes. And I'm not going to answer any more questions until you come back. I'm sure Investigator Burke won't mind if you sit in."

She got back in the car, folded her arms, and prepared to wait.

While he was walking to tent number three, Henry opened Carrie's key ring, and took off the house key. What on earth was she thinking, giving Edie a key to their house? Evidently the deputies had no idea yet that Edie was anything but extra help at the fair, and Carrie had some reason for shielding her. Well, until he heard why, he wouldn't spill the beans, but he wasn't going far enough to allow that woman time alone in their house.

When he got to Shirley's space, she and Edie were sitting on stools in the almost empty tent, chatting. As he came within hearing distance, Edie was saying, "Hobbs State Park sounds like it's well worth a visit, and . . . Oh, hello Henry, glad you're here. Did you see Carrie? Is she okay? That policeman came and took her away, and we've been worried sick."

"She's fine, and here are the keys to her car so you two can go on. She'll ride with me."

"Carrie's good at taking care of herself," Shirley said, "And, thank her for thinking of us. We will go on, if that's okay with Edie. All of us are mighty tired and hungry."

Henry said, "Edie, we'll pick you up at Shirley's as soon as we can, but who knows how much longer we'll be here while the investigator questions Carrie about *Milton Sales*." He enunciated the name carefully and stared at

Edie, making his face as stern as he could. She ignored him, slid off the stool, and went to pick up her sweater and purse at the back of the booth. She dropped her purse, and when she reached inside the box it had fallen into, said, "Oh, look, there are some of Milton Sales's pull toys inside this box. You'd better take them with you, Henry. Carrie evidently bought them as gifts, maybe for those twin grandchildren of Eleanor's she's been telling me about. She kept her purse and sweater back here, and took those with her, but evidently forgot the toys."

She handed him the box, then followed Shirley toward the exhibitors' parking lot, turning to smile and wave as she left the tent.

Henry didn't return the smile or the wave. He had an excuse not to wave, as she could see. He was holding Carrie's box. Edie could probably see his scowl, too.

Be calm, he thought as he walked back to the parking lot, put the box behind the passenger seat in his truck, and headed for Investigator Burke's car.

"Okay if I climb in back here?" he asked. At Burke's nod, he settled himself, said "Shirley is going on home, and thanks you for the loan of your car," then waited to see what the investigator would say next.

"Ms. McCrite, would you please go over the information we've discussed so far?"

She did, from discovering the wooden toy maker's booth to her curiosity about what the deputies were doing at his RV. She left out any mention of her cousin.

"And you say you don't know the man at all. Had never met him until you appeared at his fair space?"

"Right. I don't know the man at all."

"You asked Deputy Rosten if it was possible Milton Sales had been in his RV, and was somehow removed or left of his own volition before, during, or after the gas was turned on."

"Well, I didn't say it exactly like that, but I did wonder about whether or not he was there some time during that period. If he was knocked out by the gas, his removal must have been during the dark hours, because in the daytime carrying someone out of the trailer would have been noticed by a lot of people. Even at night, secrecy would have been iffy. But I also wonder now if he came to his trailer, day or night, and, seeing it torn up, maybe in conjunction with realizing the gas lines were tampered with, he was spooked and chose to bolt."

The deputy's momentary silence told Henry he was considering what Carrie had said.

"Hm. Interesting speculation. But why didn't he report what happened? Why didn't he take care of the gas leak?"

"Fear. He was frightened. Or time. He realized someone meaning harm was perhaps near by, even watching him. And, he may have opened a window to vent the gas, but was afraid to take time to re-attach the hoses. You could ask Deputies Rainwater and Rosten about the window. Also, he could have been afraid the whole thing would blow up while he was there and 'got the heck out of Dodge,' so to speak. Worst case, he could have been overcome by the gas and simply removed by person or persons unknown.

"The fact he's gone makes me think one of three things. He's afraid, and has disappeared for that reason. He's been taken captive by people who did or did not find what they were searching for in the trailer. Or he's dead. All that points to criminal activity, not necessarily, however, by Milton Sales."

There was another pause while Henry marveled, once more, at how quickly Carrie could cut to the core of matters like this. He figured Burke was probably astonished at the astute conclusions of the little, grey-haired woman sitting beside him.

Finally the investigator said, "You're thinking like a detective, Ms. McCrite. Seems your husband's profession has worn off on you over the years."

Henry wondered if he should comment on that, but stopped to ponder what the investigator's remark about his influence wearing off on Carrie signified. *He thinks we're old married folks .*

In the meantime, Carrie answered for them both.

"Actually, Henry and I have been married less than a year, friends for two years. But yes, I do know a lot about human nature, and have learned from him how to think carefully about unexpected, and perhaps criminal, activities."

"So, what do you think happened to Sales? Where is he?"

"I haven't a clue. But, with your resources, I bet you can find out. After all, Deputy Rainwater did see him and can probably describe his truck, though I don't know if he got the truck's license number. Maybe fair officials take all that down if you park in the exhibitors' lot."

Burke slanted his head toward Henry.

"Any thoughts, Major?"

"It is possible Sales was involved in something peculiar, if not criminal.

Perhaps his fair neighbors can tell you more. After all, as my wife has said, the three of them have, at their own request, been neighbors at every fair for a number of years. Those two must have observed something of interest beyond the fact Sales's attention to his booth was somewhat erratic."

"Not a bad idea, and I had intended to speak with them again tomorrow anyway," Burke said. "Okay, I guess that's all for now, Ms. McCrite. I'm sure you'll be here Sunday if I need to talk with you further. He turned toward Henry. "Will you be here too, Major King?"

"Definitely," Henry said.

And with that, they were done.

As soon as they were in the truck, Henry asked, "You intended for Edie to be alone in our home?"

"Well, I didn't like it, but what could I do? It isn't up to Shirley to baby sit her."

"Maybe not, but she is with Shirley. I am firmly against leaving her alone to use our house, our phone, and maybe even our computers as she wishes, so I took your house key off the ring. We'll pick her up now, when we get your car from Shirley."

"Okay."

She was quiet for so long that Henry wondered if she was angry about his decision. Then she said, "You're right, of course. But I knew I didn't want the law enforcement people to connect us with Edie, at least not yet. I couldn't think how else to get her out of there without Burke seeing her with you and me.

"Now, have you heard anything from Ray or the Stacks?"

"Eleanor called to say Randy's awake and able to talk, though somewhat hampered by his bandages. I told her how well things were going at both the shop and the craft fair, and that I'd been able to keep the shop open the whole time."

"How about Ray?"

"He did call, but had learned nothing. No name like Agent Arnold Frost in the FBI records Ray's contact was able to access. That's not really definitive, however. I have no idea how complete the records he was talking about are."

"Henry, do you feel like we're wading through mush? How on earth am I to think about Cousin Edith Embler? How far can we trust her? Well, obviously you don't trust her, and everything's still up in the air for me. I can't remember a time when I've been more upset about, well, what I might call one of our cases. And we aren't even in danger this time."

"Or don't think we are," he said. "We still know almost nothing about Milton Sales. He could be dangerous."

"Too true."

He decided not to mention his concerns about what the sheriff's department might be thinking of Carrie McCrite right now. Their background check on her would reveal she had no criminal record, but probably would tell them about some of McCrite and King's experiences helping local police departments with investigations in areas where they were, of all things, vacationing. The deputies might think that was odd.

He could explain it easily. Where other people ignored peculiarities and events going on around them, especially if they had the scent of unpleasantness, or might interrupt planned activities, Carrie not only noticed things, she headed right into the middle of them.

His wife could probably join Sergeant Friday from the long-ago television program, *Dragnet,* in saying "Just doing my job." Which was, as she repeatedly told him, helping people.

Caution wasn't a word in Carrie's vocabulary. Well, it was in his nature to be cautious, and to watch over her when she wasn't.

"Are you at all worried about tomorrow?" he asked.

"Hmm, not really. But I'm sure glad you're going to be with us all day."

"Last day at the fair. Maybe Edie's last day to connect with Milton Sales?"

"Yes, I know." She nodded. "I know."

Chapter Eleven

FOUR WOODEN TOYS

R oger opened the front door as soon as he heard Henry's truck pull up. "Y'all come on in. Got supper ready. Beans and cornbread. Shirley and Edie are already eating. It ain't fancy, but it's fillin'."

Carrie almost wept with gratitude. At this moment she couldn't think of a bigger blessing than an already prepared supper of beans and cornbread. She couldn't even manage a protest that she didn't expect the Booths to serve them supper. She was too tired and hungry to think of anything other than a bowl of Roger's famous bean soup.

When she turned to hang her sweater on a hook behind the truck seats, she noticed a box on the floor. It looked like one Shirley used to move things to the fair, so she picked it up, thinking Henry was returning it. They sure weren't going to need many boxes for quilts or Cuddlys coming back here tomorrow night.

Something heavy slid across the bottom of the box. "What's this?" she asked Henry.

"Oh, yeah. Forgot. Edie found them at the back of the booth. They're the wood toys you bought for Jeremy and Jemima. I figured at some point you managed to connect with Sales about gifts for the twins. You left them behind when you went with Investigator Burke."

"Oh, no! I didn't buy them. Milton Sales left them under the counter in his booth, and the guy next to him asked me to take them to the fair office. In all the commotion, I just plain forgot. I'll take them to the office tomorrow."

"I seem to recall you told the investigator you went back to Sales's booth to see if you could find toys for the twins."

"Well, I lied. I couldn't exactly say why I was really interested in him, could I?"

"Understood. And why don't we carry them inside now? I'd like to see his work, and I think Shirley and Roger would, too."

Roger said he'd clear the table after supper, but everyone insisted on carrying their own dishes to the sink for him. When he came back to take his seat, Henry was just adding the last toy, a cow, to the line-up standing on the red gingham cloth.

Shirley reached out to pull the heavy cord attached to the cow, and it rolled slowly across the table toward her. She picked it up, and said, "Whoee, these are right fancy, lots of work here. This cow must be eight inches high with the wheels. I wonder how much he's asking for these. I'd like to buy this cow, but how can I do that, since the fella has gone missing? Guess we gotta find him, that's all there is to it."

She turned the cow upside down. "Lookie there, she even has a bag and teats ready for milking. I wonder how long it took him to make . . . who-eee, this is loose . . . what the dickens?"

She grabbed at the udder as it fell off and bounced to the table, leaving a large hole under the cow that was now spilling white powder.

She'd reached out to brush at the powder when Henry said, "Wait, Shirley, don't touch that stuff."

She jerked back, and said a barely audible, "Is it anthrax? Oh, glory. In my kitchen?"

"I'm sure it isn't anthrax, but it could be an illegal drug."

"Mebee it's powdered milk and the guy is making a joke."

"Well, let's see." He picked up another toy, the horse, and, after some looking and poking his fingernail into cracks, discovered the animal's head came off, spilling more white powder. In turn he explored the chicken, which also had a removable head, and a goat, who's solid-looking feed bucket came away from the painted grass base the animal stood on.

While Roger and Shirley, Edie and Carrie sat in stunned silence, Henry took out his cell phone, scrolled through the directory, and punched the number for the sheriff's department.

At the end of a short conversation, he told them, "Someone will bring a drug test kit right out. He asks that we all wait here. Sorry, Shirley."

She got to her feet. "I'd best make more coffee."

An hour later they stood in a circle around the kitchen table, looking at the set of clear plastic drug test pouches the deputy was working with. The contents of every pouch had turned blue.

"This blue color indicates the powder in these animals doesn't test positive for any of the drugs we normally find," he said. "I'm guessing it's baking soda, but the state crime lab will tell us for sure."

Shirley went to a kitchen cabinet and came back with a plate and a familiar yellow box. She spilled some of the box's contents on the plate.

"By golly," Roger said, "the stuff does look exactly like our baking soda."

The deputy, who was beginning to nest the labeled test pouches in the chain of evidence box he'd brought with him, said, "It's not time to trust that conclusion yet. An officer will take all these samples to Little Rock tomorrow. Then we'll know for sure what it is."

He picked up the toy horse. "Whose animals are these? I need to take them with me."

"They actually belong to a missing person named Milton Sales," Carrie said, "Ask Investigator Burke about that. He knows. But for the time being, you can put me down as caretaker of the animals. What I want to know, though, is why somebody would take the trouble to hide a substance that's possibly baking soda in a way that causes us—or anyone—to think it could be a drug like cocaine or heroin?"

"Deception. Baking soda is sure a lot cheaper than cocaine, for example. My best guess is the substitution was meant to deceive. I've even known poison to be substituted for a drug when malice was intended. That's one reason we'll send this to the crime lab. We need to know exactly what we have here."

"Somebody is playing with fire," Henry said.

The deputy nodded. "For sure. I don't know how all of you got involved in this, but I'd advise caution if you have any more contact with the person owning these animals. We'll stay in touch with Ms. McCrite and Major King, and they can keep the rest of you informed.

"I understand all of you but Mr. Booth will be at the War Eagle Craft Fair tomorrow. Ms. McCrite, I know an investigator will want to hear again how you got these animals, and how you're involved with the man who made them. If someone from our department doesn't contact you at the fair, they definitely will on Monday. Actually, it would probably be best if tomorrow seemed to be a normal fair day, with no one in uniform coming near you. However, I'm thinking we might have a deputy in plain clothes on guard, just in case."

"We're Critter Quilts and Baby Cuddlys, fourth space from the front on the right. Tent number three," Shirley said. "Hours eight 'til four."

The deputy made a note as Carrie spoke up. "At least one of the exhibitors knows I had the animals. Milton Sales left them behind when he vacated his space. A man named John Harley, in the space next to Sales, said they were expensive, and he didn't want responsibility for them. He asked me to take the toys to the fair office since he was too busy. But we were covered over with customers when I got back to our place, so I put them in the box and then forgot all about them."

"Well, so far as he knows, you did take the toys to the office," the deputy said.

"Thanks for doing all the dish washing," Roger told Edie as he followed them to the door.

"I enjoy that sort of thing," she said.

Carrie wondered how anyone could truly enjoy cleaning up an after dinner mess. She had noticed Edie asked about the location of a bathroom as soon as the deputy rang the Booth's doorbell and, after her return, by-passed the table and busied herself at the kitchen sink, washing dishes and scrubbing the bean pot. In fact, as Carrie thought about it, there had never been an occasion for anyone to introduce Edie. The deputy may have even thought she was household help.

Coincidence? She doubted it. But she decided not to mention her observations while the two of them made the short drive home in her car.

"It seems unproductive to have this rental car just sitting here," Edie said when Carrie pulled into the garage. "I think I'll drive myself to the fair tomorrow. Are you going to pick up Shirley like you did today?"

"Yes, and there'll be plenty of room for you going and coming. I'm to bring back left-over stock, but we won't have much of that. Henry is driving separately in his truck. That way he can help haul things back to Shirley's, since we won't have Eleanor's van like we did when we set up. Roger is coming right before closing. He'll help take the display racks and backdrop apart and load those in the trucks."

"I'd really rather drive myself, Carrie. I'm used to being independent. I'll meet you at the fair before opening, and I can help haul things back at the end of the day."

"You aren't concerned about those two guys who've been looking for you?"

"Well yes, assuming they haven't given up and left the area. But in any case they haven't seen this car as far as I know. I can change again if I get worried."

"Okay, but you don't have a pass for the exhibitor parking."

"It won't matter, will it? I'll be there early enough that I can easily find a good place in the regular lot."

Though Henry moved his truck to let Edie out before 6:30 on Sunday morning and she left immediately, saying she'd get breakfast out, she hadn't arrived at Critter Quilts and Cuddlys by 9:30. Fair attendance was lighter than it had been the day before, so Shirley and Carrie could easily handle sales with a little help from Henry, who wrote tickets and took payments when they had busy spurts. Nevertheless, Carrie kept looking at her watch. Edie had said nothing about being late. She'd even mentioned she'd be there early enough to find a good parking place in the visitors' lot.

"I'm worried about Edie," she said to Shirley and Henry during a quiet moment. "I wonder if she decided to run an errand, or something, and it's taking longer than she thought it would."

"I wouldn't be surprised," Shirley said. "Otherwise, why drive herself? Seems dumb, since she could've just as easy come with us."

"Yes, I know," Carrie said as she watched a woman maneuver a stroller holding two children down the grass-covered aisle. Both of the kids were crying, and she wished their mother would look toward Shirley's Cuddly display. No luck, the woman was too involved in repeating "Shhh, hush" over and over to look at anything but her children and continue shoving the stroller. Carrie resisted the temptation to hand the poor woman a Cuddly for show and tell.

Shirley said, "You reckon she had an appointment and, and . . . ran into some kind of trouble?"

"But, why would she risk that?" Carrie asked, coming back to the Edie problem. "She doesn't seem stupid or foolish, and we've heard nothing about an appointment, or her wanting to meet anyone but Milton Sales."

"Could be that's exactly what she's doing," Shirley said. "Meeting Milton Sales, I mean."

"Him? But how would she work that out? " Carrie asked.

"She's got a cell phone, so could make all kinds of plans you folks wouldn't hear about. And did you notice how she hung back when that deputy sheriff was at our house last night? The woman's hiding secrets, mark my words. Haven't you been wondering why she won't tell the deputies about her search for Sales? Has she said anything more to you about that? And, how about those two guys in the dark suits who were asking about her? Find out anything about them?"

"No," Henry said. "But she's been with us all the time except now. It would have been hard for her to connect with anyone and make plans for a meeting. Most cell phones won't work where we live."

"She's been with you *except* for the time she was on break here, or was with me driving home," Shirley reminded them. "She spent most of the time going home asking about Hobbs State Park. When I told her it was the largest Arkansas State Park, she seemed mostly curious about the sections near here; Van Winkle Hollow and the visitor center. If I was you, I'd be curious to find out if she decided to have a look over there this morning, and mebee not just to sightsee, either."

After a short silence, Henry said, "Interesting. If you two can get along without my help for an hour or so, I think I will look around the area for her. Of course it's possible she decided to run for some reason, but all her things are at our house and she doesn't have a key. I'm thinking she might be meeting someone, as you suggest."

Carrie said, "I suppose it could be Milton Sales. It's possible he told her more about how to contact him than just the invitation to meet at his RV on Thursday. Seems to me asking so much about Hobbs is kind of peculiar, since she hasn't played tourist before. Her only interest in sightseeing around here was War Eagle Mill, and that turned out to be because she'd heard the name in connection with Sales. Hobbs might be a logical place for them to meet. Sales could know it well, and she'd be able to find it easily from here. It is rather public, but, assuming Sales is interested in hiding himself right now, it's also a huge place where one could remain anonymous or even hidden with little extra trouble. So, you go on, we'll be fine. I bet the crowds won't get really big until afternoon, this being Sunday."

Henry said, "I'll check around here and at Hobbs. Even if someone knows you had those hollow toys, you'll be safe, because I see the sheriff's office has sent someone in plain clothes to keep an eye on you."

"Really?" Carrie said. "Where?"

"Woman in green slacks and long suit jacket. You probably didn't notice her working with the candle seller across the way. Does the candle seller look familiar? She been here all during the fair?"

"Yes," both Shirley and Carrie said.

"But, not the woman in green slacks," Carrie added, "and all she seems to be doing is wrapping whatever sells, though I admit I didn't see anything unusual in that. But Henry, how on earth would they manage working her in without having to tell the candle maker what's going on, and getting her all excited about it?"

"Well, the candle maker could believe they're working a sting, and she's proud to have been asked to help. Maybe she was told that the couple selling leather goods is suspected of using skins from endangered species to make their purses and belts. Or maybe someone reported that those bottled seasonings over there have bits of chopped straw as a filler, and the deputy is keeping an eye out while someone at a lab tests whatever the suspect merchandise is supposed to be. They will, of course, find out there is no taint or no endangered species by the time the fair closes. So all that's happened is a doubly interesting day for the candle maker, and good cover for the undercover officer."

"I'll be jiggered," said Shirley.

"Is she carrying?" Carrie asked, indicating the woman in green with her elbow.

"Yes," Henry said. "She has a gun belt. That's why the long jacket, and why she looks rather, uh, rotund in the middle."

Carrie rolled her lips in to keep from chuckling, then said, "They are taking this seriously, then."

"You bet. Okay. I'll be back in an hour or so. While I'm gone, neither of you is to leave this space, right? And I wouldn't leave myself if it weren't for that woman in green."

Carrie and Shirley both nodded, and began saying hello and smiling at people passing by their counter.

Henry walked slowly through the crowds, stopping to look at a sign telling the history of War Eagle Mills Farm, where the fair was being held. He'd learned long ago that reading signs or looking in shop windows gave him good cover for surveillance. Next, he walked across the iron and wood War Eagle River Bridge, now more busy with people than cars, scanning the area as he went. On the mill side of the river he stopped as if to read the sign commemorating the hundredth anniversary of the bridge in 2008, and its restoration to safety and sturdiness in 2010. He saw no car like Edie's, or any woman who resembled her.

He went inside the mill, pretended to look over a display of grains and flours, climbed the stairs to study the kitchen equipment and crafts on the second floor, then went up another flight to survey the Bean Palace Restaurant as if he were looking for a friend.

He saw only strangers.

After hurrying through the aisles of fair booths fanning out from the mill, he got into his truck and headed east on Highway 12 toward Hobbs.

There was no white car in the parking lot for Van Winkle Hollow National Historic Site, so he decided to go on toward the park's visitor center and natural history museum.

Be darned. There were two men sitting in a dark blue car in the visitor center parking lot. Were these the guys that had come to their home looking for Edie? And there, on the other side of the lot, was a familiar-looking white car. He drove around as if searching for a parking place. The lot was nearly full, so what he was doing wouldn't look odd. Yes. The car was Edie's.

He pulled in a space, and sat still for a few moments, wondering whether he should wait to see what the men did, or go inside and look for Edie. When they made no move to leave their car, he decided they might be waiting for Edie to come out, so he left the truck and followed a sidewalk to the large, rustic building. Though the display and activity areas covered a lot of territory, it didn't take him long to tour all of them and decide Edie wasn't there. He even asked a woman coming from the restroom if his wife was inside. No, no one but the woman had been in there.

The Ozark Plateau Trail and picnic area were the only remaining options easily accessible from the visitor center. He hurried out the building's side door and started along the paved part of the trail. Most of the deciduous trees still held their colored fall leaves, and, though the pine trees were tall, with needles high off the ground, seeing through the forest for any distance was still difficult. There were several walkers enjoying the warm temperatures and sunny skies. Too bad he and Carrie weren't also enjoying this lovely day together.

All the benches he passed on the paved part of the trail were empty, but, on a bench at the end of a gravel side path he thought he saw movement through the trees, and paused to look more carefully. Finally he took a few cautious steps along the path. Yes, two people, deep in conversation. He wondered if what they were talking about was absorbing all their attention. If so, they evidently weren't afraid of anyone coming up on them unexpectedly.

The woman had to be Edie. Smallish, beige hair, beige slacks and sweater. She'd taken the wig off. It was probably in that tote beside her. And, who was the guy? Could this be Milton Sales? He had a ball cap on, and the hair showing in back was brown sprinkled with grey, instead of the light brown Carrie described. Didn't matter. Sales, like Edie, could own a wig. However, having that kind of thing at hand did indicate the man anticipated a need to disguise his looks at times. Curious.

Well, he was going to find out who Edie's companion was.

Henry tried to walk quietly as he drew closer to the bench, but finally the crunch of his feet on gravel alerted her. She stood, and turned to see who was coming. The man stayed seated and did not look around.

"Hello, Edie," Henry said.

Chapter Twelve

A PASSIONATE DISGUISE

F or a moment she said nothing. Then she began "I . . . ," glanced at her companion, and stopped.

Henry didn't speak either, just stared at her for a minute before shifting his gaze to the man seated on the bench, who had turned sideways. Then he looked back at Edie.

"Yes?" he said, finally.

"How did you find me?"

"Logic."

"I see."

Henry waited, watching her think her remarks into position, wondering what would come next.

"I stopped for breakfast next to the Interstate, and ran into an old friend from DC who's heading to Texas to visit his . . . daughter. I wanted to see this park, and the fast-food place was noisy and crowded, so I suggested we come here to continue our conversation. Obviously I lost track of time. I shouldn't have left Shirley and Carrie to handle sales alone, and I'm going to the fair right now. Tony has decided to stay over in this area, so he and I can get together again tomorrow."

Tony? Really? Other than the grey hair color, this man looks a heck of a lot like Milton Sales as Carrie described him. I guess Edie's afraid I'll report him to the sheriff, and the first name she came up with is from the novel by Tony Hillerman on the table by my reading chair. What will she do when she realizes where she grabbed the name?

"Henry King, this is Tony . . . Hillman."

There was a moment of awkward silence before "Tony" stood, glanced at

Henry, said a muffled "Pleased to meet you," then faced Edie. "I've got to get going, find a place to stay. See you Monday. Call me on my cell."

At that, Milton/Tony bolted off the trail and down through the hollow. He headed west—maybe in the direction of the parking lot—leaving Henry feeling helpless, muddled, and angry as he watched the man who was probably a drug dealer disappear among the trees and underbrush.

But, what had his options been? He couldn't have forced him to stay. He had no authority, no proof of any criminal activity, though he knew several people in the county sheriff's office were very interested in talking with Milton Sales. Would asking the man to stay and answer a few questions have done any good? Probably not, but why hadn't he spoken up, challenging Edie's lies?

Too late now. Years past, as a police officer, he could have forced the issue. But not today. He hadn't a clue whether or not Sales was armed. Except in extreme circumstances, he didn't carry a gun himself and wouldn't use it here, anyway.

Henry turned toward the woman who had put him in this mess. "Cut the bull, Edie. That was Milton Sales, wasn't it? The man you have barely met, right? The man who made toys stuffed with some substance that mimics illegal drugs?"

"Milton didn't make those toys. He doesn't make anything like them, and he says his counter shelf was empty after he packed up to move out yesterday. The four hollow pieces were put there later. Ask Carrie to think back over what she saw in his booth. Was there anything that looked like those four? He said proof would be that he signs all his pieces. Were those animals signed? I didn't get a good look at them so don't know, but if they were signed, the signature was forged."

"I didn't see a signature. So, why did he leave the fair?"

"Well, I . . . don't know."

"Edie, tell me the truth or I'm walking out right now. But first, in fairness, I should tell you there are two men sitting in a dark blue car in the parking lot. They undoubtedly ID'd your rental car. There's no way you can get to that car without walking by them. If they know who Milton Sales is, they may grab him, too."

He saw the troubled look on her face before she turned her back on him. In a minute, still facing the woods, she said. "I don't think they know what Milton looks like, but still, they could ruin everything."

"Ruin what?"

"Henry, can I trust you? Really trust you? I'd have to break all kinds of rules to say anything to you at all."

"Edie, I was a cop for thirty-five years. In my time I handled a lot of secrets that no one will ever hear from me, even now.

"Could those secrets put you in danger—if anyone knew, I mean?"

"Some. Possibly."

After a silence, she said, "Well, what I'm going to tell you now could, too. You ever hear of the Bureau of Drug Abuse Control?"

He drew it out of the past. "Formed under the old Department of Health, Education, and Welfare in the mid sixties. Put under HEW because, back then, drug use was considered more of a medical problem than one belonging to law enforcement, as you confirmed when you were going through the history of drug use at our home. That Bureau didn't last long, though."

"Right. It didn't. Things were changing rapidly back then. Did Kansas City ever deal with drug abuse by truckers?"

"Wasn't my department, but I heard something about it. Mainly amphetamines and barbiturates, right? I think several were caught distributing. I can see how the easy opportunity to distribute would prove a temptation to some."

"Yes. Narcotics officers were sent undercover in the trucking community to weed out offenders."

"Uh-huh. As I recall, KCPD dealt with a few of those officers. Some turned out to be of questionable integrity themselves, though Kansas City didn't get involved in proving that. Also, back then, misuse of dangerous drugs was growing so rapidly that I'm sure lawmakers' constituents felt things were getting out of hand. Something new had to be tried. Eventual result, the Drug Enforcement Administration."

"Yes. My father was one of the undercover narcotics officers said to be of questionable integrity, though that was never confirmed before he disappeared. After? He was gone, but the smudge against his name remained."

"Ahh, you know much more than you told us. And how did you learn it?"

She turned to face him again. "Because I'm part of the system, Henry. I worked as an administrative assistant in the Department of Justice. I didn't lie when I said I was retired, or that I did research and wrote speeches for people in government, but the job I held most recently, and for many years, was with the Drug Enforcement Administration, an arm of DOJ since 1973. I retired from that job three years ago, but recently I've been doing a bit of work as a confidential source for them, mainly because—having acquired the status of senior citizen—I don't look like an agent."

Henry knew laughing wasn't at all appropriate but he laughed anyway. "You mean like Emily Polifax in the novels by Dorothy Gilman? Carrie loves those, and I've enjoyed listening to a couple of them as recorded books when we're in the car."

"Yes, pretty much like that, except I don't work for the CIA." Now she smiled too, but the smile disappeared a couple of seconds later.

"Henry, I see those two guys. "

This time his brain clicked into action immediately. "I guess they got tired of waiting for you. Have they seen you yet?"

"I don't think so, they just turned onto one of the sections of trail running parallel to this about fifty yards away. Your body is shielding me from their view."

"Put on your wig quickly, and don't be surprised at what I do."

As soon as the dark curls were in place, he took her in his arms.

Murmuring into the prickly curls, he said, "Tell me now why they're looking for you and who they are."

"I don't know, I—don't—know."

She lifted her face and he bent his head as if he were kissing her. Would this pose seem plausible to those men? After all, he and Edie didn't exactly fit the image of young lovers using a private place for a quick interlude. But, maybe with that wig . . . and Edie's face was hidden against his chest now. Older man, young bimbo?

He heard their shoes crunching on the gravel behind him, and still keeping his body between them and Edie, he turned to look over his shoulder, following the look with a growled "This area is taken guys, buzz off."

"You seen a woman with dyed blond hair around here?"

"Nope, haven't seen or heard anyone but me and Phyllis. Like I said, buzz off. Go find your blond somewhere else." He moved away from Edie a couple of inches, took one arm from her back, and gave his pants an obvious tug, as if settling them in a more convenient location. While he was doing this, she managed to unfasten the beige slacks and let them drop around her feet. She uttered an exaggerated gasp as they fell, and, without thinking, he bent his knees slightly, preparing to retrieve them for her.

It took only a second for him to realize she had entered into the charade, had meant for the slacks to fall, and his responding movement only added to the reality of their pretend activities. *Oh, crap.*

Edie lifted her arms from his waist to around his neck, pulled his head down, and the kiss he had pretended became real.

He wanted more than anything to jerk his head back, but stayed where he was as heavy footsteps crunching gravel came closer. Then the second man said, "We're only half way around this trail, come on, let lover boy alone. We're wasting time. She's probably up ahead."

As soon as he heard that, Henry turned his head to break the kiss, but held the rest of the pose for several minutes, occasionally moving as if to touch or caress, while thinking the responding moves by Edie were more personal than necessary.

Then, at last, the footsteps faded away.

His reaction to the appearance of the two men, and the desire to protect this woman by acting out a scene he had played as a disguise in years past, had been automatic. But now he felt only disgust with himself, and, as soon as he thought it was safe, he pulled completely away from her.

"Leave that wig on while we go to my car. If there is any evidence those two guys are around there, we'll have to leave yours in the lot."

"Yes." She re-fastened her slacks, then put her arm around his waist as they walked along the path. Knowing it was safest, he rested his own arm on her shoulders.

"Are you going to tell Carrie about the scene we just played?"

He kept moving along the path with her, but let his words express the distaste he felt. "What I discuss with my wife is none of your business, and right now I am feeling only regret for that scene, necessary though it may have been. Assuming what you had begun to tell me was the truth, it was important to protect you, but only because we don't know who those men are. At the moment a romantic charade seemed our only option. I've used it once or twice in years past with success."

"I'm sorry, Henry. It was stupid of me to meet Milton here. I suggest you think of what happened back there as something you did only in the line of duty. Then forget it."

"You still haven't told me what part Milton Sales plays in all this. The rest of the story?"

"Later. For now, we'll forget what just happened."

"You know that's not in the cards. Carrie, Shirley, and I agreed I needed to look for you, and they know I was looking here at Hobbs. Whatever I do, I am not lying to my wife."

"Your choice, Henry, your choice. I say you found me here with Milton. The men came. We hid in the trees until the men left. That's enough to explain. Then forget it."

Sure, he thought, then quickly switched to planning options if the men showed up again.

As soon as the parking lot was in view he said, "The dark blue car is still in the lot but, since it's empty, I suggest you go to your car immediately. Drive out. I'll wait a few minutes to be sure they don't show up and follow you. Got your cell phone?"

"Yes, in my purse."

"Turn it on and lay it on the seat. If you don't hear from me, it's clear and you can go straight to the fair. If they follow you, I'll phone a warning. In that case, continue down the highway into town. Go to the Harps Grocery located on the corner where you turned to come to War Eagle. Park in an open area, walk inside, always being sure people in the lot can see you clearly. Take a cart, and head for the produce section. Stay in that section, maybe picking up one or two things as you browse. It's nice and open there, with a view to the deli and bakery. People will be around. Wait in that area until I come."

She nodded, and hurried toward her car.

He headed across the parking lot, wondering if the love scene and her overly warm response was something Edith Embler really planned to forget. He didn't want to hurt Carrie, but if he didn't tell her how he had protected her cousin . . . well, would Edie spill the beans? She might even threaten to tell Carrie later, especially if the two of them didn't continue helping her with the resolution of whatever was going on here. And that would be blackmail.

Nuts! He was probably making too much of this. As soon as he and Carrie were alone, he'd just share the straightforward facts, how he hadn't had an option. Carrie would understand, in fact, since she was more interested in aiding her cousin than he was, she'd probably approve.

But, Edie? Whatever degree of truth she'd told him, whatever her job was, he still didn't trust her. A confidential source for DEA? Well, maybe, but in his experience, such people were sometimes so used to manipulating facts while working to achieve a goal that it was hard for them to tell full truth about anything.

After he got in his truck he sat without moving, watching Edie drive out of the lot and turn west. He wished, oh how he wished she'd turned east and headed out of their lives.

No sign of the men. Time to go back to Carrie and Shirley. Time to protect his wife from this woman's self-focused quest, but first . . .

He dialed Carrie's cell phone. "Found her. She's on her way back to you. She probably won't say anything by way of an excuse, but if she does, don't believe a word she says until I get there. Everything okay? Good. Love you, too."

He turned the key, listened to the motor catch, and wondered if there was any way he could keep the events at Hobbs from either haunting him, or causing hurt.

If he told all, would Carrie really understand? Women, including his Cara, could sure be unpredictable.

Then another unsettling thought startled him, and he pulled his hands away from the steering wheel.

Was there lipstick on his shirt?

Chapter Thirteen

FOLLOWING IN HER FATHER'S FOOTSTEPS

B eing caught with lipstick on a shirt sounded like a joke, but those jokes must have some basis. Obviously men had been caught when wives or girlfriends found an unfamiliar lipstick smear on their clothing. He couldn't see enough in the little rear vision mirror to be sure he was unsmudged, therefore it would be best to take time for a trip to the Men's, just in case. A lipstick smear was no way to introduce the interlude with Edie to his wife.

He slammed the truck door and hurried toward the building.

Yes! A good mirror. He was completing his inspection of a totally clean shirt when the door opened and the two men in dark suits came in, exchanging looks when they saw him. They were way too close before he had time to move.

"Well now," the largest one said, coming to stand on his left, "Get finished with your playtime?"

Henry's response was a low, growling hum.

The other man stood on his right. "Y'know, Arnie, this is a public park. A *very public* park. Odd place for such private activities."

Both men moved even closer until they were pushing at him from either side. Henry contemplated his options. Probably better to stand still and find out what was going to shake out here. Besides, they outdid him in muscle, and didn't look more than forty. And, from what Carrie had said, he assumed both of them were armed.

The larger of the two—Arnie—said, "Tell me, *Sir,* what your name is and what's going on here?"

Henry said, "Move away from me. I don't know who you are or what your game is, but my watch is from Target and I probably have forty bucks on me, tops. My credit card is at home. If you hassle me, all I have to do is shout. As you say, this is a very public park."

Arnie's companion said, "Hey, we're the good guys, just looking for a very bad woman. Maybe your friend is that woman. Dumb of us not to realize she might be wearing a wig. So, where did she go? If we're to assume you're one of us good guys, why are you protecting her? Or, are you a bad guy we should be checking up on?" His hand suddenly shot out, and he grabbed Henry's right wrist. "Let's see your wallet, *Sir.*"

"Not until you prove to me who you are and why you want Phyllis."

Arnie took a leather badge holder from an inside jacket pocket, held it toward Henry briefly, shoved it back in his pocket. He had just clamped his hand around Henry's left wrist when the room door opened and five teens bounced in, jostling and laughing. As soon as they were inside, all five went silent. "Whoa," the tallest one said. "What's goin' on here?" The other four came closer, obviously scenting adventure.

The men let go of Henry's wrists, and Henry eyed the kids, hoping no more serious confrontation was pending. They were big guys, maybe part of a high school football team.

However, what one of the boys said next was more unsettling than the presence of Arnie and Company.

"You two messin' with this old guy?"

Henry looked around at the boys. Then, waking up enough to take advantage of the unexpected backup, he said, "They are. I think they were planning to rob me."

He moved behind two of the boys as if he wanted to use them as a shield, and quickly lifted his cell phone over their heads, thinking he might get a photo of at least one of the men. Then, jamming the phone in his pocket, he hurried out the door, hoping he could make it to his truck before the two men untangled themselves from the kids.

He made it out of the building, jogged down the sidewalk and across the parking lot. So far, so good. But, *old guy?*

While half-wondering if he should have stayed to find out more about who those men were and what they wanted, he jumped in the truck, turned the key, and jammed his foot on the gas. *Old guy?* He wouldn't tell Carrie what they'd called him.

The truck leapt out of its parking space. He didn't see any sign of the men, and no dark car followed him down the highway.

They called me an old guy.

Forget it, King. Those boys are young.

Come to think of it, when he was in high school, most of his teachers looked ancient to him. He remembered how surprised he'd been when he saw his math teacher, maybe twenty-five years later, and learned he'd just retired.

When Edie arrived back at the fair tent she slipped smoothly into helping customers with only a smile and brief apology, but no explanation. Shirley and Carrie, prepared by Henry's call, said nothing, but did exchange eyebrow-raising glances when Edie turned away to pull one of the few remaining baby quilts off the display for a customer. Business had picked up, so the lack of time for any private conversation wasn't awkward. When Henry arrived about forty-five minutes later he, too, went into work mode, writing tickets and making change without comment.

Carrie, bursting with questions, worked absently, once even forgetting which of the women in front of her wanted the pale green Cuddly. Something about this situation was weird, she sensed that, and had no answer to her *"Why?"* Part of the problem was that Henry seemed as distracted as she. There were undercurrents swirling inside him, and it was maddening that she had no opportunity to ask what was going on.

Though they hadn't been together for a lifetime, as Investigator Burke had assumed, she realized now that her ability to pick up mental currents from Henry was surprisingly well developed. She wondered if it was the same with him.

The afternoon rocketed by. All the baby quilts were gone, and only a few Cuddlys hung on display stands as the four o'clock closing time approached.

Shortly before closing, Henry took time to call Jason's cell phone, and learned Randy was definitely on the mend, Patricia was her old happy self again, and the twins were, well, feisty. Randy's mom had arrived and could help with care of the twins, so the grandparents were now spelling each other for hospital visits.

After telling Jason about the huge selling success the fair had been for Shirley, Henry asked when the Stacks contemplated coming home. He got no definite answer, though Jason said Eleanor was beginning to miss her shop and realized keeping it open could be a burden for her friends.

Since so much was happening at present, Henry secretly agreed about shop-keeping being a burden. However, he said only "We'll be glad to see you," when Jason informed him they'd probably return home some time during the week, now that Randy's mom was there to stay for a while.

Roger appeared at four and he, Carrie, Edie, and Henry began dismantling the booth while Shirley finished filling out forms and went to join the long line of exhibitors waiting to turn in paperwork and fees at the fair office.

And that was that. The War Eagle Craft Fair was over.

After the trucks were packed, Roger decided to wander around, watching exhibitor break-down, leaving Carrie, Edie, and Henry alone to sit on stools remaining in the booth space.

"Edie, what are you going to do now about finding Milton Sales?" Carrie asked.

"She's found him," Henry said, and began the story of his search for Edie, seeing the car with the two men in the parking lot, and finding Edie with Milton Sales at the end of a secluded path at Hobbs.

"How did you know to meet him there?" Carrie asked, seeking verification for Shirley's guess that Edie and Milton had made plans for more than one get-together when they met at his booth on Thursday morning.

"We exchanged cell phone numbers last Thursday."

"Well then, I assume your quest is ended." Carrie said.

"More complicated than that," Edie replied.

Henry said, "As soon as I properly identified Sales he hurried off, and there was nothing I could do about that. I did hear him say he and Edie plan to meet somewhere tomorrow. But, in the meantime, Edie had just begun to tell me her story when the two men showed up on the paved part of the path behind us. I'd heard enough by then to know it was important to keep them away from her, at least for the time being, so I did the only thing I could think of at the time. I put my arms around her and pretended we were deep in a romantic session. Fortunately they were looking for a blond and she had her wig on."

Carrie began laughing, then glanced at Edie, said, "Sorry," and patted Henry's knee. "Quick thinking," she continued. "So what happened then?"

She thinks it's funny? Then he got it.

She laughed at my romantic scene with Cousin Edie because it was so obviously play-acting and, well, ridiculous, and she's right about that! I suppose she apologized to Edie because the laugh might be considered insulting to a woman.

"When the men approached and asked if we'd seen a blond woman on the path, Edie kept her face buried in my chest. I acted gruff, said we hadn't seen the woman, and warned them off. After they left, the two of us headed for the parking lot.

"Since the men were nowhere in sight, I felt it was safe for Edie to drive her car back here. Obviously they'd ID'd it, or else they knew who Sales was and had some reason for following him. I gambled that they wouldn't know to look for Edie here at the fair, and stayed in the Hobbs' parking lot for a while to see if they'd return to their car. When they didn't show up, I went back in the Visitor Center to double check, and ran into them in the men's room."

"What happened then?"

"A bunch of teen-aged boys ended up getting me out of a mess." He described what had happened, leaving out the term "old guy."

"Oh my. Thank goodness for those boys."

"I think I got a picture of at least one of the men. I held my camera over my head from behind the kids and gambled on what it would get." He took out his cell phone, checked the photo, then handed it to Carrie. "It's blurry, but does either of those guys look like Agent Arnie?"

"Yes, I'm sure that's who the one on the right is. Since he stayed in the car, I didn't see enough of the other man to identify him." She held the phone toward Edie. "Do you recognize either of them? Could they be the men you saw at the motel?"

Edie squinted at the picture. "I don't know. Since it was dark I didn't get enough of a look at either of them to be able to say for sure, though there are similarities."

Henry put his phone away and Carrie said, "Okay, then, what's the rest of the story? There must be a reason why Cousin Edie is worth protecting in this elaborate manner."

Henry and Carrie both looked at Edie, who had said nothing, and was now staring at the ground.

"She says she works as a confidential source for the Drug Enforcement Administration under the Department of Justice. It's something like being undercover. That's as far as she got in her story before the two guys in suits showed up."

Edie looked up, fire in her eyes. "I didn't give you permission to tell this."

"Carrie and I are a team, I don't keep secrets from her, and she is as able to respect confidences as I am. Understand this. You tell either of us something, you have told it to both."

"A source for what purpose?" Carrie asked Edie, ignoring the break.

"Hoping to help close down a pipeline for drugs feeding into the three corner Ozarks area of Arkansas, Oklahoma, and Missouri. One suspected cover for distribution here is craft fairs. I wondered if Milton, in addition to possibly having information about Dad, might be either a connection to dealers, or a distributor himself."

"Makes sense," Carrie said. "And your job makes sense. It's a connection to your father, isn't it?"

"Yes," Edie said. "That's a big part of it. It's a connection to him."

"Is there more? Did you find out anything from Sales?"

"He says Dad was killed in McAllen, Texas, by men who were supplying drugs to American truckers. Milton told me he, like Dad, was undercover at the time, but hadn't been exposed. He actually saw Dad's body, but doesn't know what happened to it after he left. Since the body was never found, perhaps they buried him. I hope they did."

She stopped, lapsing into silence. Carrie and Henry were silent too while she dealt with her own thoughts.

Finally Carrie said, "I'm sorry, Edie."

Henry nodded, then said "Is there any progress on uncovering drug sources here? Do you think one of them could be Milton Sales?"

"I'm not sure where he fits in, but he actually doesn't seem likely. For one thing, he says he didn't know about the RV gas lines being disconnected, and he seemed really worried about that."

"Odd," Henry said. "Whoever did it had little concern for the safety of people at the fair, which indicates the person is dangerous. Or, of course, it could be more than one person. And, I'm sure you realize Sales himself would be a likely person."

"Well, I guess that's possible though, as I said, he was terribly concerned. Acting? I don't know. For whatever reason, after I told him I knew his RV had been trashed, he said it worried him, but he wouldn't say more. However, concern about protecting vital information is why he removed his personal possessions from the place on Friday morning, including his laptop, clothing, and toiletries. He hid them in the boxes he uses to transport his toys, and stowed everything in his truck. He says he couldn't find a motel room in the area, so spent most of Friday night in the truck, which he parked in the exhibitor's lot at some distance from the RV. But he decided to make sure he'd gotten all that was important and, about eleven that night, went back into the RV."

"So, his stuff was out when the gas lines were disconnected," Henry said. "Don't you think that suggests Sales himself knew there might be an explosion and fire?"

"I guess it does," Edie said, looking troubled, "even though he said he didn't know about it. I . . . well, I don't know."

"What about the security guards?" Carrie wondered. "Where were they when he went back in his RV?"

"I asked that. He said the guard had just passed by and all was quiet when he decided to check the place."

"Seems to me he took a huge chance, " Henry said. "So, what, of such importance, was he worried about? Was it still there in all that mess, or did the searcher find and remove it? Another thing, whoever trashed the place and, ultimately, unfastened the gas lines, took a chance with the security guards too. It would sure be simpler if that person was Milton Sales himself. Only one entry."

Edie said, "He *says,* after seeing what had happened at the RV, he decided to leave the fair completely. He packed up his unsold toys early Saturday morning, as you know. He found a motel room that had just been vacated, stowed his stuff, and, I suppose, has been there since."

"I wonder about the RV, and his counter and display shelves," Carrie said. "The sheriff's people aren't going to let him waltz in and remove those."

"He seemed surprisingly unconcerned about them when we were talking at the park."

"Odd," Henry said. "The big question then is how he fits in all this. His actions are peculiar, to say the least, especially since he seems to be on the run now. Maybe his laptop holds whatever the searchers were looking for. It is possible the searcher or searchers unhooked the gas lines in anger as you suggest. So, is Sales a good guy or a bad guy?"

Edie said. "He's involved in something of course, but is he a drug dealer, or looking for drug dealers himself? I haven't heard anything about him from my office, so I don't think he's working for us."

Henry looked at his wife. "Edie says he told her he didn't make those toys with the powder in them, and his booth was empty when he left on

Saturday. Do you remember seeing anything like those pull toys when you bought my police car?"

"N-no. I guess I didn't."

"He said he signs all his pieces. Were those signed?" Edie asked.

"I didn't notice. I do know the police car is signed, though."

They sat silently for several minutes, ignoring the on-going hubbub around them. Finally Carrie asked, "I wonder about the birdhouse man, John Harley. He made sure I knew those toys were part of Milton Sales's stock. Now it seems he made a point of calling my attention to them. Could we consider that suspicious?"

Edie was looking thoughtful but had said nothing when Shirley re-joined them, waving a handful of papers. "I'm done," she said. "Where's Roger got to? Let's grab him and go find us something to eat."

Chapter Fourteen

SHIRLEY SHARES SUSPICIONS

"I need to change rental cars," Edie told Carrie and Henry as they were taking the stools they'd been sitting on to Carrie's car. "I'll get supper on my own and be back at your house by eight."

As Henry lifted the hatchback he said, "Edie, I don't think that's a good idea. Those guys certainly know it's a rental car, and probably where you got it."

"It won't be truly safe taking the car to your house, either," she said, "even if I park it in the garage. We already know those men have discovered a link between Carrie and me. So, I might as well exchange the car they've identified for a different model."

Carrie looked at her husband, wondering if Edie was going to win this one and go off on her own. *Hmmm, from the look on Henry's face, I'm betting on him.*

"All right," Henry said, "but if you want to return the car, we'll follow you to the rental place and wait while you turn it in. Don't get a replacement yet. You can ride with us for a day or two, unless you plan to move on right away."

"No, and I need a car. Don't forget, I have an appointment with Milton sometime tomorrow."

"You're going to have company for that," Henry said. "As for now, Carrie and I will go to the agency with you after we eat."

"How do I know you won't notify the sheriff's department about the meeting? It's no secret they're looking for Milton."

Carrie watched the exchange, trying to pick up nuances. *Milton? She's calling him Milton now. Is that a familiarity she hasn't admitted to us, or simply the common way many address each other these days, especially on the Internet?*

"Yes," Henry was saying, "I might notify the sheriff, but I won't do it before I see what Sales has to say. Think about it. If I turn him in up front, then—in their minds at least—all three of us get tangled further in whatever his business is. No guarantees after we talk, however. His disappearance, the destructive search of the RV, and the disconnected gas lines are enough to keep their interest in him lively, not to mention the four powder-filled toys Carrie picked up. I'm sure they'll want to keep their hold on that RV for a while, but it's a pretty expensive piece of equipment for him to walk away from. He'll want to show up and claim it eventually, and that's assuming he's cleared of any wrong-doing."

"Well, yes, but he's hardly going to show up and claim it now. As you say, they wouldn't let him take it away, though I'm not sure what they think it's evidence of. No one was hurt."

"Leaking gas?" Carrie said. "Possibility of an explosion or fire?"

"Okay, okay. So there are problems all around. But, you think he'll meet with me if he knows you'll be along? He's suspicious of everyone right now."

"Why would you tell him?" Henry asked.

Edie didn't answer, merely shrugged her shoulders.

Carrie thought, *Seems like Henry won this round.*

The rental car was returned without incident, and nothing more said about Monday's meeting with Sales.

At six a.m. on Monday, Carrie and Henry were sitting at the kitchen table drinking coffee when the phone rang. Carrie answered, and a male voice asked for Edie. When Henry mouthed the question "Milton Sales?" she nodded, shrugged, and went to knock on the guestroom door. When Edie, fully dressed, opened it, Carrie pointed to the phone on the nightstand. "For you."

Back in the kitchen she said, "He asked for Edie, so I assume he knows her voice well enough to recognize she wasn't the one answering."

While she was up she poured more coffee for both of them, and had just returned to her chair when Edie appeared.

"That was Milton. We're meeting for breakfast at War Eagle Mill. Nine o'clock." She lifted her chin and stared at Henry. "I assume we can make it by then."

Carrie looked from one to the other and took a sip of coffee to conceal her smile. *She's still miffed about who's calling some of the shots. Henry knows that, and he's ignoring it. Evidently he doesn't believe our presence is going to endanger her real mission—tracing a drug source into this part of the Ozarks.*

Keeping her expression bland, she said, "Coffee?" and, when Edie nodded, went to pour it.

Henry asked, "Did you tell him you had turned the car in?"

"Yes. And I told him I would be depending on you for a ride to the mill."

"What did he say?"

"Pretty skittish at first, so I had to say I trusted you . . . both of you," she finished, looking at Carrie. "I told him you were my cousin and we were tight. But don't you have an appointment with a deputy sheriff today?"

So we're suddenly tight? Best buddies? Carrie thought as she said, "The deputy who came here to test the powder said something about an appointment, but I don't want to talk to anyone official until after the meeting with Sales. Don't know what direction to go, or who I'm possibly covering for."

Edie winked at her. "Careful. You might get caught doing something illegal, or even working undercover."

Carrie ignored that. Her mind had moved on to another problem. "Odd he's chosen the Bean Palace. It's kind of boxed in, steep stairs to the third floor, no other exit. What if someone, law enforcement or not, follows either Sales or us? Catches us all there together?"

"You *are* thinking like an agent," Edie said. "But Milton says if someone is keeping tabs on any of us they'll know how to find us, no matter where we choose to meet. He also told me there are little-known back stairs for a quick and easy exit to the parking lot, if needed. We'll be right by the stairs if we park at the side of the mill facing the river."

"Remind me," Carrie said, "Why are you so interested in meeting him again when it obviously could invite more trouble for all of us? You found out what you wanted to know about your father, didn't you? So I'm guessing your continuing interest is only in Sales's possible connection to drug distribution. You want to clear up the issue of whether or not he's involved, right? On the other hand, why does he want to meet with you? Does he know what your job is? Otherwise, what possible reason could he have for a meeting this morning?"

Before Edie could say anything Henry spoke up, "She—and we—want to know how he's connected to those powder-filled toys. Even if we weren't curious about events at the RV, you and I are now part of this because of the toys. As for his reason for wanting to schedule a meeting? That's murky, I admit, and it could be because he's suspicious of Edie. He might wonder if her interest in finding him was truly because she wanted information about her father. Is she in danger from him? I doubt it. He could easily have killed her Sunday morning, but that's one reason we're going with her now. On the other hand, I wonder if he doesn't want to affirm his innocence of any wrong-doing through Edie, and now, through us as well."

"Us?"

"Yes. Yesterday I learned that Edie and Sales had exchanged cell phone numbers. Her cell phone doesn't work here, so how did he call?"

"Ohhhh. He used our land line."

"And, assuming she didn't give that number to him, how did he find the number?

"Phone book. He met you at Hobbs. He knows our names."

They both looked at Edie, and she nodded.

"So, he probably knows a lot more than our phone number. Thanks to the Internet, few of us have secrets any more. It is quite possible for any diligent searcher to learn our recent past connections to several criminal cases on the side of the law.

"Another reason we want to meet with Sales, Carrie, is that you're possibly suspected of connection to a crime because you had those powder-filled toys in your possession, and also showed a peculiar amount of interest in Sales while you were at the fair. We need to learn the history of those toys."

Carrie said, "Okay, I see all this. But, Edie's the only one who can clear me on the reason for my interest in Sales at the fair. And she hasn't chosen to do so thus far."

Edie had been turning her coffee mug around and around on the tabletop. She now pulled a paper napkin from the holder and concentrated on blotting a drip of coffee on the side of the mug.

Henry watched in silence while she did this, then said, "Here's something else. We really don't know who those two men followed to the park. Was it you, Edie? Or Sales? Both, maybe? The only way Carrie and I can get rid of the men as far as our own lives are concerned is to solve your mysteries. And of course both of us want to be sure you're not in any danger. By the way, I'm convinced those guys are not part of the FBI, no matter what badge Arnie is flaunting. The fact Ray found no evidence of an FBI connection is suggestive, if not final confirmation."

He reached out and took Carrie's hand across the table. "It looks like we've become part of another investigation, like it or not."

Carrie smiled at him. "Does anyone think it's odd Sales chose to return to the same neighborhood where there's been trouble? Maybe that should tell us something?"

"Tells us he knows the area at least," Henry said, "and maybe he wants to check on his RV from a safe distance—see what's happening there. I doubt the sheriff's department has bothered to tow it away, assuming the people who run the fair are okay with it being left on their property. They live right next to the fairgrounds, and would be able to see the RV from their front windows."

Carrie said, "Phooey. He could check on it less noticeably without three more people around to draw more attention to him."

The phone rang again and, before answering it, Carrie looked at the Caller ID. "Unidentified number, but the prefix is the same as the sheriff's office."

She waited until the answering machine picked up.

"Ms. McCrite, this is Detective Investigator Burke. Please call me as soon as you hear this message." He gave the number and hung up.

"I have an idea," Carrie said. "Let's ask Shirley if we can borrow her car for the drive to the mill. No one involved in this investigation has seen it yet. It was in the garage all during the fair."

Henry nodded. "Good idea. Call her. My truck still has their stuff in back, and it's the more distinctive of our two vehicles, so leaving it at their house for a while makes sense."

"This is getting out of hand," Edie said. "I don't like so many people knowing what's going on."

"I understand your concern," Carrie said, "but Shirley and Roger have been part of several of our investigations already. They're close-mouthed. Not even their son, who works with them on the farm, knows much about their side activities with us. Besides, they aren't aware of your current DEA work, and we don't need to mention that."

"Okay, I give up," Edie said as she took her coffee mug to the sink. "I can be ready to leave in less than thirty minutes."

Shirley's car sat in front of the house, and the large workshop door was open when they drove through the farm gate. After Henry's truck was closed inside the shop, Shirley came off the porch to hand him her car keys.

"I hate to ask another favor," Henry said, "but, Eleanor's shop . . ."

"Yep, I thought of that. I need to go into town to pick up some things at the store so I'll stop by, check everything, and put a sign on the door. Already got the sign made. 'Closed for a family emergency.' That do it?"

"Yes, great. Thanks, Shirley. I'd planned to put up a sign myself, since I wanted to be with Carrie when she was questioned today, but when this appointment with Milton Sales came up, there wasn't time."

"Y'know, she said, "I've been doing some serious thinking about that man. He seems crooked as a dog's leg for a lot of reasons, including those powder-filled animals. But, on the other hand, could he be law enforcement of some kind? Undercover, like? What do you think?"

No one said anything.

Shirley continued, "Henry, you having law enforcement savvy, could you guess the truth about someone who's doing that kind of work? Does anything they do give them away? I see stuff on the television about the county's drug task force, and just last month there was that big sting pulled by undercover deputies. Could Sales be in on something like that? I think this whole thing sniffs of secrets, and people being tricked. Was he trying to catch someone by using those toys and the powder? Did he light out because bad people on the wrong side of the law found out what he was doing?"

Carrie and Edie stared at her, and Henry looked thoughtful.

"Well, by golly, I didn't mean to shock y'all into total dumbness. And, what's so crazy about my idea anyway? Why wouldn't it be possible? Might explain some things about Mr. Sales. Let's say he's law enforcement, and the bad guys suspect it. Wouldn't that fit in somehow with his messed up trailer and the unscrewed gas lines? Someone wanted to scare him, or even kill him? Makes a reason for those powder-filled toys, too. Decoys of some kind?" She looked at each of them in turn, but, Carrie noticed, her brow-wrinkling study spent the most time on Edie's face.

"Well now, don't y'all talk at once."

Edie was the one who broke the silence. "Shirley," she said, "that's certainly one explanation. And it does have logic."

"Yes, it does," Shirley agreed, bobbing her head.

"We have a lot to think about when it comes to Milton Sales," Carrie told Shirley as the three piled into her car. "We'll report when we come back. Probably around noon. Thanks for the loan."

"Y'all be careful now," Shirley said. "That car is only ten years old."

Chapter Fifteen

MILTON'S STORY

"Interesting woman, Shirley," Edie said as they drove out of the valley.

"And my dearest friend," Carrie said. "Never in my life have I admired a woman so much."

"After what she came up with, and since she is your best friend, I'm not sure I believe you haven't said anything to her about my current work."

"Beyond being insulted because you suggest I revealed that, Edith Embler, I am insulted on Shirley's behalf. And you can't discount what she suggested about Sales. She beats us all in intuition and smarts."

"Yet you said she couldn't read anything but her own name until her oldest child started school and shamed her into working with a literacy tutor."

"That's right." Carrie turned in the Cadillac's front seat so she could look over her shoulder at Edie. "That has nothing to do with her intelligence, only her life circumstances."

"Okay, if you say so."

Carrie faced front again, tightening her lips because, to her, the "if you say so" clearly revealed prejudice. Then the pique dropped away and she grinned as she heard Edie scuffling her feet on the car floor, making a crunching sound.

"What's this . . . stuff . . . on the floor of the car? Looks like someone dumped a box of . . ." The crunching continued. "Cereal? Is it crumbled cereal on the floor back here?"

Face still front, Carrie explained. "Oh, that. A couple of years ago, Roger took the truck and went fishing without telling Shirley, forgetting she needed to go into town to get some special feed for their dairy cows. So she took off for the co-op in her Cadillac, and had the bags loaded in the trunk and back seat. One bag in the back seat broke and spilled. Shirley cleaned up most of it, but not all. Irritates the heck out of Roger whenever he sees it, and neither of them has ever been inclined to finish cleaning it up. He's too proud, and she thinks it reminds him to keep her in the picture when he plans to leave the farm."

Carrie hoped the sounds she was hearing from the back seat now were caused by suppressed laughter.

Conversation died then, and everyone stayed with their own thoughts until they reached the mill's parking area.

Edie leaned on the back of Henry's seat and reached her arm across to point. "According to Milton, the stairs start over there. If you pull up next to the mill by that door, we'll be near the exit for the secondary stairs."

"Yes, I can see that," Henry said, and, chastised by the tone of his voice, Edie leaned back in her seat and said only, "I don't see Milton's truck."

"Look across the river!" Carrie said as Henry pulled up and parked.

"What? I don't see anything." He got out of the car and looked.

"That's the point. Look way to the left. The exhibitors' parking lot is empty. Less than sixteen hours since we left here, and Milton Sales's RV is gone."

"Sheriff must have impounded it, after all," Henry said.

"You think so?" Carrie asked.

"Well, at least it will be safe from more vandalism if they did impound it," Edie said. "But, I wonder, does he know? Let's go inside. Maybe he's driving something other than his truck and is already here."

"Whew," Carrie puffed as she led the way up the stairs. "There's something to be said for stopping to look around the second floor gift shop on your way to the restaurant. A straight climb up these steep stairs is a bit much."

"True, but hunger helps push," Henry said as they lined up to study the Bean Palace breakfast menu posted on the wall. "Ah. Sausage, eggs, wheat germ biscuits and gravy for me. What about you gals?"

"I don't see Milton," Edie said. "Aren't we going to wait for him?"

"You can wait if you want, not me, I'm too hungry," Carrie told her. "I'll have the Buckwheat Waffle Supreme with blueberries and whipped topping."

"Done," said Henry. "Edie?"

"Well, I'm hungry too. Since he's late, I'll go head and order their biscuits and gravy. Never had that, and I've wondered what it's like. I see it on about every breakfast menu these days." She pushed ahead of Henry and told him, "I'll order for us. I'm paying."

"I'll get a table," Carrie said. "How about that one by the window? Place for four, and no one is seated nearby if we need to talk privately. We can see the road and parking lot from there."

Edie and Henry nodded, and Carrie went to secure their place and wait for her food.

Except for exclamations of pleasure, not much interrupted eating for the next twenty minutes. Finally, after a bit of conversation about probable recipes for what they'd eaten, Edie came back to the business at hand and said, "I'm worried. Milton is over forty-five minutes late. How long can we occupy this table after we finish?"

"Do you suppose he hooked up his own trailer and just drove off?" Carrie asked. "Perhaps the sheriff didn't post anyone to guard it after all. But Sales would have had to move it in a short amount of time, since there was only a two-and-a-half hour window between when he called you and when we got here."

"I guess I shouldn't have told him you were bringing me," Edie said. "That may have spooked him, and he decided not to come."

"No, it didn't spook him," Carrie said, looking out the window. "I see him getting out of his truck right now. Let's each order a biscuit to put honey on. That way we have something to do while he eats, and he won't feel uncomfortable eating alone."

Milton Sales nodded briefly to them, went to order his breakfast, and took the seat next to Edie. He said, "Sorry I'm late, couldn't be helped." Then he looked across the table at Carrie and Henry. "First thing I want to tell you is that I had nothing to do with the powder-filled toys Edie describes. In fact, I've never seen them."

He went to pick up his breakfast tray, and, after taking a few bites, continued, "I understand John Harley supposedly found them on the shelf under my sales counter, said I'd forgotten them, and gave them to you, Ms. McCrite?"

"Calling me Carrie is fine. And yes, that's exactly what happened. Since we're talking about the drug business here, and you claim you never saw those toys, I begin to wonder about John Harley."

"Uh-huh. Did you see anything like them when you came to my booth on Thursday morning?"

She shook her head. "I don't remember seeing toys like that, no."

"As you think about the cars and other toys I do make, and those four animals on wheels, does the style of craftsmanship, the wood used, and anything else you remember look the same, or even similar?"

"No, but many artists work in more than one style."

"Perhaps, but I assure you I never saw those animals and never touched them, as any fingerprint expert can learn if someone cares enough to test them. Edie said they had a smooth finish. Probably take fingerprints well.

"What's more to the point, John Harley knew I didn't make them when he gave them to you. Even if I'd decided to branch out with new items since I saw him last, the first thing we always do when we meet here each year is show off any new items we'll be selling. Conclusion? He knew those wheel toys weren't mine. They were a plant and he knew it."

He looked around the table as if expecting someone to say, "Of course you didn't make them," while he ate a few more bites, but no one spoke until Henry said, "The whole situation with those toys does raise questions. Any ideas about the powder inside them?"

"Maybe to cast suspicion on me—to confuse the real issue of who is bringing in drugs to sell in the Ozarks. Now, I don't mean the primary dealer has to be John. He'd almost have to be involved, but the real boss could be someone he fears, or owes allegiance to."

Carrie said, "Well, at least it looks like he knows something about the drug business."

Henry added, "Yes, and I understand he's been a friend of yours for a long time."

"That's true, he has. Ergo, why should you believe me? I'll give you that. I don't blame you for being cautious."

He chewed in silence while looking at each of them in turn.

Henry asked, "I'm curious about why you chose to meet Edie here. Odd location under the circumstances."

Sales laughed, and gestured toward their plates. "What about that, really? How could you wonder after you've each finished one of their meals? I eat at the mill whenever I get a chance."

"Hmmm," said Carrie, licking honey off her fingers.

Henry said, "Okay. We'll assume for now that you had nothing to do with those four toys or the powder in them. What about John Harley?"

"Major King, I . . ."

"Ah, so you know something about my history in the Kansas City Police Department?"

"Yes, I did pretty thorough research which, along with what Edie tells me, makes me think I can trust you and your wife."

"Trust us? For what? Not to turn you in on suspicion of being a drug dealer?"

Sales's smile faded, and he mashed a piece of biscuit, stirring it into his gravy.

Watching him, Carrie thought, *He's wondering what to say next.*

"No, not that, but I'd like to believe I can trust you. You must keep what I'm about to say in total confidence. Will you do that Edie? Ms. McCrite? Major King?"

Carrie thought, *More secrets. This is high drama. Maybe we should all prick our thumbs and smear a drop of blood on paper.*

Henry said, "You must realize that depends on what you plan to tell us."

"Okay, I concede that. But at this point you need to know that, like you, I'm connected to law enforcement. In that capacity, I've had my eyes on John Harley for a couple of years, though I've known him much longer. In fact, I was chosen for this current job because of my attachment to craft fairs, and a long-time friendship with him, as well as a background in drug interdiction.

"My history as an undercover agent for the old Bureau of Drug Abuse Control came to the attention of the sheriff's department in this county, and you might say all things worked together. They approached me, and I agreed to join the effort to curb drug distribution in this part of the Ozarks, with my special focus being craft fairs."

Carrie looked at Edie. Was her cousin surprised? Did she know? Hard to tell. She had a blank look on her face.

Henry asked, "So you live in this area?"

"Yes. I normally only use the RV to travel to other craft fairs around the Ozarks. Crafting is my full-time business these days, and it provides good cover for research into drug trafficking. I had the RV here this year in order to keep a full-time watch on what seemed like a rapidly developing case centering on John Harley. But things are more complicated now that it seems John—or someone—suspects my law enforcement connection."

Henry gestured in the general direction of the fairgrounds. "Did you know your RV is gone from the field over there?"

"Yes. Deputies had it towed in last night. They'll keep it safe for the time being."

"What were the people or person who searched the RV looking for?"

"Probably something that showed I was either part of the drug trade or an agent against it. They wouldn't have found anything because I never keep paperwork, computer files, or other information that would connect me to law enforcement where it could be located by a searcher. I'm guessing the vandalism was more because they were angry they hadn't found what they were searching for than a product of the search. There was sure no reason to cut up bed sheets, though I can understand dumping out boxes of cereal and dry food."

"What about tampering with the gas lines?"

"That could be part of the same thing, a kind of vengeance, or they could have unfastened the connections in the hope I'd come back, and, in spite of finding the mess, try to light the stove to make tea or coffee. I guess they might also think I smoke, but that would mean they don't know me well, and I think the people who did this know me very well. Or it could just be they thought law enforcement would suppose I had unfastened the gas lines myself to destroy evidence of drug-dealing, or injure someone I expected to come in."

"How come you didn't either fix the leak or report it?" Carrie asked.

"I didn't know about it until after deputies discovered it."

"Oh? Really?"

He looked at her but didn't seem angry. "Yes, really. The excessively destructive search and the gas leak could not have happened at the same time. I saw the results of the search but I didn't know about the leak. After discovering the vandalism, I decided the best thing I could do was remove myself completely from the scene before a more intense attack ruined all the undercover work done thus far. Better for someone to think I'd skipped and wonder why, than for me to stay and perhaps risk exposure, or a more dangerous personal attack. I'm guessing the disconnected gas lines were one form of personal attack."

Carrie said, "Did you have a chance to check and see if anything was missing?

"There was only time for a quick look, but I didn't see anything. I had my laptop, memory sticks, and a few important papers with me in the truck since an RV is not really a secure place."

Edie said, "What next?"

Sales put his hand over hers. "One important thing now is for me to testify that your father was an honest man, trying to do his job. I hope to clear his name for you."

"And yours as well?" Henry asked.

"Already done as regards the past, I assume, or they wouldn't have asked me to be part of the current task force working to shut down a pipeline of drugs into the Ozarks."

"Maybe. Also a good way to keep an eye on you."

Sales laughed. "That, too," he said, "though I'm sure it wasn't their reason."

Henry finished the last bite of his honey-smeared biscuit and asked, "What evidence have you found in the way of drug distribution through craft fairs?"

"Nothing at all until this peculiar incident with Harley. As soon as sheriff's deputies learned about the powder-filled toys on Saturday night they contacted me, then went to the fairgrounds and did a thorough search through John Harley's booth and his stock of bird houses and feeders. Everything was clean, maybe only because he's very careful."

Carrie changed the subject. "Did you know Edie before this past week?"

"Only by name and reputation, though, in a way, I feel like I've known her for years. Her father and I worked together—spent a lot of time together. He talked about his Edie a lot. He often said she was near my age, and that he'd like me to meet her. I am so glad to have finally accomplished this, though it's been more than forty years since he died. Meeting her brings me back to those days with him. For a while we were good friends. Once this is over, I hope to go east with Edie, meet her mother, and give her news about her husband."

Carrie noticed Milton's hand was still curved over Edie's on the tabletop. "So, what next?" she asked.

"I have a date to meet John Harley and his wife for dinner at the Crescent Hotel in Eureka Springs tomorrow. John and Liz Harley and I are old friends, remember? They're from Little Rock, but he told me Thursday that they'd decided to stay in this area for a few days to go antiques shopping, sightsee, and relax after the intensity of the fair. Of course that may also mean they have drug business to accomplish in this area. If they do, I'd sure like to catch them at it."

Carrie said, "His wife? If she was here, why didn't she help him out in the booth? He was alone every time I saw him and could have used some help."

"She has helped him off and on in other years, but he said she aggravated a back problem carrying some of his merchandise in on Wednesday. Other than a visit to a chiropractor, she didn't leave the motel until Sunday night, and supposedly spent a lot of time in the motel's hot tub."

"What motel?" Henry asked.

Sales looked at him for a long minute, then grinned. "Well, well, you're on the same track I am. It was Ozark Suites, and the housekeeping staff I talked to said Mrs. Harley wasn't in the room when they cleaned it on Thursday, Friday, Saturday, or Sunday, and no one saw her anywhere in the building during the day, though of course they couldn't be everywhere. And, get this, the hot tub was emptied for cleaning and repair last week."

"How did you find that out?" Carrie asked.

"Desk clerk. I hit it lucky. This morning I went there and asked about a room later in the week. I said one thing I'd heard recommended was their superior hot tub. Clerk told me it had been out of service for repair and cleaning for several days, but would be ready to go today. Had a hard time keeping a stone face when she told me that."

"What about other information?" Henry asked.

"Ah. Well, they provide breakfast, but only coffee the rest of the time. There had been no food deliveries during the day for several days, according to the clerk."

"I see," Henry said. "How did you get her and the housekeepers to talk to you without raising suspicions? I assume you didn't want to show any official identification, faked or not. That could call attention to you and might get back to the Harleys through gossipy staff."

"While I was at the front desk, I said I would have a lot of office work to do if I stayed with them, and asked about order-in meals. She handed me a list. I pointed to one name on the list at random, said I had heard that one was closed, had any of the others delivered in the last few days? She said no, because the guests last week were mostly craft fair exhibitors or fair visitors, and all of those were away during the day."

"I speak some Spanish, and I gave the housekeeper on the Harley's floor the impression that I have a romantic eye for Elizabeth Harley, who's husband is a beast and demands she stay in their room all day while he's gone. She said the lady had not been in her room when it was cleaned on any of the days they stayed there." He laughed. "I think she suspects the woman has more than one boyfriend on the side."

"Good work," Henry said.

Edie said, "Milton, I think I should go with you to the meeting in Eureka Springs."

He answered her immediately. "Edie, that's not a good idea."

"Y'know, Milton," Carrie said, "When I first talked to John Harley about you, and made up a story about my cousin being a friend of yours, he said if my cousin came back, I should tell her that Milton wasn't married. The implication was that my cousin and you should become better friends."

Henry said, "Carrie, please forget this whole idea. It's potentially dangerous. Remember John Harley himself may have been responsible for the RV search and gas leak, and he surely knows the source of those powder-filled toys. He isn't likely to continue accepting Milton Sales as a true friend."

"Ah. We'll see about that," Edie said. "That's one reason I want to go along."

Carrie, excited by a new idea, said, "What about this? I'll buy a wig, and that, with high-heeled boots, my tinted glasses, and one of my older pantsuits should conceal me pretty well. John Harley and his wife, so far as we know, have never seen you, Henry, but we'll think of something to change your looks a bit anyway. We can be in the dining room when Milton and Edie go there. We could keep watch and provide back-up."

"*WHAT!*" Henry said, then looked around the room to see if anyone had noticed his outburst. Everyone seemed absorbed in their own conversations and food.

"I'm not involving civilians," Milton said.

Edie moved her hand, put it on his arm, and stood. "My friend, I have something to explain to you. Let's go for a walk."

Chapter Sixteen

WHO'S IN DANGER NOW?

"**W**ell, why couldn't they talk in front of us?" Carrie asked as soon as footsteps on the wooden stairway died away. "I suppose she's going to tell him about her work as a confidential source for DEA, so what's up with the secrecy?"

Henry shrugged. "Maybe a little romance mixed in? Otherwise, there may be things about her work—and his—that we don't need to know."

Carrie huffed. "Guess they don't fully trust us."

"Nor we them," he said. "And, speaking of that, we are not going to any meeting between Milton, Edie, and the Harleys. That whole adventure could be dangerous for them, assuming we have heard nothing but the straight truth this morning. It's out of the question for us."

"But, Edie's safety . . . "

"I know, Cara, and I understand your concern, but she's working for the DEA by choice, what she does in relation to the Harleys is her decision alone. I'm sure she doesn't expect us to provide back-up. I also understand Sales's reasons for going to the Crescent Hotel, and why Edie would want to go along. Again, assuming the truth of what they've told us, both of them are stuck in a difficult position, with the Harleys possibly knowing or suspecting Sales is connected to law enforcement. I think Sales believes they were responsible for the wreckage and gas leak in the RV, and I agree it's likely they were. Of course the way Harley gave those toys to you pretty much nails him as involved in the drug trade, assuming it's true that he would have known Milton Sales did not make them."

"Yes, I understand all that, Henry. I'm not stupid."

He frowned and spent a silent moment just looking at her. "Carrie, my dear, I never said you were, let alone thought it."

"Well, but . . . but you were explaining things I know as if I didn't know them."

"I'm sorry, I didn't realize I was offending you. I was just repeating suspicions and facts as I see them, partly to think them over myself."

"Oh."

When she said nothing more, he went on. "It's a volatile and dangerous situation, with the advantage being on the Harleys' side for the moment. Profitable craft fair undercover work by Sales is pretty much out of the question from now on unless he can convince them he has no connection to law enforcement. Since they probably don't suspect Edie, she could help by playing girlfriend and, in the conversation, bring up fictionalized details that prove his ordinary citizenship, or even details of his drug use, past or present. That may be what the two of them are talking over right this minute. In any case, the meeting at Eureka Springs is going to be difficult, and for us to be there in any capacity would be extremely foolish, especially if the Harleys learned we were there and who we are."

She nodded her head, and stared into her empty coffee cup.

"Cara?"

"Let's go downstairs and see if Edie is ready to go home with us."

There were several more cars in the parking area, and one man had just finished unloading fishing gear from his van. While Henry watched him from the mill porch, he headed across the road to the river area below the stone dam.

Huh, never thought of fishing the War Eagle. Might be interesting to try it out.

There was no sign of Edie and Milton at first, but then Carrie, who had walked out into the parking lot, pointed toward the bridge on the opposite side of the mill. Henry joined her, and saw Edie and Milton leaning on the bridge railing overlooking the millrace and wheel. Edie was talking and gesturing while Milton listened, shaking his head slowly and staring down into the churning water.

Henry wondered if this had been going on since the two left the restaurant. Well, it didn't matter. No way he and Carrie were going to get in any deeper. Time to head for home and schedule Carrie's interview with Investigator Burke.

Now Sales was shaking his head more vigorously. It would have been interesting to hear what they were saying. He wondered whether Edie or

Milton would prevail when it came to plans for future undercover work.

"Should we walk over there?" Carrie asked.

"They wanted privacy. We'll give them what they want."

"For how long?"

"Good point. I assume they've seen us. If we simply stand here as if waiting for them to finish, I'm sure that will speed things along."

"You can stand here. I'm going back inside the mill and do more looking around. They have a lot of interesting cookware on the second floor. If those two aren't finished when I get back, then I'll go closer and see if that reminds Edie I need to get back home and call Investigator Burke."

"Go ahead. I'd like to watch that guy who came here to fish. Think I'll walk to the river where he's setting up. I might decide to try my luck here some time and maybe he can give me some pointers. I'll find you in the mill if Edie and Milton break loose before you're back."

Carrie spent more time looking at jewelry and crafts on the second floor than cookware. Before long she tired of even that, and decided to go back to the first floor for a closer look at mixes and flours she wasn't familiar with. Just reading instructions for using some of that stuff could be entertaining, and, come to think of it, they had recipe books, too. Maybe she'd add a second cookbook to her kitchen.

But first . . . a trip to the restroom. She went out the front door of the mill and saw Henry standing with the angler. He wouldn't miss her. Crossing the parking lot, she opened the door to the women's side of what she thought must be the fanciest pit toilets in Arkansas.

She heard someone come in while she was still in a stall, and, when she opened the door to come out she gasped, and said, "This is the women's rest . . ."

"I know."

The man had a gun, and, in the close quarters, it was easy for him to push it against her neck. "We are going to walk out of here quietly, go to the van across the lot, and you are going to get in, also very quietly. If you don't, my partner, who is playing at fishing across the road, will kill your friend so quickly he won't know what hit him. Do you understand this?"

Oh God, oh dear God, Henry . . .

"Yes, I understand."

"Then let's go. Walk beside me. I'll have the gun right here. Do you see it?"

"Yes."

There had to be something she could do. Drop to the ground? Yell? But, what about Henry? And, where were Edie and Milton?

She dropped her purse.

The two of them continued walking. It seemed like miles, but it was only a few yards. Because of the bridge approach she could no longer see Henry, or the man who had supposedly been fishing. Where were they? Where were Edie and Milton? *Oh God, help us all.*

Then she and the man were next to the van and the man was opening the sliding door, pushing her up and across the seat. He got in, sat next to her, shut the door. The gun touched her side.

Who's the man fishing? Could it be Arnie? This guy could have been the one who stayed in the car when the two of them were at my house. I wish I'd paid more attention to the picture on Henry's phone. But, if the other man is Arnie, why didn't Henry recognize him?

The driver's door opened and the man next to her said, "She dropped her purse on the way to the van. I was hanging on to her so couldn't get it."

The man at the door grunted, left, and came back to toss her purse on the passenger seat, following it with large sunglasses and a floppy khaki hat that had drooped around his face. Instead of the suit, he wore jeans and a dirty, over-sized canvas jacket.

The man turned toward them and asked, "Guess all went okay?"

Arnie! That name fits him better now than Agent Arnold Frost, and she understood why Henry hadn't identified him. She probably wouldn't have recognized him herself. The dirt, rough clothing, and day's growth of beard in contrast to a slick, clean-shaven man in a well-tailored dark suit sure made a difference.

But now Henry was out of danger, and probably in the mill, already looking for her. What, what could she do to signal him?

"Yup, all okay. Best get out of here before hubby gets wise."

The van began moving in slow motion. Carrie's thoughts also seemed to be coming in slow motion, including the words to the Ninety-first Psalm she'd read in the New Living Translation of the Bible just a few days ago:

He alone is my place of safety . . . he will rescue me from every trap.

The gun poked her side and she almost laughed aloud. This sure was a trap, and she sure needed rescuing. It didn't matter whether the thoughts about safety were three thousand years old, or had been written yesterday, they sounded good to her.

But why did they take her? Why would Carrie McCrite be of any use to them? Did they think she knew things they needed to learn. *Oh. She knew Edie, and now, Milton. But why not attempt to take one or both of them, instead of me?*

Because you were alone—vulnerable and easy?

So, what should I do right now?

WAIT, a voice inside her head said.

Okay, she'd wait. She didn't really have a choice about that anyway.

The van turned onto a side road, bounced along for a few minutes, stopped. Arnie got out, came around, and opened the sliding door. The man next to her said, "Arnie has a gun, too. You are going to come outside with me now, and stand beside the van. No funny business." He backed out, yanking on her arm to pull her across the seat.

"Owww. Let me go. I can get out on my own."

"Then do it. And don't forget, both guns are pointed at you."

As soon as Carrie was out and standing next to the van, the second man, as Carrie had come to think of him, held her while Arnie pulled her hands together in front and put on handcuffs. He then pulled a pillowcase over her head. She heard some kind of sturdy tape being pulled off a roll and soon figured out why. Tape was wrapped loosely around the pillowcase, keeping it from sliding off her head, but leaving enough of an opening to allow free passage of air. Duct tape? Electrician's tape? Electrician's tape was stretchy, and would probably be easier to remove than duct tape.

"Get back in the van."

Feeling her way, Carrie obeyed. When someone held her feet together and lifted them, she tensed, preparing to kick out. Then she held back. *Wait.* She didn't want to make them angry. She sat quietly while they taped her ankles.

I don't suppose they plan to kill me. After all, they could have cuffed my hands behind me, which might be safer for them, but would make it impossible for me to sit comfortably. So they think I might be of some value to them. Alive.

Doors shut. The second man sat down heavily on the seat next to her. The van backed, bouncing on the unpaved road. Then, eventually, it moved forward onto smooth pavement.

She fought terror—but any sense she was winning that battle seemed remote and incredibly tiny. *I can't give in to this. I can't, I can't. I need to think clearly . . . I need to think.*

She gritted her teeth. *Don't cry, don't you dare cry. You can't blow your nose.*

Instead of crying, Carrie began giggling. Feeling incredibly stupid, she tried to quit, but the giggles kept bubbling out.

Until the second man's hand smacked across her face.

T urning his back to Henry, the guy getting ready to fish put down his rod and opened the tackle box. Henry heard him rummaging around, then a muffled exclamation before he headed back toward the parking lot.

Must have forgotten something.

Henry looked out into the river. Good place for spin casting. He'd call the Arkansas Game and Fish Commission and find out more. This guy was ignoring him, and obviously wasn't one to share information. But he was a trusting soul to walk off and leave his equipment at the feet of a stranger.

Henry looked down at the fishing rod the man had dropped on the ground. *What the deuce?* The rod didn't have line in it. The grip was dirty and pieces were missing. Alarm began to stir, and, without even considering fingerprints, Henry jerked the shabby tackle box open. It was full of junk, bits and pieces of nothing.

He headed toward the parking lot at a trot, and came up over the bridge approach just in time to see the van pulling away.

It took too many minutes to search the mill, and the clerk on the second floor said a woman of Carrie's description had gone downstairs several minutes ago. Henry rushed out into the parking lot, shouted at Milton and Edie that Carrie was missing, and then barged into the women's section of the outhouse without any hesitation. *Empty.*

No, NO!

Edie and Milton were standing by Shirley's car when Henry ran back into the lot.

In jerks, he told them, "Abducted. Carrie. Probably those same two guys. Should have been more alert. Should have looked more carefully at the man who got out of the van. Might have been Arnie Frost. Should have known. Dark windows on the van. We have to follow. When we get to the highway I'll go left, you go right. Van was white, dark windows."

"Wait," Milton said. "Talk to the sheriff first."

Henry snatched the cell phone from his pocket, scrolled to the number, and got Investigator Burke immediately, without remembering the man might be alert to a phone call because he was expecting Carrie to call him back. Henry tried to give details coherently, but there was too much to tell. He shoved the phone toward Milton. "You tell them the danger. You get them on the road, searching for that van."

Looking stunned, Milton Sales was silent for a moment, and then, as he began speaking, Henry turned to Edie. "This is *your* fault. You involved her in your mess. You put her in this danger. If there is anything more you haven't told me, you do it now, and you *will* tell the deputy that Carrie's only interest in Sales was because of you. She thought you needed him to clear your father. That's all! She has no connection with drug dealing or distribution. *You will tell them ALL the truth!*

"NOW, Edie, WHO are those men? Why have they taken Carrie, and how did they know we were here?"

Behind him, Milton said, "She doesn't know, and I'm not sure, but I suspect they're either part of a cartel in competition with the Harleys, or higher-ups in the group John Harley was with. They probably took Carrie because she was easily available, and with the thought they could use her as leverage to get at information they think Edie or I may have. It's also possible they think Carrie is somehow involved in all this mess. As to how they knew we were here, I haven't a clue. There was a tracking device on my truck last week, but I removed it, and there's nothing there now. I am so very, very sorry."

"It's a bit late for being sorry," Henry said, shutting his eyes. He wanted to hit someone—including himself, for being so blind. He wanted to roar down the road to find Carrie. He wanted to *do* something. He had to find Carrie, he had to see to it that she was safe. There must be something, something . . . .

He had to do something.

His brain went numb, and he stood in frozen silence beside Edie and Milton, trying to breathe evenly. Had to be calm. Had to. *Oh Carrie, Little Love.*

Couldn't just stand here.

He began pacing back and forth in the parking lot and was still at it when a deputy sheriff's car, coming a bit too fast, slid into the lot, raising a cloud of dust.

In a minute both Investigator Burke and Deputy Olinda Rosten were out of the car, asking him to repeat his story and describe the van. Henry shut his eyes to focus on forming a picture, and was surprised at how much he had noticed without realizing it. When he finished giving details, he said, "Talk to these two. They can tell you how all this got started, and how this woman drew Carrie into it."

While Deputy Rosten returned to the car to broadcast Henry's description of the van, Investigator Burke turned to Edie. "Guess there's more to this whole situation than we've learned so far. I know how Sales is connected, but what about you, Ms. Embler?"

"I'm Carrie's cousin."

Henry glared at her and had about decided to say, "Tell it all, blast it," when Burke spoke instead.

"Yes? And?"

"I came here to look for Milton Sales because he, along with my dad, was an agent in the old Bureau of Drug Abuse Control back in the sixties. Dad disappeared in 1968 while tracking down dealers who were providing drugs to truckers in the United States. Mother and I have known for years that Daddy was suspected of being a double agent, possibly even selling drugs to truckers himself. Doing research on my own, I learned about Milton Sales. I hoped he could help me clear my father's name and tell me what really happened to him. When I learned Sales had retired, moved to Arkansas, and was selling his woodcarvings at craft fairs in the area, I came here to see if I could find him. The fact I have a cousin here was fortuitous."

"And?"

"That's all. I found Milton Sales. I learned the truth about my father. Milton is going to be able to clear my father's name."

Henry said, "Edie . . ." and took a step toward her. She didn't flinch or even look at him.

Burke said, much to Henry's surprise, "Ms. Embler, your connection to the DEA is now known to selected people in the County Sheriff's Office here. I am one of them. We work closely with the Drug Enforcement Administration office in this area." He put his foot on the bumper of Shirley's Cadillac and, his voice cold, said, "Now, do we understand each other?"

Henry hadn't a clue what Edie would say next, and Olinda Rosten saved her from needing to answer when she slammed the door of the Deputy Sheriff's car and trotted over to rejoin them, frowning. "I have news that complicates things," she said, voice quivering. "About two hours ago a housekeeper at the Ozark Suites Motel found the body of John Harley in the room registered to him and his wife Elizabeth."

She stopped to catch her breath and Henry wondered, briefly, why she was so upset by this news. The Harleys, whatever they did, shouldn't cause a skilled law officer this degree of agitation.

Olinda went on, "He was in the bathtub. He'd slit his wrists. Only been dead an hour or so."

For a minute no one said anything. Then Milton Sales asked, "What about his wife? What about Liz?"

"No sign of her," Deputy Rosten said, voice shaking again. She took another deep breath and continued more steadily. "Her clothing and toiletries are still in the room. No sign of their SUV, or the enclosed trailer it was towing."

This deputy is too tender hearted, Henry thought.

Carrie had been trying hard to identify sounds as the van hummed over paved roads, listening for anything that said where they were. Eventually she heard a train whistle, and then, when the van stopped, the easily identifiable sound of train cars on tracks in front of them. It didn't take long for the train to pass, so it couldn't be one of those hundred-car-plus coal trains on the Kansas City Southern tracks. They probably hadn't gone far enough to cross those tracks anyway. It must be a freight run on the Arkansas and Missouri line.

After the train sounds faded and they bumped across the tracks, the van spent what seemed like a long time in city traffic, with pauses for stoplights, until things were quieter again and they turned off on an unpaved road. The van rattled along for probably three or four minutes before it turned left and paused, engine idling.

She heard the hum of a large truck engine nearby. Eighteen wheeler? On this road? The sound wasn't rough enough for a dump truck, though that would be more common on a road like this. Maybe a live-haul chicken truck, but nothing here, including the smell, told her they were anywhere near chicken houses.

The noise stopped, a door slammed, and male voices shouted greetings.

She could distinguish only "Smooth," and what sounded like "Cash." Then silence.

Where was she?

The man next to her got out of the van, there was the sound of a large door opening, and they rolled onto a hard-surface floor. The door shut. She heard more voices, and one of them belonged to a woman. *A woman?* The female voice was easier to hear than the men's had been. Carrie understood "Hurry," and "Get her to tell you."

Then the woman said " Use the car. They'll be searching for the van by now."

Second Man returned and dragged her toward the van's side door, bouncing her out and onto the building's floor. Carrie tried to anticipate his moves so she could brace or bend her body and minimize injury, but she hit her knees on the metal step and began to fall. Male arms grabbed at her, catching her under one arm, and she was pulled forward several feet until a voice she recognized as the second man's said, "Get in and sit." She leaned toward the car, judging with her shoulder and the side of her left arm where the door opening was. Then she turned her back to the opening, bent forward, and moved down cautiously until her rear end touched the seat and she could scoot in. *Now what?*

The man got in beside her, and two car doors slammed. She assumed Arnie was driving, and the woman had been left behind. The car backed, and then they were moving forward on the unpaved road.

"Get her to tell you," the woman had said. *Tell them what?*

What do they want to know? How much do they know already? Will I need to lie? Can I lie and get away with it? What's Henry doing? Is he looking for me? And, how did they know we were at the mill? Who told them?

Too many questions. This isn't productive.

She blocked the questions out and began praying.

It seemed no time at all before the car stopped. Someone, probably Second Man, pulled the tape off her ankles and she was told to get out. He took her arm. She heard a key in a door, then was shoved across a threshold. *No, it couldn't be.*

Her key. Taken from her purse?

It felt and smelled like . . . home.

Second Man released the pillowcase, yanked it off, and Carrie was dragged to a seat at her own kitchen table.

Arnie stood beside her, saying nothing, while Second Man disappeared.

Taking a quick look through the house, she supposed. Or, maybe, using her bathroom.

When he returned, both men stood over her, and Carrie noticed they were both wearing surgical gloves.

"Where are the toys?" Arnie asked.

Careful, careful.

"Toys? What toys?"

"Where are they?" Arnie struck her across the face and she tasted blood where a tooth had cut into the inside of her cheek. She wanted to spit, but didn't. They were in her home. She swallowed, and wondered what would happen if she asked for a drink of water and a paper towel.

"Tell us where they are. Harley said he gave them to you. He never lied."

For some reason, both men laughed.

The past tense of lie stuck in Carrie's head. *Why "lied?" What has happened to John Harley?* She shook her head, and hoped she'd misunderstood.

"Don't shake your head. We'll rip this house apart if we have to. *Tell us!"*

Wouldn't telling them she knew about the four pull toys get her into more trouble? Then they'd understand she knew powder had been hidden inside.

"I don't have any toys here but the wooden police car I bought for my husband at the fair." Tears were stinging her eyes, running down her cheeks, dropping unhindered on her jacket. She swallowed again.

Arnie and Second Man looked at each other.

"Where is it?"

"In a drawer in the bedroom. If you will take these things off my hands, I'll get it for you."

"Tell us where."

I don't want them touching my things.

"TELL us!"

"Chest of drawers. Bottom drawer on the right. Under my sweaters."

Arnie disappeared, and came back with the little car.

"Too small Arn. It was a bigger haul than that for sure. Can't be it."

"I—know—it," Arnie said. Taking her iron skillet off its hook, he put the car down on the kitchen floor and smashed the bottom edge of the skillet against it several times, finally splintering the car and leaving dents in her vinyl flooring.

Arnie advanced toward her, swinging the skillet. Holding it over her head, he said, "I'm getting angry. If you don't want me to treat you like I did that car, tell me where the toys are." He hit the side of her face again with his hand, not the skillet. "Tell me!"

Carrie spoke as slowly and calmly as she could, talking through the pain banging in her face and mouth. "I don't have any other toys here. The guy who makes bird feeders did give me some pull toys he said belonged to Milton Sales. Said he was too busy to leave his booth, and asked me to take them to the fair office so Sales could pick them up later. We got busy at the booth where I was working, and I forgot. They were loaded in my husband's truck by mistake, and we ended up carrying them to a friend's house and taking them inside to show her. The cow's udder came off on her kitchen table and spilled white powder all over. There were four large toys, and all of them had white powder inside. So we called the sheriff, and someone came out and made tests on the powder. He said it was probably baking soda. Anyway, it wasn't drugs."

Arnie stopped her with a growl. "Not drugs?"

"Definitely not drugs. The sheriff's deputy took the toys away. Said he would send them to be tested in Little Rock."

"Bull."

"No. Truth. What possible reason could I have for lying to you? You can rip this house apart if you want, but I am telling the truth. The only toy I had here was the little police car I bought for my husband." She looked at the mess on the floor and then lifted her chin and looked straight into Arnie's eyes, repeating, "I am telling the truth, and I wish I'd thought to tell you about those stupid pull-toys first. Then you wouldn't have smashed the gift for my husband."

Second Man said, "Arn, I don't think she stole our goods. Doesn't fit. Hell, she's a grandma. Got Bibles and church stuff all over the house."

While Arnie and Second Man looked at each other, she said again, "I am telling the truth. The sheriff's deputy took the toys, and they were never in this house anyway."

Finally Arnie nodded, and Second Man went outside, returning in a couple of minutes. "Cell phone doesn't work here. How about the land line?"

"No, they'd find the records too easily. We'll have to drive to where the phone works. But first, maybe we can find that information the boss wants, and we'd better hurry at it. No telling how long before hubby comes back."

"Nah, he'll be out looking for this one for a while yet. We've got time, then we can report to the boss when we get to where there's a signal."

Carrie said, "There are some bananas in a bowl over on the counter. Could I have one, please? And feel free to take one for each of you if you like. Also, I'd like a drink of water. Glasses in that cabinet to the left of the sink.

Without comment, Second Man brought her water, and put a banana in front of her on the table. "Banana, Arnie?" he asked, peeling one for himself.

"No." He looked at Carrie. "Embler's staying here. Right?"

She chewed on a bite of banana and nodded. *No use lying now.*

After taking a final sip of water, Carrie said, "I need to go to the bathroom,"

Arnie said "Just hold it."

"Arn, we don't want her to pee in the car." Second Man walked her to the bathroom and stayed with her, though at least he turned his back. Getting her slacks and panties down and up worked pretty well in front, but she had to be content with turned-under elastic in back. She wasn't about to ask her guard to straighten her underwear.

When they returned to the kitchen, Arnie said, "Okay, where is Embler staying? Where's her stuff?"

"In our guest room. She wasn't here when you came before, but she moved in the end of the week."

"Well, isn't that handy. She's got papers the boss has been looking for. Which room?"

Carrie told him. What did she care if they searched Edie's things? She was pretty sure they wouldn't find anything important. Whatever else she might be, Edie wasn't stupid.

"Bring her along," Arnie said, as Second Man started to follow him.

Second Man taped her feet, dragged her down the hall, and pushed her into a guestroom chair before the two men began tearing the place apart.

They were down to pulling mattresses off the beds when Carrie, crossness beginning to overcome fear, said, "If you tell me what you're looking for, maybe I can help you find it."

"Shut up." That was Arnie.

Second Man said "Wait, Arn, maybe she knows something about this."

Arnie snorted, "Why would she help us?"

He probably didn't hear Second Man mumble, "To keep her furniture from being torn apart," as he bent over Carrie, coming so close she could smell the banana on his breath. "So," he said, "Here's your chance to be friendly to us. This Embler woman is the daughter of a guy who was sort of related to our boss's parents many years ago. Boss wants some important paperwork from that time, and thinks Embler might have it."

Be nice, a voice inside her said. *You can be nice without telling them anything that might put one of us in more danger.*

"Well, I honestly don't think she does. I helped her unpack, and didn't see any business files or paperwork at all. She drove a rental car here and has since turned it in, so there was nothing concealed there.

"She told us she came here to find out what happened to her father over forty years ago. He disappeared during a business trip to Texas or Mexico, and she and her mother heard only that he was some kind of double agent, dealing in drugs. They never heard where or how he died. Her mother is still living, and Edie wants to find out what really happened to her father for her mother's sake, as well as her own. She wants to learn where he's buried and take her mother there if possible.

"She's never revealed to me that she knows any more than a few basic things from forty years ago, and, if she does, why bother to come here at all? Just to look up a cousin she hasn't seen since she was seven, and never bothered to visit for over fifty years? I don't think so. Coming here makes no sense if you're searching for someone who disappeared in South Texas or Mexico.

"Then the question is, why here? What ties to her father could possibly be here?"

Arnie had stopped dumping and was now listening. "She say anything more about him dealing in drugs, other than the double agent thing?"

"No."

"So, why did she come here? You got any ideas about that, smart mouth?"

Carrie could see no way around telling a small lie if she wanted to protect Milton Sales. Now was not the time to debate whether or not he was worth it.

"Not really, but I think she was told John Harley might know something about her father's disappearance, and she traced Mr. Harley here."

Arnie began laughing. "Boss is gonna love this, and lady, if you're giving us a true story, John Harley won't be any help." He dropped the drawer he was holding on a mattress and said, "Let's get out of here. Whether she's telling the truth or not, I don't see any papers."

"What about her?" Second Man asked.

"We'll keep her with us until the boss gives further instructions."

This time Second Man didn't untie her feet. He simply dragged her to the car and, before they were out on the road, he'd fastened the pillowcase over her head.

Chapter Nineteen

TWO PLUS

Without any conscious thought impelling him, Henry began pacing again, his feet and legs lifting and stepping, lifting and stepping, moving him back and forth in the parking lot.

Nothing. They still knew nothing.

He ignored Milton and Edie, who now sat with Olinda Rosten in Shirley's car. Detective Burke was in his Deputy Sheriff's car, probably talking to various officials about events here. Henry wished he could hear the conversations, but he'd been firmly, though kindly, excluded from that possibility.

So far there was no news of the van, or of Carrie, and no additional information about John Harley or his wife.

Henry's thoughts had been bouncing wildly, wondering why Harley would commit suicide, wondering if he could have been murdered, and the suicide faked. He couldn't shake the thought that Milton Sales might have killed Harley. After all, Sales had been very late meeting them this morning and he'd never explained why.

His mind also raged at Edie, who, after all, was the one who pulled Carrie into this danger, pulled her into whatever was happening to her now.

He stopped during a turn at the edge of the parking lot, and looked across the river to the fields where Shirley and John Harley had displayed their wares only one day ago.

Now, workers were dismantling the tents while a truck collected trash.

Henry watched the activity, watched people going about their jobs. None of them knew of the events that had taken place over here. None of them knew, and, ignorant of his anguish, none of them cared.

He turned to look around him in the parking lot. On this side of the river, only the skeletons of display booths remained. A crew had been working to take the booths apart when he, Carrie, and Edie arrived for breakfast this morning. He'd barely noticed them then. They hadn't been important. Yesterday's bright fair trappings were today's wooden skeletons, important only to those who tore things down and collected trash.

Now he wondered why the workers here had quit so early. That meant none of them were around when Carrie was abducted.

He turned back toward the river. Where was Carrie right now? What was she thinking? He couldn't, wouldn't dwell on any options but that she was okay, maybe even free. He would find her; someone would find her. She would be all right.

He heard footsteps coming close behind him and turned eagerly to see if there was news. Edie, walking alone, stopped, and held out a wrapped sandwich and a cup of something.

"It's 2:00. Time to eat. Hope you like ham, and this is sweet tea. Sugar energy will do you good. Come, sit with us in Shirley's car."

"I can't."

"Yes, you can. Come on now, eat with us." Her voice was untypically gentle.

"Has there been any news?"

She shook her head. "Not yet. After we eat, maybe we should go back to your house. Right now, there's nothing more we can accomplish here."

"They might bring Carrie back here."

"They might. But they might drop her off at your house, too." A half smile decorated her face.

Is she trying to be funny? I can't, can't sit with this woman.

"Come on, Henry. Let's begin thinking what we can do to find Carrie. To help her, you need to begin thinking like a cop, and right now, it's time for the cop to eat lunch."

As they walked toward the car, she asked, "I've been wondering, should you phone Shirley and tell her you're running a little late returning her car? Or, have you already done that?"

"No." Reluctantly, he thanked her for the reminder, and punched in Shirley's number. After a short explanation, he sat in the back seat of the big old Cadillac, listening to the crunch of crushed cattle cubes whenever he moved his feet.

Edie was beside him, Deputy Rosten and Milton in front. Rosten said "Wish we'd kept an officer with you today, but who could have seen a reason for it? Yesterday at the fair, yes, but today? We didn't think, and, of course, didn't know you were coming back here. At the least we should have warned all of you to stay close together."

That's exactly it. My fault. I was okay with coming here because I wanted to get to the truth about Milton Sales and those confounded hollow animals. But I should have stayed alert, should have kept Carrie in sight all the time. This place, its very familiarity, got to me. For a while, the danger didn't seem real.

He took a bite of his sandwich, chewed, swallowed. "That's it," he said aloud. "I didn't think about there being danger, or that Carrie would be targeted when she really knows so little about what's going on. If only she had talked with Burke first thing this morning. We shouldn't have come here at all."

His thoughts flashed back to what Carrie said this morning, that she didn't want to talk to the detective until she knew more about Milton Sales. She'd even said she needed to know who she was covering for, though it was possible she meant that to be tongue-in-cheek.

Trying to think like a cop, as Edie had said, separating emotion from common sense, Henry admitted both he and his wife had been eager to come here. Thinking further, he wondered if there was any chance good would somehow come out of this. If he had been the one abducted, and Carrie left behind to cope, would she still be thinking about their need to be involved? *We're meant to help people, to find the truth for them.* He could hear her saying it right now.

He took another bite of his sandwich. He hated sweet tea, and wished for plain water.

"No point beating yourself up," Deputy Rosten said. "We work with the situation as it's presented to us. That's all we can do."

Investigator Burke knocked on the driver's door of the car. When the deputy opened the window, he said, "News. It's possible John Harley was murdered. Crime scene techs found a couple of spilled pills under the bed in the Harley's motel room. Best guess so far is that they're sleeping tablets, though no one can be sure without more testing. The housekeeper insists they weren't there yesterday morning, but of course that could just be CYA. Murder is only surmise at this point, but it is possible Harley was drugged, moved to the tub, and his wrists slit. Razor blade in the tub, no distinguishable prints. They'll have to examine the cuts more closely and check for drugs in his system." He leaned in, looked back at Henry. "No news of the van yet. Sorry."

While the detective could still hear him, Henry said "Milton, where were you this morning? You were quite late to our breakfast meeting."

He was met with silence until, finally, Burke spoke. "Milton late to breakfast? Hard to imagine that."

No one said anything more, and Henry wondered what Milton Sales was thinking of him at the moment. He couldn't have missed the implication.

Well, so what. The timing was perfect. Any law officer might be suspicious, and I still don't know where he was.

Finally Investigator Burke said, "I don't think we can accomplish anything more here at the mill. Major King, because of the circumstances, Deputy Rosten will accompany you and Ms. Embler home and remain there with you, perhaps even through the night if you can accommodate her.

"Milton, I suggest you drive to the motel and go in as if you planned to meet with the Harleys. Deputies will take you into custody shortly after you arrive. If anyone is watching, the action might help conceal your involvement with our Drug Task Force. You will, of course, be released after a reasonable amount of time. Our jail isn't too bad." He gave a little chuckle, slapped the side of the car, and stood erect.

Henry got out of the car and went to throw his cup of tea and sandwich wrapper in the trash container. Burke came up to him there. "Do you know anything more about what happened at the fair? I was going to ask Ms.McCrite to give me every little detail she could remember about her encounters with Milton Sales and John Harley, and how she got those four animals."

"I can tell you all I know, though there may be nothing new." Henry imagined Carrie standing beside him as he repeated all she had told him about activities at the fair. Remembering her excitement gave him so much pain that he stumbled several times in the telling, but finally got through it.

Burke thanked him, put a hand on his arm, said, "We'll find her," and was gone.

Milton Sales had already driven away, and Edie and Deputy Rosten were waiting for him in the back seat of Shirley's car. Henry got in, started the engine, and, as he headed toward the road, said, "Keep your eyes open for a white van with dark windows. Arkansas license is the one with the picture of a diamond on it. First letter of the plate identification is an A. That's all I noticed. No easily visible dents or scratches on the white part of the van, but I did see a crack and dent in the rear bumper on the driver's side."

"We'll watch," Edie said, and that was the end of conversation except for small talk until he got to Shirley and Roger's house and pulled up by the front porch.

Shirley hurried out before Henry got to the porch steps. "Any news?"

Henry shook his head.

"Carrie's a sharp one, she'll figure a way out of whatever's going on, so don't you worry too much." She glanced at Edie and Olinda, who were climbing out of her car, and said, "I know y'all probably want to stay close to the phone, so, instead of asking you here, I'll bring supper up about 5:00."

Henry said, "You don't need to do that, Shirley, I . . ." He shrugged.

"No trouble. Gotta cook for Roger, Junior, and me anyways."

Henry saw possible reprieve from a silent dinner with Edie and Olinda Rosten, or worse, from having to listen to their chatter during the meal. "You and Roger plan to stay and eat with us then."

"Well now, we might if we can put it off until 6:30. We've got the milking duty this evening; Junior's going out. She nodded at Edie and Olinda. "See y'all then. Plan on fried chicken and potato salad. Sort of a picnic. Made an apple pie this mornin'."

Henry left Carrie's car in the drive and hurried to unlock the front door for Edie and Olinda. He didn't go in the house, just pushed the door open for the women, and returned to put the car in the garage.

As he locked the door from the garage into the house he fretted about the long evening without Carrie, and wondered what he was supposed to do as host to these two women. Was the deputy here only to help guard them from harm, or was she guarding them as suspects of some kind? He wondered if they had been completely cleared of any suspicion by now. Surely Carrie's abduction would . . . he stopped in mid-thought. Was it possible Investigator Burke thought Carrie had left of her own free will?

Not possible. These were smart people.

Excited conversation from the hall stopped his musing. Sounded like Rosten on the phone, almost shouting.

When he came around the corner and looked through the guest room door, he saw why. The room was chaos. The searcher or searchers hadn't cared what kind of mess they made. Edie stood in the hall, looking stunned. At least she was smart enough to know she shouldn't go in the room yet.

"Edie, what were they looking for?"

She shrugged, and shook her head. For the first time, he felt sorry for the woman.

WAIT, oh wait! What if . . . ?

He hurried down the hall to his and Carrie's bedroom. Neat as always, except for her sweater drawer, which had been emptied on the floor. Was that where Carrie had hidden his little police car? Were they looking only for that car? Otherwise why hadn't they tossed this entire room like they did Edie's? And why Edie's? Were they somehow aware of her current work as a confidential source for DEA?" *But how did they know where to look for the car? Only Carrie would have known that.*

"Carrie was here," he shouted to Rosten as he rushed through the rest of the house. Carrie's purse was on the entry hall table, contents spilled out. Her house key, as he had suspected, was missing.

In the kitchen he found two banana peels on the table with a partly empty glass of water. The splintered car was scattered across the floor, its tiny red-painted roof light lying next to the edge of a counter as the only remaining evidence of its identity. There were dents in the floor. He felt a chill when he saw the iron skillet that had obviously made the dents. Such rage. And Carrie had been here.

Without touching anything or stepping into the mess, he looked for signs of blood, and felt some relief when he didn't find any. He saw a scrap of what looked like electrician's tape but didn't touch that either. Had it been used to secure Carrie's hands and ankles?

He sat at the kitchen table next to the banana peels. *She was right here.* He looked at the peelings, and saw a smear of blood on one of them. Oh, dear God! *Little Love, what did they do to you? Hit you in the face? Did your lip bleed?*

At least they gave you water and something to eat.

She had been in this chair.

Be quiet. Think. What happened here?

He shut his eyes and put his hands on his knees, bumping a knuckle on the curved table skirt. He thought about the time he'd hurriedly stuck his gum on the under side of the family breakfast table when he was only seven or eight. One of his mother's firm rules had been against chewing gum at the table.

Carrie's hands were probably tied. Still, if she could manage to peel and eat a banana, that means they were either tied in front, or they freed her hands so she could eat. Is it remotely possible she tried to leave me a message somewhere?

Tentatively, slowly, he got on his knees, bent to look under the table, and, to the astonishment of both Deputy Rosten and Edie, who had just followed him into the room, turned on his back and slid beneath it. "Flashlight!" he said. "Quick. Drawer below the phone."

When the flashlight was handed to him he studied the wobbly scratches. They didn't look like anything that had been caused by manufacturing or moving.

He said, "Looks like a number 2, a plus sign, and then letters. Probably W O M A, a space, then what looks like C and maybe an A or an R."

"Let me see." It was Deputy Rosten. Both she and Edie, in turn, slid under the table to study the marks, then sat at the table with him.

Edie said, "I think you're right on the two and the letters, but what made those marks? That's hardly from a fingernail. How could she make marks like that? If she was tied up in some way, *how did she do it?*"

"Is she wearing a large ring?" Rosten asked.

"Simple wedding ring," Henry said. "No stones in it, and I never gave her an engagement ring. She does have other rings, but rarely wears them. I'm fairly sure she had only her wedding ring on today."

"I don't think a simple wedding ring could have done that," Rosten said.

They were silent for a minute before she continued. "If she was tied, and I believe we all assume she was, they must have fastened her arms in front rather than more painfully in back. And she had enough free movement, I assume, to eat one or two bananas. So, she sat here for some time, and could have moved her hands and wrists under the table without being observed.

"Oh, wait! Suppose they used metal handcuffs. Those have fairly definite edges. Metal handcuffs could have made the marks."

"You're right, that is possible." Henry went to get a cooking spoon out of the drawer. Holding his wrists together to simulate handcuff confinement, and keeping away from the original marks, he tried making scratches with the spoon. Then he got down to look under the table again.

"The spoon cut through the wood stain and made clear marks. Metal handcuffs could do that too. It wouldn't have been hard for her to make the marks undetected, assuming she was restrained with metal cuffs. Painful and awkward, maybe, but possible."

Rosten said, "Two, a plus, then W O M A, and CR."

"Two . . ."

"Got it!" Henry said. "What about the two men she'd expect us to know about, *plus* a woman!"

Rosten said, "A woman? Has a woman now joined up with the two guys? What woman? I wonder . . . " She stopped, and shook her head.

"Well, anyway, I'll go with your idea about what she tried to write. It sounds logical. So, what's the *CA* or *CR*?"

Edie spoke up, sounding hesitant, Henry thought. He decided the abduction of Carrie had trimmed her cousin's sails considerably. "If she'd written a *and* r it would be car. So, what do you two think? Maybe she started to write *car* and got stopped before she could finish. But, if that's it, what's the significance of *car*?"

"If it's car," Henry said, "it probably means they've switched from the van to a car, which would make good sense from their point of view. And that means there's a home base located somewhere in this area, a place where the van could be left and a car picked up, unless they simply ditched the van and stole a car."

"I need to report this," Deputy Rosten said, pushing her chair back and heading for the phone.

Chapter Twenty

THE END OF THE RIDE

A s soon as the pillowcase was secured over her head and Second Man had leaned back in his seat, Carrie said, "I've been wondering how you knew we were at the mill. Pretty smart, however you did it."

"You bet," he said. "We did it the old fashioned way. We followed you there."

"But, how?" We were in a car you'd never seen before."

"We were parked up the road a bit, where that house is being remodeled. We knew we could be there a long time, but the guys working on the house let us sit in the drive when we told them we were supposed to bid on a tree removal job, and the folks weren't home yet. We almost missed you at that, but the Caddy has nice clear windows. We didn't know the car, but saw you all inside."

"Ah," Carrie said. "You sure must have wanted to get ahold of me—or someone.

"You were our current interest. Harley said you had those pull toys. Besides that, Embler was now staying in your house and the boss says she has important old papers."

"Ah," she said again, and went back to figuring out where they were headed. Since they'd started from a known place, she was having little trouble understanding where the car was in a landscape that, so far, was familiar.

Finally Second Man said, "Reception good here. Stop at the next easy place and I'll phone."

When Arnie pulled off the road, Carrie was sure they were in the parking lot of her nearest town's grocery.

"I'll call," Arnie said, as his door opened. After it slammed shut, Second

Man puffed out a breath in a sound easily recognized as frustration.

The "*Be friendly*" voice inside her mind was still there, so Carrie, ducking her head to avoid getting the pillowcase in her mouth, asked, "Are you married? Do you have children?"

"My profession makes family life tough. Was married once. Didn't last long."

"Oh, I'm sorry. How about parents, or sisters and brothers?"

She thought he wasn't going to answer, then he sighed, and she could tell he was looking away from her, probably staring out the window. "There's Mom. She's about your age. Had a younger sister when I was a kid. Don't know what happened to her. I was, uh, away from home for a couple-a years and when I came out—came back, she was gone. Mom never said what happened to her.

"Pop disappeared when I was seven, and Mom was expecting Laurie. Guess he didn't much care for little kids."

"Pretty name, Laurie."

"I always thought so."

"What about you?" he asked, after a pause.

"I have a son near your age. Only the one. My first husband was killed a few years back."

"Oh yeah? How'd that happen? Some kinda accident?"

"No. He was murdered. Shot."

Carrie could tell Second Man was thinking that over.

"Shot?"

"Uh-huh. Guy who did it had once been a friend."

"Guess he really wasn't."

"I guess not," Carrie said, as the driver's door opened.

Second Man asked, "So, what's up?"

"We'll talk outside," Arnie said

"What if someone comes near the car and sees this woman with a pillowcase over her head?"

"We can stand right here by the window and that'll hide her. I'll put the kid lock on so she can't get out."

Carrie felt a cold draft as both car doors opened. She heard a grocery cart banging into the cart rack, then the doors slammed and she was alone.

She thought, *I never knew what being truly alone was like. Until now.*

Muffled sounds and garbled voices, near and far, continued all around her as what seemed like endless time passed. Finally, she reached again for thoughts and prayers that came from within, calling on calmness and protection as companions instead of Arnie and . . . she wished she knew Second Man's name.

Would Henry find her scratchings under the table? Would he be able to figure them out? Probably not. How could he? Wouldn't matter anyway. She hadn't known enough to be of much help. Now she knew the car was silver, but she hadn't seen it then.

Feelings of panic shot in and out of her mind as she waited. She had no doubt they were discussing her fate. Considering the fact she'd heard so much and could easily identify them, it was pretty certain what kind of fate they planned.

Henry, I'm sorry, my love. I should have listened to you a long time ago. Now I'm the one who needs help, and there's no me to help me. I know you're trying to find me, but, how could you know where I am? Only God, Arnie, Second Man, and I know that.

So, who do I trust with my fate?

She began giggling again, then remembered Second Man's slap, which had stopped her earlier hysterics. This time she stopped herself, and began thinking the words of The Lord's Prayer, as Arnie and Second Man got back in the car.

"Oh-kay, off we go," Arnie said.

Second Man was silent.

At first Carrie didn't pay much attention to where the car was going. She was too involved in her attempts to overcome both panic and sadness. But then something clicked in her head. They had turned back in the direction they'd come from. The car turned right, not left. *Why?*

The ride continued in silence while Carrie tried to judge locations. They were most likely near her house, but hadn't made the final turns that would take them there. Instead, it felt like they were going on into the wooded area that stretched for some distance along Walden Valley beyond the Booth's pastures and the bluff caves. It was a bit of remaining wilderness that everyone in the area cherished.

The car turned off the valley road, bumping uphill on what Carrie suspected must be the old logging road, a remnant of major tree harvesting in the 1950's, and still used occasionally by hunters.

So, this is the place.

NO. I won't accept that. Dear God, I told Jason Your love and care are with us every moment. Do I—can I, really believe that right now? Believe it for me, too?"

The car stopped. Arnie said, "Be sure it's out of sight."

Second Man grunted, opened his door and pulled her out. She fell on her knees and folded to the ground while the car door slammed. One slam. She was alone with Second Man.

He pulled her up, tugged her off the road, and then they were in the woods, with underbrush, rocks and fallen tree limbs attacking her as she was yanked between rough-barked trees. Her mind went numb. No comforting thoughts came, only an apology to Henry.

I can't endure any more painful bumps without crying. Well, who will care? Who will hear? I can cry all I want.

No, I will not die with tears running down my face. Our Father, which art in heaven, . . . this is my sufficient guide to eternal life."

Second Man dropped her, and her head hit a log. She was fading into foggy oblivion when she heard a shot. Two shots.

I feel so fuzzy. Where am I shot? Don't you feel something besides fuzzy when you're shot?

All she felt was someone taking the handcuffs off. Then she heard Second Man's voice saying, "Lady, you'd better play dead until I can get out of the country, or I'm dead."

After his footsteps faded away, Carrie shut her eyes and let herself fade away too.

Chapter Twenty-One

NOT QUITE DEAD

C old.

That's all Carrie was aware of for what seemed like a long time.

Silly, pull the blanket up. She reached out and tried to close reluctant fingers around . . . *what?* Leaves? They rustled when she touched them. *Leaves.*

In the woods. I'm in the woods.

She was lying on the ground, and she was supposed to be dead.

Not dead?

She heard a noise. *It's me, Carrie McCrite, laughing and crying.*

Not dead. Not . . . dead. *Oh, thank you.*

But she had to play dead until Second Man got out of the country. She must do that. He'd saved her life.

And she had to tell Henry she was alive.

Using her arms to lift the weight of her upper body, she moved stiff muscles into sitting position. After a few moments spent wiggling feeling back into her hands, she reached for the tape around her neck, found an end, and pulled, passing the tape from one hand to the other to unwind the several loops that held the pillowcase in place.

At last she breathed clear air. Cold air.

It was still daylight, but the sun was in the west. Both the golden light and her rumbling stomach told her it was near suppertime, and lunch had been only a banana.

I'm hungry. I'm alive.

She took another breath of cold air, then surveyed the woods around her.

No sign of the road, but Arnie had told Second Man to pull her far into the woods so her body wouldn't be found quickly. She shuddered, and said a prayer of thanks.

Bless that man. Nameless, but he'd become a real person to her, a human with a living mom and a missing sister named Laurie.

Just so, she'd obviously become a flesh-and-blood human to him, someone he couldn't kill, someone he'd been willing to trust with his own life. He knew Arnie and his boss wouldn't tolerate a living witness to any part of their criminal activities.

Carrie took several breaths and thought about the man who had not shot her. She'd be grateful to him for the rest of her life. Her instinct to be friendly, rather than show anger or fight her captors, had probably helped save her, but she'd never sensed the mind or heart of a killer in Second Man. There had been too many tiny kindnesses, though they were well hidden under the tough guy façade.

Her feet felt like lead weights when she bent her knees to reach the tape around her ankles. She found the end of the tape and began unwinding until the last bit came loose. Her feet were free, though not ready to support her.

She'd made it through the first step toward safety.

Step two was to find the road before dark. Thank God this was fairly familiar territory for her, though possibly Arnie, at least, hadn't thought of that. But then, what difference would it make if she were dead? He'd just headed for the nearest heavily wooded area he knew about.

Had Second Man suggested this place? Did he understand that familiarity would help her find a way out? If so, that meant he may have known, back in the grocery store parking lot, that he wasn't going to kill her. Was it simply luck he had been the one chosen to take her off into the woods? Maybe it was just that Arnie didn't want to be tagged as a murderer, should he ever be caught. She drew a breath in, blew it out in a long, wavering *whoosh*.

Her body felt numb and wobbly, it would help to have a walking stick. She looked around, saw a small branch that looked possible, and crawled toward it. It broke in her hands. Too rotten.

Several years ago she'd seen a man parked on the logging road when she was out hiking. He sat on the tailgate of his truck, carving a walking stick. Several small, uprooted trees were stacked next to him in the truck bed. "Dogwood," he'd said, and showed her how the dogwood trunks in his stack had turned to the side just underground, forming a natural handle for walking sticks and canes.

Well, had she the strength, she'd uproot even a dogwood tree right now; though, back then, the waste and loss of spring beauty in the forest had made her angry at the wood carver.

She spotted a low branch on a nearby tree that looked dead. Maybe she'd be able to break it off. She crawled forward and reached up to grab the branch with both hands, testing its strength by cautiously lifting her weight. She caught herself just in time when the branch broke off.

It would do.

Carefully, she stood, leaning heavily on her stick. Then she thought back through the last horrible moments before Second Man fired his gun into the forest floor. Which way had they come? She stared at the place where she'd been lying. Yes, she was sure she'd fallen facing away from the road, so that meant the road was . . . over there. Carrie started walking, picking her way carefully over debris on the forest floor.

Henry was keeping busy in the kitchen. Working here helped keep the "what-ifs" at bay. If he thought about Carrie and "what-if," he came close to losing control of any and all his emotions. How did other people cope? How had crime victims and waiting families he'd dealt with in Kansas City managed to live with anything like what he was feeling? He'd seen the jitters, the rages, the crying, the terrified and sad and hopeful faces. He'd never been to that edge himself. Until now.

Henry pulled the kitchen table away from the wall so there would be room for two more chairs, and began putting out plates and silverware.

Drinks. Should he make iced tea? Roger and Shirley would drink coffee; he and Carrie usually drank water with supper. As he recalled, Edie drank water with all meals except breakfast, so he wouldn't bother asking her about a preference.

She was busy straightening up in the guestroom. He'd helped her put mattresses back on the twin beds and drawers back in the chest, then showed her the linen closet and left her to put clean sheets on the beds and return her possessions to wherever they'd been before the search.

Detectives, who had come promptly after Olinda's call, uncovered no evidence of any outside presence in the room other than the mess itself, and Edie hadn't found anything missing. So, what were searchers looking for?

Arnie and Co. had undoubtedly worn gloves inside the house, and hadn't, insofar as anyone could discover, left other identifiable evidence of their presence. The banana peel with a smear of blood on it had fingerprints—probably Carrie's. The other had none. The water glass displayed the same prints as the one banana, and the detectives had taken both peelings and glass with them.

So, that was it. All evidence of criminal activity inside their home depended on Carrie's eventual testimony.

Olinda, who'd been doing a walk-around search outside the house, came in the kitchen and, when he looked up, shook her head. "Not even a tire track. Too dry."

"I guess I expected that. Do you want iced tea with supper?"

"Water's fine."

She sat at the table and watched him take celery, carrots, a turnip, and a cucumber out of the refrigerator. "Making raw veggie sticks? Good idea. Can I help with that?"

He sighed. "Thanks, but no. Gives me something to do."

"Ah, yes." After a pause, she said, "So tell me about the Booths. I've not met him yet, but she sure seems a sharp cookie. According to Edie, she nailed Milton Sales's true involvement in all this before we did. It's almost like she has second sight."

He chuckled as he began peeling a turnip. "Typical Shirley. She is sharp, especially when it comes to anything related to human nature; and she's not afraid to speak her mind. It can be ticklish if she uncovers some supposed secret a bit too close to home, but you soon get used to that, and what she says is never really harmful. She and Roger are good and valuable friends of ours. Shirley has saved Carrie's bacon more than once."

"Tell me more."

"Well, the first time was right after Carrie and I met. A friend of ours had been murdered near here in Walden Valley, and . . . "

The logging road hadn't been hard to find, but her strength was waning, her shoes weren't meant for heavy walking, and increasing shadows made it difficult to see hazards. Recent rains had uncovered rocks and left ruts in many places, and she had to watch carefully to avoid them.

At last she reached the valley road and paused to rest, leaning heavily on the tree branch. She wished she dared sit down somewhere for a few minutes, but darkness had begun closing in. She had to keep moving, she had to let Henry know she was okay.

She began walking again, chanting to herself, *Left, right, left, right.*

No, she had that backwards. She was leading with her right foot. She stopped, lifted her left foot, and started again, *Left, right, left.*

She knew she wouldn't have enough strength to make it up the hill to their home. Besides, who would be there? Edie? Maybe even Milton Sales or Inspector Burke, waiting to interview her. Who could she trust with the information that she was still alive?

Left, right. At least this road had been graded recently.

It was getting darker. *Step, step, step, step. Keep moving, left, right.*

She was shaking with cold as she trudged past the Booth's pastures, and saw, at last, bright lights shining through the windows of their milking parlor. Roger's truck was parked by the side door. So probably Roger and Shirley were taking the milking duty tonight.

Left, right, left, right. She was moving more quickly now, drawn by that beacon of light.

She stopped by the farm gate, hovering in the shadows while she studied the landscape for possible dangers.

She didn't see Junior's truck, so he'd already left for his rented house up on the ridge. There was no sign of the hired man's car either, but Shirley's Cadillac was parked beside the house. So Henry, and probably Edie, had come back from the mill, left Shirley's car, and picked up Henry's truck..

Carrie opened the gate, stumbled, then steadied herself and headed toward light and warmth.

Henry looked at the kitchen clock. 6:35. The phone hadn't rung. It hadn't rung to bring news of Carrie, and it hadn't rung to tell him Roger and Shirley were going to be late.

Roger and Shirley were never late. In fact, they were usually painfully early, arriving before you were quite ready for company. So, where . . .

The phone rang.

"Yes." He'd said it too loudly.

"Something has come up." It was Shirley.

"Yes?" Did he sound as frenzied as he felt?

"Everything's okay, but could you come down to pick up your dinner? Come alone, and don't let on to the girls that anything might be unusual. Tell them we have to stay here because one of our cows is having twins.

Okay? Keeping a stone face is important, very important, but everything is fine now. You got that? *Everything is fine.* See you in a few minutes."

He licked his lips, and turned toward Edie and Olinda. "News?" Olinda said.

"Not really, I just need to go and pick up our dinner. One of the Booth's cows is having twins and they need to stay with her. I'll hurry, I know we're all hungry."

He got his jacket and headed for the garage, his head buzzing with hope that was based on nothing but Shirley's confident statement, "Everything is fine now."

Chapter Twenty-Two

SECRETS TO SAVE A LIFE

All of Henry's conscious thoughts during his drive down into the valley were on Shirley's four words, playing over and over, "Everything is fine now."

He stumbled up the Booth's front steps and had just raised his hand to knock when Roger opened the door.

"What?" was all Henry could manage.

"Carrie's here. She's okay."

The room began to spin, and Henry barely made it to the nearest chair before his legs gave out. "I . . . how? *Here?*"

Roger chuckled. "Here. The two men who had her all but brought her home. She was left in the woods off the old logging road. Walked here."

"Where is she?"

Roger sobered. "In Junior's old room, finishing supper. She's had a rough time, Henry, and is kinda bruised and battered. She'll tell you all about it later, not now, I think. She told us a bit, but the telling was hard on her. Two men drove her up there, one of them took her into the woods and was supposed to kill her, but he didn't, or couldn't. He shot into the ground, took off her handcuffs, then walked away. Thing is, she says he saved her life, so his life is in her hands now. If they find out he didn't kill her, he's dead himself. He trusts her to stay hidden until he can get away, maybe even out of the country. So we thought we'd keep her here for a while—at least until everything gets sorted out."

"Oh God, oh my God."

"Yes, you owe Him plenty of thanks. Come on back now. Shirley saw to it that Carrie had a hot bath, partly so she could look her over and see if she was hurt anywhere. She's just finished supper now, and looks some better than she did when she got here. Shirley says there are bruises on her body, but her face is the worst. Get ready for that, and don't let on.

"We all know you can't stay long. Those girls will expect you back up the hill with a picnic basket pretty darn soon. Carrie understands, and doesn't expect you to stay."

"Why didn't you call me right away?"

Roger stopped and turned to face him. "Well now, our first care was for her. Sorry my friend, but it took a while to sort things out here, and Shirley was immediately mother-hening, seeing to a bath, finding pajamas for her, and so on. Guess we coulda called and said she was here and safe, but we didn't know anything more than that, and we didn't know what was going on up at your house. Carrie warned us first off that we weren't to tell anyone but you she was alive and safe. We didn't know why she said that; we didn't know anything." He repeated, "Our first care was for her."

"I'm sorry, Roger. It's just that . . . "

He stopped when Roger put a hand on his arm and said, "Come on now, she's waiting for you down the hall."

Henry couldn't figure it out. Suddenly he felt as shy as a kid on his first date. *She's alive. She's safe. But what will I say to her?*

Carrie was sitting at a desk with an empty plate in front of her. She did look battered, and in spite of Roger's warning, Henry had to muster all his remembered policeman's stoicism to suppress an exclamation. There were greenish bruises beginning to darken on her face, and her cheek was swollen. Shirley's pajamas, rolled up at the bottom and sleeves, must hide other damage.

She started to stand, but he hurried across the room and almost fell against her as he knelt by the desk chair.

Neither of them said anything. He looked up at her and then, for the first time in memory, Henry King began to cry, while Carrie stroked her hand across his hair, over and over.

After a couple of minutes Shirley said, "Well, this is sure some happy reunion, what with everybody getting all weepy. Gosh almighty, you'd think you two had been separated for weeks instead of a day. Come on, Henry, say a few nice words, kiss her goodnight, then go in the bathroom and put cold water on your face. You've seen she's okay, and you've got two hungry mouths to feed waitin' at home. Can't be gone long."

Henry stood, said "Olinda came home with us, like a guard or something. She'll be there all night." Then he choked to a stop and turned away. When he turned back, he bent to kiss Carrie on top of her head, since he didn't know if he dared touch her face.

Carrie said, "Goodnight, Henry love. We'll make plans tomorrow. I assume Roger explained how things stand. Right now I don't know who we can trust with the knowledge that I'm alive and well. Who can keep the information to themselves and help save the man who saved me?

"Therefore, we need to consult and make plans. Maybe you can tell Olinda and Edie you've got an already scheduled morning meeting with the mayor or police chief in town, or somebody really important, but you'll have your cell phone with you. If any news comes in, they can call you. Don't forget to show how worried you are." She grinned. "Or at least you'd *better* be worried. If you can manage to get away in the morning, drive down here.

"I could use some fresh clothing. Put clean jeans, several pair of underpants, a bra, socks, the blue sweatshirt, matching turtleneck and jacket, and my flannel nightgown in a sack, and bring them with you. I keep basic make-up supplies in the travel case in my closet, so please bring that, too. Since your truck will be in the garage, they won't see you put that stuff in it. If there's a hitch, just call here in the morning and say you can't make whatever meeting you've told them you were scheduled for.

"Sorry you can't stay, but, as you can see, there's only a twin bed." She laughed, and blew him a kiss. "Oh, I forgot. Stick my wooly house slippers in the sack."

She stopped talking, but her wonderful teal-blue eyes said enough, and Henry was comforted. She really was going to be all right.

He swallowed all comments and questions and walked out of the room after one last, long look at her. In less than five minutes he'd put the picnic basket on the seat beside him in the truck, and was headed back up the hill.

"Here 'tiz," he said when he walked in the kitchen with the basket. He sat it down on the counter and let Olinda and Edie survey the contents, oohing and ahhing as they lifted out a plate with three pieces of apple pie, a large bowl of potato salad, and what looked like a complete fried chicken. The veggie sticks and drinks were already on the table, so they sat down to eat without wasting time.

"Did you get to see the calves?" Edie asked.

"No. They weren't born yet."

"Maybe we'll get to see them later. I hope so."

"Uh-huh," he said, thinking his own thoughts. He hoped his distraction would be put down to concern for Carrie.

"Detective Burke called," Olinda said. "It isn't an expert opinion yet, but it seems increasingly clear that John Harley did not cut his own wrists. There were no trial cuts like one usually sees on a suicide, and both cuts were made from the inside out. Unusual, since the common way would be to slit one wrist, then change the razor to the other hand and cut the second, making the cuts initiate from the outside in each case." She illustrated with her dinner knife, holding each wrist, palm up, in turn. "See. You have to do some almost impossibly awkward twisting if you cut from the inside out. Why would he do that? Also, there's a mark on the back of his head, which may have been caused when he was put in the tub by someone." She shook her head once, and looked down at her plate.

"Hmmm," Henry said, still thinking about Carrie.

"I can tell you're dead tired," Olinda said. "You go on to bed as soon as we finish eating. Edie and I will clean up. Do you have a household alarm system that needs to be set?"

"No alarm system," he said.

"Well, then be sure the doors and windows are secure before you go to your room, since Edie and I wouldn't know where to check. We'll leave the guestroom door open so we can hear any unusual noises during the night. Is there a phone in your bedroom?"

"Yes, and in the guestroom."

"Good. If there's any news, we'll all hear the phone ring. You go on now. We'll see you in the morning.

"Oh, yes. We found cereal in the cupboard. We can have that for breakfast, don't need anything fancy."

So, after checking the house and saying "goodnight," he left them cleaning up in the kitchen, went into the master bedroom area, and shut the door.

Henry awakened at 5:30, and realized with consternation that he had slept soundly through the night.

He had expected to be awake, puzzling over what Carrie would reveal about yesterday's events, and wondering if she truly had to play dead for some unknown amount of time. Sleeping soundly seemed disloyal to her.

But then, he knew she was safe, and that had obviously been enough, no matter what tough times might still face them.

Okay, new problem. How would he tackle the need to be away part of the morning? Would a fictitious meeting with someone important sound reasonable, when concern for his wife should be the most important thing? Maybe he could say he was going to talk with the police chief in town and bring him up to date on current events. Olinda, at least, knew city police wouldn't normally be investigating out here in the county, but maybe his feeling that the nearest police force should be brought into the picture would sound convincing to her. On the other hand, would it sound so convincing she'd want to go with him?

He sure wished he knew who could be trusted with information about Carrie.

The phone rang. He slid to the side of the bed, reached out to pick up the receiver, and heard Edie's voice, then Milton's. Not wanting them to think he was listening in, he said a quick "Hello, see you got it, Edie," and hung up.

So Milton probably hadn't spent the night in the county jail. It would be nice if he came and got Edie out of the way for the day, and Olinda went back to duty anywhere else but here. Might happen. Who knew?

Then he came back to earth on the realization that Edie probably wasn't safe yet. Going off alone with Milton would be the height of foolishness.

Almost as foolish as going to the mill yesterday and not being alert to potential danger.

He sighed. Time to tackle today.

Olinda and Edie were finishing bowls of cereal when he walked into the kitchen. "Smells like you found the coffee," he said. "Sorry, I forgot to get it out for you."

"No problem," Olinda said, "by now we know the contents of your kitchen pretty well." She was studying him as she continued, "I didn't hear the phone during the night, so I guess you didn't get any news about or from Carrie?"

He shook his head, and remembered to look and act frantically concerned.

Still studying his face, she went on, "I checked in at the department this morning, and none of the deputies had any updated information. I'm sorry."

"I didn't get any news," he said. "I didn't make any calls out—didn't know anyone to call who could help us beyond those already doing so, and you know the phone didn't ring until Milton called this morning. Is he okay, Edie? I guess he didn't end up in jail."

"No, though deputies did pretend to take him in for questioning yesterday. He said he plans to spend today talking to the organizers of the War Eagle Fair, and those who run other fairs as well. He wants to tell them about our updated suspicions. That hasn't been done so far, partly because past investigations didn't turn up any organizers who were involved in activities that seemed remotely suspicious. Besides, no one knew enough to warn them about specific individuals or types of crafts that might be suspect until Shirley discovered the contents of that pull-toy cow, and we realized John Harley could be hiding drugs in bird houses. Now, the idea is to enlist them to help us in the future.

"He also plans to ask if they might, by chance, have observed something at this year's fairs that will help us."

Henry nodded. "Sounds good."

He wished Olinda would stop looking at him so intently. He stared back at her while he said, "I need to keep busy or I'll go nuts with worry. I think I'll head for town and talk to the police chief. I'll bring him up-to-date on this. You never know."

"Good idea," Olinda said, finally ending her intense stare, "but eat something first. I'm still assigned to you and Edie, so I'll be here if news comes in about Carrie, or we learn more about the people who abducted her. They are, we assume, connected to our drug case. I should phone the Sheriff, give him an update, and tell him about your plan. It would be smart to let him know you're going into town and get his okay."

"Don't bother about that," Henry said. "I'll have my cell phone with me, and I'll go straight to the police department. I plan to drive Carrie's car, since it's less recognizable. I promise to lock the doors and keep my eyes open."

He tried a half smile, since she was staring at him that funny way again.

Chapter Twenty-Three

SOMEONE NEW STEPS IN

Henry was startled to see what looked like the county sheriff's unmarked car parked in front of the Booth's porch. He pulled up beside it and rushed toward the door. Why would someone so high in law enforcement need to be here now?

It took a couple of minutes for Shirley to answer his knock, and Henry immediately heard an unfamiliar male voice say, "Good. Now tell us . . . ," then lapse into silence when Henry walked in the room.

Initially he had eyes only for his wife. She looked okay, and was smiling at him. *Thank God!*

He put down her make-up case and the sack of clothing and went to kiss her on the top of the head before he turned toward the man who'd been speaking. He recognized him immediately from newspaper photos. The county sheriff himself, a new one since he and Carrie were in touch with the sheriff several years earlier. The stocky build, greying hair and mustache were certainly familiar enough. So was the poker-stiff posture that spoke of his former life in the military.

"Norman Cook," the man said, standing and holding out his hand. "I'm glad to meet you, Major King. Your name, and your wife's, are known to me, as I have just explained to her. Our previous sheriff shared information about a retired police major from Kansas City who, with Ms. McCrite, helped uncover facts that led to solving a couple of murder cases in this area. I've also learned about your recent involvement in a case in Kansas City from a friend in the police department there, since that case had a link to Arkansas. I think you know my friend—Doug Boinevich?"

Henry nodded, and said, "For many years."

The sheriff continued, "Doug said your wife was wounded during the resolution of that case." He looked at Carrie, and said, "Madam, you need to keep yourself out of harm's way."

Henry thought "Amen to that," then realized he'd spoken the words aloud.

The sheriff smiled at him, and sat in his chair again, saying "But, that's past. Now you're in time to join my conversation with Ms. McCrite, and hear any information she has to share."

Still addressing Henry, he said, "You may wonder why I came in person, and alone. Roger phoned me at home early this morning, explained a few details, and the sensitive situation Ms. McCrite finds herself in. It therefore seemed best that, at least initially, I tend to this myself.

"I should disclose a connection here. Roger is a second cousin on my father's side of the family. He and Dad spent time together during family picnics when they were kids. The family is increasingly scattered now, and, sadly, those big gatherings have stopped, but the family connection meant he felt he could safely appeal directly to me."

Still standing, Henry nodded, but his thoughts were in turmoil. Who was this man, really? *Okay, Roger's cousin, and a friend of Doug's, but is that enough to know?*

Since Norman Cook's election he'd read articles in the newspaper concerning activities in the county sheriff's office. Those mostly concerned budget items, or were comments about on-going cases. He hadn't seen anything openly critical. But wasn't it odd that Roger never mentioned the man was his cousin?

Well, maybe not. Roger might think saying he was related to a man elected to this responsible position constituted bragging. If anything, Roger and Shirley would brag about how ordinary they and their families were.

Now they're trusting this cousin enough to put Carrie's life in his hands. That has to count for something, but he's still an outsider, an unknown element.

Henry felt Roger's stare, and realized his friend was possibly aware of what he'd been thinking. Both he and Shirley had an unsettling ability to understand other people's thoughts. Now the corners of Roger's mouth lifted almost imperceptibly. He gave a slight nod, and said, "Have a seat, Henry. Join us."

Was there a special emphasis on *"Join us?"*

Henry took the nearest chair, and both he and Sheriff Cook looked toward Carrie, who was seated on the Booth's couch with Roger on one side and Shirley on the other. Henry wished the Booths would move so he could be next to his wife, but he thought a request for that might sound out of place to everyone in the room but Carrie.

He sat silently, waiting. He was probably even more eager to hear her story than Norman Cook might be.

But, how would the retelling affect her? As a former police officer, he knew she'd have to speak about it soon. But, he also knew quite well how this retelling could cause pain, even increased trauma, to victims and witnesses. In Kansas City, he'd seen that many times, and hated having to do the questioning, especially when the person was answering from a hospital bed. Was this too soon for Carrie? Surely Roger could have waited at least another day before calling the sheriff?

He came back to earth in time to hear Roger say, "When she learned Norm is my cousin and could be trusted to keep her secret, she insisted I call him right away."

"I was afraid I might forget details," Carrie said, "and I really wanted to have the telling over with so I could start thinking about something else, if that makes sense to you."

She was addressing the sheriff, but looked at Henry, who nodded, and said, "It does." *It's important for her peace of mind that she shift part of this burden to someone who can take positive action. That's typical of trauma victims, as I know all too well. Oh, dear God, I'm sitting here analyzing my own wife!*

"Go ahead, Ms. McCrite," the sheriff said. "Don't be afraid of repetition. I do know something about the case, and the unique position of Milton Sales with the department. I've also heard about Ms. Embler's probable connection to the DEA, though I haven't verified that yet. However, I am not as familiar with other details as Detective Burke and Deputies Rosten and Rainwater. So, if you'll begin at the beginning, please."

She did, starting with Edie's phone call, repeating details Henry already knew, until she got to her capture in the restroom and the abduction following. He could have verified that her recitation to that point was accurate and complete. Evidently the sheriff found it so. He'd not stopped her once to ask a question.

Now Henry kept silent with some difficulty as she described being put into the van and driven away. He looked down at the braided rug on Shirley's floor, following its pattern around and around with his eyes. What was past couldn't be changed. Raging about it now would be futile.

He nodded in appreciation as she gave her account of listening for sounds that offered clues to where she was. When she got to the unpaved road part, and the sound of what she assumed was the tractor of an eighteen-wheeler, the sheriff stopped her.

"You're sure?"

"Pretty sure. It sounded like that to me. I can't say whether or not there was a trailer attached, but since the driver changed gears several times I assumed he was backing a trailer into place. After the motor noise stopped, what sounded like a truck cab door slammed, and I heard men shouting. I couldn't distinguish much of what they said. Only the words *smooth*, and *cash* came through."

"Ah," the sheriff said. "So there's no way you could know how many men were involved?"

"No, other than the two voices I could distinguish and, of course, the two men with me."

"Okay, go on."

Henry broke in when she mentioned hearing a woman's voice, and what she had heard of the woman's conversation. "Could you repeat that, Carrie?"

She did. "Hurry. Get her to tell you. Use the car; they'll be searching for the van by now."

"Sounds like she was the one in charge," he said.

"Yes, it definitely sounded that way. Several times after we left there, the men referred to 'the boss,' and I wondered if that woman might not be the person they were referring to." She stopped speaking for a moment, and her voice faltered when she continued, "I am sure she's the one who gave them orders to kill me."

Henry flinched, and fought to control a compelling urge to go to her.

"It does sound like she was in charge of events," the sheriff said. "Go on."

The rest of her story had Henry feeling horror and awe alternately. To lie there, expecting death, and then your adversary shoots into the ground? He could barely comprehend what it would be like. Bravery under fire? As far as he was concerned, she'd managed that with the best.

The sheriff said, "He was supposed to kill you, didn't, and before he walked off, asked you to protect him by playing dead, so to speak, until he could get away?"

"He said, 'get out of the country,' but I don't really know how he meant that."

The room was so quiet after she spoke that Henry heard a cow bellow in a distant pasture. Neither Roger nor Shirley paid any attention, so Henry assumed such noises were common enough to be ignored, and the bellow didn't announce the pending birth of twin calves.

Finally the sheriff said, "It is your intention to honor his request?"

"Of course. He saved my life. I don't think he has the heart of a killer."

"My deputies are spending their time searching for you and your abductors."

"I don't see any need to stop them from doing that. It seems to me searching for abductors is legitimate activity, no matter where I am, or whether I'm dead or alive. Arnie Frost is still a criminal, as is the woman, and possibly others."

Henry said, "Exactly. And there is also a drug case to pursue, as well as the death of John Harley, and the disappearance of his wife. She may well be dead, too."

"Yes," the sheriff said, then fell silent, obviously pondering the serious matters facing him. Respecting this, no one spoke.

Finally he said, "What we really have here is a witness protection situation. I've got to figure out how to take care of that, since I'll also be covering up the fact the witness—a woman we are using officers to search for—has been found."

Roger cleared his throat. "The point is, how safe is your department for keeping Carrie's escape quiet? How many of your deputies might want to blab to others just because this is a really great story? Besides that, are you darned sure every officer you have is—how do you guys put it—clean? Drug money talks pretty strong. I, for one, am not willing to risk Carrie's life on trusting that no one in your office has been dirtied. I believe she's safe as long as Arnie and his boss continue to think she's dead. We need to keep it that way."

"Exactly," Henry said, and thought, *Hooray for you, Roger, you've pinpointed my concerns about the whole situation, and bringing your cousin into it. Since it's important for Carrie's safety and mental peace that we keep her escape a secret, that's exactly what we're going to do.*

The sheriff shook his head, looking worried. "It's your life that could be in danger too, Roger, and the lives of everyone here. If you read the news today, you know drug lords, terrorists, and similar criminals can kill scores of people to reach one person, or prove a point. If that applies here, you are no more safe than Ms. McCrite, so I certainly understand how important it is that no one finds out she's here."

Roger said, "Now, Norm, if we all keep mum, how will the bad guys find out? And, where else would you like her to be?"

"In a safe house we can guard, but that would mean some in my department would have to know she's alive."

The sheriff turned to Carrie. "Are you sure you want to protect this second man, as you call him? He may be guilty of many crimes, including murder."

"Yes, I am sure, for the reason I have already stated."

"Are you familiar with the Stockholm Syndrome?"

Henry shifted in his chair, and watched his wife's expression change from surprise to anger to ice. He could see the emotions easily, even on her damaged face, and he understood the reason for them. To suggest she was sympathetic to her captors because she had begun to identify with them was an insult.

He said, "She was in their presence for less than a day, Sheriff Cook. I hardly think that would be enough time for her to identify with those men or want to protect them. That sort of thing isn't in her nature anyway. What she is asking is in response to a very singular event, that one man has risked his life to save hers. In the name of humanity, she owes him something. She wants to pay that debt, and her experience must be seen as unrelated to his past activities. If he is a killer, then his actions toward her are even more striking, and more likely to signify a change in his outlook. I won't go so far as to suggest character reformation, but it is possible, no matter how remotely."

"But, as a former law officer, you would know that . . . " the sheriff began.

"That does not negate my humanity, Sheriff, nor that of the man who saved Carrie's life at great risk to himself."

Carrie broke in. "Both of you are getting off track. As Henry knows, I have always been a keen observer of people, and I've lived long enough to add depth of experience to that. When I said I did not feel the one I named Second Man had the heart of a killer, it was a result of observation, not sympathy. I had surmised this about his nature very early, and that helped convince me it would be a good idea to remain pleasant and submissive when I was with the two men. I sensed that would be more productive on my behalf than anger or resistance. I am sure you can follow my logic. I can't affirm my actions made any impression on Arnie, but I think they did on Second Man, and that probably helped save my life."

Henry said, "Carrie, after you were switched from the van to the car, then driven to our house, how far did it seem?"

"Not far. I didn't hear any sounds I recognized after we left there, but I did keep track of turns. We drove back to the paved road, turned right, went probably a couple of miles—unless my judgment of distance was way off— and then turned left. After a mile or so we turned into our lane, so the only big unknown is where the unpaved road we were on is located. By then I was getting kind of disoriented, but I am sure about the turns, and it didn't seem like we were in the car very long."

Shirley, who had been untypically silent, spoke up. "Jo Marshall, one of the ladies in our County Extension Homemakers' Club lives on an unpaved road about three miles that way." She pointed. "Isn't that the direction you think you came from, Carrie?"

After Carrie nodded, she continued, "It's called Marshall Road, since her family has been there long enough to have the road named after them when the county went from rural route box numbers to real addresses for the 911. I've been to Homemakers' Club meetings at her house, and a place I pass on her road sometimes has big trucks around. I always thought it kinda odd for such a business to be off a paved highway, but Jo said it had been in the same place for more years than she could remember, and most county roads weren't paved back when it first set up there. She said she thought they did some kind of freelance hauling.

"Last time I was at her house for a meeting they'd just put up a couple of new-looking metal buildings at that business. When I said something about it, Jo told me the place had new owners, and she'd been watching to see what they were going to do there. She was hoping it wouldn't be more trucking, since the heavy rigs churn up clouds of dust in dry spells, and the dust turns to muck when it rains.

"Y'know, I think I'll pay a call on Jo this afternoon. I seem to recall she was interested in the recipe for a casserole I took to our meeting there back in August. I think I'll write out a copy and take it to her, apologizing for forgetting to do it right after the meeting. It doesn't matter that she won't remember asking for my recipe. She'll probably think she did ask to be polite. We all do that sometimes. I can stay for a chat if she seems to welcome it. That okay with you, Norm?"

"Yes, see what you can find out, but be your usual canny self and don't stick your nose into anything that might fall down on you. I suggest you drive Roger's truck instead of that noteworthy Cadillac."

"Better 'n that, I'll drive Junior's pickup."

"Good. Call me on Martha's phone at home this evening to tell me what you learn. In the meantime, we'll see what we can find out about any business located along Marshall Road. I'll have one of our guys follow up and go by in his personal truck like he's looking for something further along. He could get lost and stop to ask directions. I can tell the deputy I've had an anonymous tip about a business on Marshall Road that's a suspected front for drug dealing.

"Heck, I might just go by there myself tomorrow. I could drive my truck to work."

Roger said, "Can't do it, Norm. Everyone knows your face. You want to look things over, send someone else."

Cook nodded. "I keep forgetting about being known on sight. New thing for me."

Roger spoke up again. "Why don't you stay for a bite of breakfast with us before you go to work? Seems to me what we have here is more than a protected witness to a crime. She's given you a clue, and you'd be smart to follow up on that, rather than worry about whether or not some woman named Carrie McCrite has been found, and your guys are still out looking for her." He laughed. "Truth be told, she really hasn't been found. If anything, she's found herself. "

The sheriff looked at his watch, grinned at Roger, but didn't respond to the breakfast invitation. Instead, he said, "Ms. McCrite, It would be helpful if you could show me about where those bullets went into the ground. Do you think you can locate the general area, and maybe at least point to it from the car if we drive up that way?"

Carrie looked thoughtful and didn't say anything. Henry supposed she was wondering if her wish to protect Second Man extended to protecting bullets from his gun. She knew, of course, that testing them might reveal crimes the gun had been used for in the past.

He decided to help things along. "Let's go up there in the car I have out front. Plenty of room for the three of us, and everyone's used to seeing it around here. As Carrie knows, it will save time for your deputies if they have some idea where to start searching for those bullets."

He looked at his wife and continued, "Won't take as long as if they have to sweep the entire area."

Carrie stood. She'd gotten the message. They'd eventually search for the bullets whether or not she helped define a likely area.

"I'll get a couple of things from my car, then let's go," the sheriff said.

Chapter Twenty-Four

WHO'S BEEN HERE?

s the car turned onto the old logging road after a very short drive,
Carrie thought about what had seemed like such a long walk the
evening before. Being in the same place again, however, did not
cause any residual feelings of horror. She only felt gratitude that her life
had been spared.

As soon as they reached the location she'd walked away from, she
realized it probably would have been easy for the sheriff to identify the place
without her help. There hadn't been much breeze during the night, and
accumulated branches and leaves marking where she and Second Man had
gone into the forest were still disturbed. Not only that, she could see a scrap
of white in the distance. Probably a tissue that had fallen from her pocket
when she made her way out.

"This is it? The sheriff asked.

"Yes. Arnie stayed in the car, which was parked about where we are now.
The other man and I headed into the trees where the disturbed leaves are.
I remember that fallen tree because I saw it when I walked out last
evening."

"Smart of you to leave your hanky here."

Carrie said nothing, since the tissue's presence was a surprise to her.

"Will it be difficult for you to show me the exact location where the gun
was fired? I'll understand if you say it is. But, I'd like to find those bullets
now, or at least one of them. Because of our circumstances, I need to be
the one searching. I can't send deputies up here with better equipment until
you've been returned home officially."

She said, "I'll go with you, and glanced at Henry, hoping he couldn't read her thoughts. She didn't want those bullets found, but her own honesty—which right now seemed a burden—meant she'd help the sheriff.

She didn't remember ever being so torn between two sides of a criminal case, or, for that matter, between two parts of any life circumstance.

Henry said, "I'll go along too, if you don't mind."

"Okay," the sheriff said, "Doubt any of us will disturb clues, but we'll stay away from where they walked and keep our eyes open."

"Of course," Henry said, squeezing Carrie's hand.

They walked into the woods, led by Carrie. When they came to the scrap of white caught on a fallen branch, Carrie saw that it was a man's handkerchief, not one of her tissues as she had supposed, and she was sure there had been no cloth handkerchief here last night. That meant someone had come to this place since then. She walked on, saying nothing. Sheriff Cook would have to discover the implication by himself.

Both Henry and the sheriff passed the white cloth without comment, though Henry, at least, would know it wasn't her's.

When they came near the place where Second Man had fired into the ground, she couldn't hide an exclamation.

Since neither of the men knew the exact spot they were headed for, it took both of them another moment to notice what she had.

She'd stopped moving, but the sheriff hurried forward, beating Henry to the newly disturbed piles of rocks, dirt, and leaves.

"I guess I was wrong about anyone coming back to get those bullets," he said. "Obviously they were important, and would have told us something. Your Second Man—or someone—came back, found the place, and most likely dug them up. I doubt there's any point to me searching now. If by chance he didn't find them, I doubt I can without more workers and equipment. We'll come here later with a metal detector, but he probably found both bullets unless one ricocheted wildly."

Henry looked into the woods. "I assume he's long gone."

"The man is certainly no fool," the sheriff replied, "I'd bet he was gone shortly after first light this morning."

Carrie still said nothing. *And I hope none of us ever sees him again.*

The sheriff poked around in the disturbed spot with the camping shovel he'd brought with him. It was obvious from his desultory movements that he thought there was no point to further searching, and he soon stopped. Without speaking, he stood, and turned back toward the road.

On the way he paused by the handkerchief. "This yours?" he asked Carrie.

"No, it isn't. I carry paper tissues, and I didn't see it here last night." Maybe he'd think she hadn't heard him when he told her it was smart to leave a hanky to mark the spot.

"Man's handkerchief," he said, as he took out a pen, lifted the handkerchief, and dropped it in a bag he'd pulled from his pocket.

As soon as they were back in the Booth's living room, Shirley appeared from the kitchen. "Everything go okay?"

Norman Cook said, "Looks like Second Man came back and got his bullets, so it didn't exactly go okay. That avenue of investigation is closed off, though he did drop a handkerchief and I have that."

"Ah," Shirley said, glancing at Carrie. "Well, that's too bad, Norm, but now, who wants coffee and cinnamon rolls?"

"Can't stay," the sheriff told her, "much as I regret it. Thanks for the invitation. However, if you happen to have any of those rolls extra . . . "

"Got a plastic bag, too," Shirley said, as she disappeared into the kitchen.

"So, what's next for you, Norm," Roger asked

"For now, I'll go along with your plan to keep this woman's presence here quiet, but remember that, given the parameters you've laid out, the sheriff's department can't visibly guard her or any of you. If someone involved in this finds out you're alive, Ms. McCrite, you'll be in danger again, and once more I'll say that the rest of you will share the danger. It's already touched all of you through the craft fair connection, and don't forget, Edith Embler and Milton Sales are included. As to whether or not there's someone in our department connected to Arnold Frost and Co., well, I hope not, but right now I can't assure you of that. You've raised some serious questions.

"First thing back at the office, I'm going to check into Ms. Embler's assertions she's a confidential source for the DEA. I'll let you know what I find, but I'll call from my wife's unlisted line at home.

"So, Ms. McCrite, for now, you stay out of sight. Your husband shouldn't be visiting you, and you can't talk to him on the phone. Create a code for Shirley or Roger to use if the two of you need to communicate. These days, almost no method of communication is safe if someone really wants to break in, and we haven't much of a clue yet as to how sophisticated these folks are. I do think Martha's unlisted number is safe enough. Still, Roger or Shirley, keep in mind what you say, even there."

"I'll be thinking about a new place to move you, Ms. McCrite. Other than take you to my own home, I don't know of any yet."

Shirley stuck her head around the corner. "We have friends up the road, Jason and Eleanor Stack. They've been gone, but plan to be back soon. They have no connection to any of this so far. Would Carrie be safer there?"

Both Carrie and Henry shook their heads, and Henry said, "Not fair to involve others."

The sheriff said "Let me check up on Ms. Embler. Given what I've heard, she's most likely in as much danger now as Ms. McCrite. It would he helpful to find out what papers 'the boss' those men talked about thinks she has."

Henry said, "Since the room was torn up when we came home, it will be safe for me to ask her again what the reason for that search might have been, not mentioning we know they were looking for papers. I can point out the search may prove she's in danger, because obviously the bad guys think she has—or had—something they want. Maybe she told me she has no idea what they were looking for because she doesn't trust me yet. I'll push at her harder now."

The sheriff nodded and Henry continued, "As an increasingly anxious husband, I can ask tough questions because I think the answers might help us find Carrie."

"Good. I value your experience and your help. If we learn enough to decide Ms. Embler can be trusted, it might be best to keep the two women together at your house, and well guarded. Let's see what I come up with. I can always assign Deputy Rosten to some other case if needed, but I really must find a safe deputy or two to help out, and maybe she fits. For now, though, it seems we need you, Roger, along with Shirley, as citizen guards, much as I'd like to relieve you of that duty."

Carrie said, "I should go home as soon as possible. I don't want to bring danger to Shirley and Roger."

Shirley came back in the room in time to say, "Carrie, you're the one who might be in danger, so hush that talk. Both you and Norm listen to me. Us here make a good team, and we've proved it before, but we do want to know if Edie and the deputy are safe with this. We'd sure like to have Henry free to help out, for one thing, and I know he wants to be with Carrie, wherever she stays. So Norm, you go find out about those two women."

She walked past Henry to hand the sheriff a sack.

"I'll do the best I can as quickly as I can, Shirley." He kissed her on the cheek, said, "Thanks," went to the front door, and was gone, leaving the scent of fresh-baked cinnamon rolls floating behind him.

As soon as they heard the sound of his shoes going down the wooden steps, Shirley said, "Let's the rest of us sit at the kitchen table. I've got more rolls, and we need to make us a plan."

Chapter Twenty-Five

RED HAIR RULES THE DAY

"Seems to me we pretty much need to leave things like they are 'til we get more information," Roger said as Shirley set out the pan of rolls and Carrie dispensed plates and cups of coffee. "So, Henry, you'd best head into town the back way, say a quick howdy to Chief Trent to prove you've been there, then go home to your two women."

"Hey," Carrie said, "wait a minute. I'm his *only* woman. Those two are house guests, and there better be no monkey business up there."

She laughed after she said it, and realized the heaviness she'd felt since yesterday was mostly gone. Time to move forward.

Henry reached over and took her hand across the table. "Cara, you are, now and forevermore, my *only* and most special woman, never doubt that. Roger misspoke."

"Yes, I reckon he did," Shirley said. "I reckon no male nor female could never come between you'uns."

"Hmpf," Roger said, "silly women. They know they have us hog-tied."

Henry took a bite of roll, chewed, swallowed. "Well, your *woman* does make terrific cinnamon rolls. Maybe she'll share her recipe with me."

Carrie said, ignoring the bantering, "I wish we knew whether or not Edie and Olinda are safe, and that's safe two ways—safe from harm, and safe with the knowledge I'm still alive. I am sorry to be causing all of you this trouble. Having them in with us so I could go home would relieve some of that. Besides, I'd like to be working toward solving our problems. Just sitting here, waiting for Sheriff Cook and others to move things forward is not easy. I want to be accomplishing something."

"Here's my idea for a bit of action," Shirley said. "Let's fix up some kind of disguise for you, and you can go with me to Jo Marshall's this afternoon.

Maybe someone will be outside at the truck place that you recognize. Anyway, I bet Jo can tell us more about what she's seen there, and it's my thought you should hear anything she says first hand. I'm sure she'll be safe with this. Jo's no gossip.

"I don't know about Carrie being out and about," Henry said.

"I'd like to go, and it's probably at least as safe as hiding here."

"I'm not sure," Henry said. "No one is aware you're here but us."

"Well, yes, so far as we know." Carrie wondered what was really safest for her now, and stared past Roger at the calendar on the kitchen wall. It had a picture of an old mill with vines growing over it, and suddenly she was back at War Eagle Mill, coming out of the restroom booth, seeing Second Man for the first time. For a minute there was a flash of yesterday's terror. Was it only yesterday? And, had Second Man gotten away yet?

Henry squeezed her hand. "Bad thoughts, Cara?"

"Not so bad. I was thinking about Second Man, wondering where he is now."

"I'm first, and I'm right here," he said.

She had started to smile when she noticed how hurt he looked.

The sheriff mentioned the Stockholm Syndrome. Could I really have . . . ? No, that's nonsense.

She held his hand more tightly. "Yes, Love. I thank God for that every day. And now, we have work to do because, when Arnie and the others are arrested, all of us can go back to normal." *And by then, Second Man will be away safely.*

"Shoot," Shirley said. "Not normal is more exciting."

Roger chuckled. "She's right on that. I go into town now, folks at the feed store and barbershop want to know all about our latest adventures and, if nothing new is going on, then they want to hear a re-do of an old one. Can't remember how many times I've told the story of Van Buren. When this is all over, I'll have something new to talk about."

"Reason they don't get bored at his re-telling is because the story changes every time," Shirley said. "Who knows what those folks think of our adventures by now."

"I wondered why people look at me kind of funny when I shop in town," Carrie said, and was pleased when Shirley and Roger laughed.

Henry didn't laugh. He was silent for so long that, finally, Carrie said, "What is it?"

"This is not a game or something to entertain people with. It's serious crime. Drug trafficking is involved. Lives have been and are in danger. One man has died."

"Oh my," Shirley said. "We've really gone off base. We didn't mean . . . we don't want . . . Roger and I both know this is serious. It's just that . . . "

Carrie was still holding Henry's hand. Now she turned it over, and began running a finger around and around on his palm, noticing the lines, a scar, and a spot of stain. The stain was probably from when he re-finished that rickety old table she was fond of. He hadn't said it should be discarded. He'd repaired and refinished it, presenting it to her proudly only a few days ago.

Without looking up at Roger or Shirley, she said, "He's right, we shouldn't make fun and games out of this. But I understand what Roger and Shirley mean. We expect a happy ending, even though this is not fiction. We have had happy endings before, but we've been through tough trials getting there. Caution is good, but worry can cloud reasonable thinking. Worry sometimes keeps people from seeing their way to solutions."

She looked at Roger, then Shirley. "You must remember something, though. Henry has seen all too many criminal cases that did not come out well. People were hurt. People died. Criminals went unpunished. That's tough for him now. His life is in the middle of this criminal case, even if unofficially. People he knows, and those he loves are involved, and may be in danger. We can't be unaware of what happened to me yesterday.

"Why don't we blend our viewpoints? Henry, accept our optimistic outlook, but we'll let your caution guide us too. Okay, everyone?"

Now she looked up at her friends. Roger and Shirley were both nodding solemnly. Interrupting each other, both started to speak: "We're powerfully sorry," Shirley said, as Roger started, stopped, and then, following her words, added "I sounded terrible, and I'm sorry. This isn't happening so Shirley and me can have adventures to brag on. Henry, you tell us what next."

Henry was silent again while they all waited.

Finally, he said, "I guess disguising Carrie so she can go with Shirley to Jo Marshall's and check out that truck place might move us forward. Roger, will you or Junior go along in the back jump seat in Junior's truck as re-enforcement? You'd be pretty much out of sight there in the back, and could stay on guard while Shirley and Carrie are inside the Marshall's talking. Is that okay?"

"I'll keep the girls company and take my shotgun along," Roger said. "Junior can stay here and watch for anything peculiar while he's tending the cows."

"Okay," Shirley said, "Let's figure out a disguise for Carrie. How about starting with a hair cut and color? I used to cut the girls' hair and I'm pretty good at it, if Carrie trusts me."

"I do, and I need a haircut, but color? I don't know."

"They got temporary hair color. Our girls used it for fun when they lived at home, Sally, the youngest, especially. I know they still make the stuff. Haven't you seen kids, even adults, with green or orange or purple stripes in their hair?"

"Oh, hey, wait a minute."

"Don't worry. What the girls used came out—mostly—the first time they washed their hair. And not all of the colors are gaudy day-glow stuff. They got ordinary colors, or did when the girls used it for Halloween and such. How about being a red-head again, Carrie? Henry ever seen you with red hair?"

"Uhhh, well, no. "

"Gimme a minute. I'll call Teasley's in town, see what they have in stock. If something sounds good, Henry can pick it up when he goes to see Chief Trent, bring it back here, and we'll get you disguised in time to go visit Jo Marshall. You'll look real different with the grey covered up and maybe wearing one of the girl's old dresses."

"I bet I will," Carrie said, and sighed.

Two hours later Carrie stood in front of the cheval glass in Shirley and Roger's bedroom. "I feel like *Anne of Green Gables* with this wild red hair," she said.

"Wasn't that older lady's name Marilla? Matthew and Marilla, the folks who took Anne in?" Shirley asked. "Not sure, never read it in a book, though the name sounds right from what I remember seeing on the television. It's a pretty name—Marilla. If I'd learned to read before the girls were born and read that story, one of 'em would have been named Marilla."

She studied Carrie, looking over her head into the mirror. "Well, anyway, the hair color is pretty, and that dress is long just because Sally's a few inches taller than you. Was your hair anywhere near that color when you were young?"

Carrie poked at the orange curls. "Not so bright."

"Here, put this hat on, It'll cover part of the brightness. I called Jo, and she's expecting us. All I gotta do is corral Roger."

"What about my glasses?"

"You've got those sunglasses. Did the two men who took you ever see you in sunglasses?"

"No, they had my purse the whole time, and the sunglasses were in it."

"Okay, put 'em on and we're ready to go."

Chapter Twenty-Six

THIS MUST BE THE PLACE

A fter Shirley turned the truck onto Marshall Road she slowed to fifteen miles an hour. "They'll think I'm driving slow because of the rocks and dust," she said. "Only makes sense on these roads anyway. Now, you can look out the front window kinda slanty, and, as I pass, still see out of the corner of your eyes, can't you? That way you won't seem to be paying too much attention. The place is just ahead. Roger, you look too."

"Oh, yes," Carrie said, "This could be it. I see the trailer from an eighteen-wheeler in back of those buildings. I don't see any tractor, but the largest metal building would hold it easily. Too bad there are no people about, it would be helpful if I could identify either of the two men who abducted me. However, remembering when we pulled in and stopped, all I see here now fits with what I heard and felt then. The second building could well be where they parked the van and moved me to the car."

"Looks to be some kind of office at the side of the smaller building," Shirley said.

"Uh-huh."

"Okay, here we are at Jo's place."

Carrie was almost instantly ashamed by her surprise when she saw the elegant house. Well, why shouldn't people out here have lovely homes? But on this road? She'd expected a simple farm house. A generous amount of money had paid for the large two-story home with shutters and a pillared front porch. The wide porch held a hanging swing, and there was wicker furniture, undoubtedly left out now so the Marshalls could enjoy pleasant fall days sitting there. There was even a ceiling fan to chase away summer heat and mosquitoes. Scarlett O'Hara would be comfortable in this home.

"Shirley, did the Marshalls move here before the trucking business came in?"

"Yep. I don't exactly know how long they've been here, but I don't think they would have chosen this land—pretty as it is—if any business was close by. No zoning out here, though. You can't pick your neighbors."

"Both their families had big cotton plantations in Georgia before the war," Roger said. "Lotsa money. His family sold out after the war and came to Arkansas, her's stayed in Georgia. Them that stayed didn't do well at first. The daddy was a bitter man, and had lost one son in the war, but the younger son accepted the change, and caught up after a few years."

Experience had taught Carrie what war they meant. "Slaves?" she asked.

"Yes," Roger said, "a terrible thing to do to anyone, but they must have been among the better owners, because Ben Marshall told me most of her family's slaves stayed on. They were given bits of land for a garden and materials to make a house, and then paid to work for the son. Thank the good Lord those times are behind us now. The Marshall people here are great-great-grandchildren of the Marshalls that left Georgia, and Jo and Ben have one daughter-in-law who's African-American. The two grandkids are the color of honey. Both have big brown eyes and brown curly hair."

"Plenty cute," Shirley added.

"Where do the son and his family live?" Carrie asked.

"Seattle," Roger said. "Ben Junior and his wife are engineers that have something to do with the airplane business. Jo can tell you about it. Good place to start conversation if you need a starter, which, with Jo, I doubt you will."

Shirley pulled into the asphalt circle drive in front of the porch, tooted the horn, then got out.

Carrie, suddenly embarrassed by her fiery red hair, pulled her hat down as far as it would go, and was sliding out of the truck when a generously-sized woman came out on the porch. *Picture-perfect grandma.*

"You'll explain about the disguise, won't you?" she whispered to Shirley.

"Already have, on the phone," Shirley said, "and I forgot the dang recipe. No matter, she knows we're here on more serious business."

"Welcome. This is sure a nice surprise," the woman said as she jiggled across the porch. "I see Roger's here, too. Come on along, Roger, unless you object to some girl talk. Ben's away. He's got the idea he wants a new baler, so he's visiting dealers." She bent, peering in at Roger. "I have fresh applesauce cake."

"Mighty kind, but I'll stay out here. Catch up on my reading."

"Oh-oh, oh, my," Jo said, "I get it, you're the watch dog. Well, since the sun's warmed the porch, why don't you sit up here? I often do that of an afternoon. I'll bring some cake out."

"I'm okay here for now, thanks, Jo. Maybe in a bit."

The three women went into the house and Carrie's amazement deepened. Furniture in the entry hall and parlor might, indeed, have come from what she imagined Scarlett's Tara to be like. Some of the pieces must be quite valuable by now.

"This is beautiful," she said, speaking more from her respect for antiques than an admiration of actual beauty, since heavy, dark wood and horsehair were not her taste. Her nose even detected the faint mixture of mothballs and mustiness she associated with antique upholstery.

As Jo Marshall directed them through the parlor and into a more comfortably furnished sitting room, she said, "Thanks. That furniture came west from Georgia in 1866. We don't use the room, so it's mostly a family museum. The couches and chairs are terrible to sit on, but, well, who could get rid of family antiques?"

She shrugged, and her whole upper body wobbled.

"Sit," she said. "How about some applesauce cake and coffee?"

Carrie said "Thanks, not for me. We just finished a delicious lunch at Shirley's."

Shirley spoke at almost the same time. "No thanks, Jo, though I do remember how good your cake is." After a pause, she said, "You understand that no one must hear of our visit and its reason. Truth be told, people's lives may well depend on secrecy. Might be best if you didn't even tell Ben, if that doesn't bother you."

"It doesn't. We're close, as you know, but I don't run to him with every-thing that happens in my day, and he can keep secrets, too. Such doesn't bother either of us."

"Okay, then. I told you some of the story on the phone, but here's all of it. Carrie has experienced the worst part, and can correct me if I go wrong. Things are bad enough that we had to disguise her to even think of letting her out of my house, but I thought she should see your neighbor's business and hear your account of what you've noticed about the place. She's already told us that what she now sees fits with what she felt when they took her there, blindfolded."

"Okay, go on," Jo Marshall said, and wiggled herself into a more comfortable position on the couch she had chosen for her seat.

Shirley told the story, emphasizing safety for Carrie as the reason no one must know she hadn't died in the woods, rather than any need to protect the man who saved her. When she finished the story, uninterrupted by Carrie, both women looked at Jo expectantly, and waited.

"What a truly terrible thing to endure. Carrie, I feel right honored to have someone I'd call a heroine visiting my house. I don't know if I can help you much, but I'll try to recall all I can, as well as what I've seen the last few days, which may be of some interest to you.

"It's my practice on pleasant days to enjoy sitting in the swing on our porch with a bite to eat and a glass of sweet tea. Ben often joins me there of an evening, since we aren't big on watching television.

"Most of the trees between here and the truck place have leaves that drop in the fall, so we can see it pretty well for much of the year. Ben keeps saying we should have planted a row of some sort of evergreens as a screen years ago, but we just never got around to it, which, for your interests today, is a good thing.

"The business was called "Specialty Hauling" for years, and all we ever saw was trucks coming and going. I reckon customers phoned the office here and arranged for someone to pick up their load and deliver it where they wanted. I think it was short hauling, since we could tell trucks weren't often gone more'n two days, and most just one. The rigs were all painted the same yellow, but we could see differences in them after a while watching from the porch. It kind of got to be entertainment for Ben and me, guessing what they were hauling, and so on."

"Sounds like you're good observers," Shirley said. "Did they ever bring loads back here?"

"Not often. You can tell from the sound of a truck whether it's loaded or not. We got to know how to tell that. Most of the time, the trucks were empty when they came and went from here.

"Well, a few months ago it was obvious the business had changed hands. All the yellow trucks left, and those two new metal buildings went up. They have only one big truck there now, and two smaller ones—you know, the kind that has a separate cab in front with a big closed-in box on the back like furniture stores might use. They have a couple of big vans, too. All of them are painted white. No company name anywhere and, as you saw, none on the buildings.

"The big truck sometimes goes away for a week or more, and we've known the two smaller ones to be away for several days. The vans stay pretty close, but, on occasion, they are gone overnight.

"I've seen four different men around the place pretty regularly, most of the time getting in or out of trucks, or backing a smaller truck or van into one of the buildings. They also get a few visitors. Most are men, a few women, and they come in SUVs or pick-up trucks. The trucks usually have covers over the bed or large tool boxes behind the cab. Most of the time they drive into one of the two new buildings so we never see what they're picking up or delivering. Ben says some kind of repair work or vehicle enhancement, like adding darkened windows or lifts, could be what goes on inside, but we haven't seen evidence of anything like that driving away yet. Most of the time the visitors don't stay more than an hour, so I think he's wrong.

"UPS stops there almost every day, and the driver goes to that office door on the side of the smaller building to leave packages. Sometimes there are a lot of boxes in a shipment, which is kind of unusual for UPS, isn't it? Don't they mostly carry smaller shipments?"

"Ones I've noticed or received are small," Carrie said.

"That's what I thought. Well now, all this activity picked up speed about the middle of August, and has stayed steady ever since. And, here's something that will be of special interest to you since Shirley mentioned you hearing a woman's voice. Over the last week or so I've seen a woman come out from that small door several times. Looked like she came out to talk with people who'd just driven in. After a few minutes the big door there would open and they'd drive inside, the women walking in behind them, then the door would go closed. I never saw her before last week, though she could have been in and out before then, and I missed it. But for sure she wasn't around as much as she is now."

"What's she look like?" Shirley asked.

"Oh, well, let's see. Dark, straight hair, cut short, almost manish. Hard to tell from this distance, but my guess is she's around forty-five and good looking. She's skinny except for big bazooms. Kind of tall, maybe five foot eight or nine."

"What time of day have you seen her?" Carrie asked. "Or does it vary?"

"Varies. I think she's been there most all the time since I first noticed her. I never saw her drive off, so I figure there must be a living space inside that smaller building. I haven't smelled food cooking, but, who knows, she may live on microwaved dinners. Or the wind could have been a direction to take the smells away."

"What does she wear?" Shirley asked.

"Oh, just jeans and a shirt that looks like a man's dress shirt with the sleeves rolled up. I bet she wouldn't wear a polo or t-shirt any more'n I would. There are those bazooms." Jo laughed. "A shirt suits her better. She never has on anything like a mechanic's overalls, if that's what you're thinking about."

"Not really, just tryin' to get a picture. I guess you've never seen her dressed up—you know, like going to church or out to dinner?"

"No, but I could have missed something like that."

"What do you remember seeing during the late morning and early afternoon yesterday? Was she around then?"

"I didn't spend much time on the porch yesterday, Shirley, and I'm sorry, because I know what you're getting at. Did I observe anything around the time you think Carrie was there? No. I was inside, working in the kitchen and tending to laundry. Ben was working in the pastures, except for having lunch."

Carrie asked, "What about the four men you mentioned? When you see them, what are they doing?"

"Before the woman showed up, they talked to those that came, and directed them inside like she's doing now. But they didn't hang around all the time like she is." Jo laughed again. "After all, someone has to do the grocery shopping, even for TV dinners, right? Maybe she has them go shopping for her. It's almost like she's hiding out here."

"What about nighttime? Is anyone around then?"

"We aren't on the porch after dark this time of year, but if our lights are out and I'm near the front windows upstairs, like when I'm going to bed, I've noticed light over there, and, one or two times, headlights coming or going."

"If you don't mind," Carrie said, "could we go sit on the porch? I'd like to look the place over more carefully "

Shirley shook her head. "Uhh, I don't know about that. Might not be safe for you."

"There's still some spotty cover from the trees, especially at the north end," Jo said, "and they never pay any attention to us anyway. I took over a box of cookies right after they moved in, partly because I was curious to see what was inside those buildings. No one was outside, so I knocked on the small door. One of the men came, and I told him I wanted to welcome them to the neighborhood, which, of course, was baloney, more-or-less. The man did act real glad to get the cookies, and he thanked me, but he sure didn't invite me in, and I haven't gotten so much as a wave from any of them since. Anyway, I think it will be okay to sit there, since guests during the day often sit outside with me in pleasant weather like today. I insist on bringing out some coffee, though, unless y'all want sweet tea."

Both Carrie and Shirley accepted the offer of coffee, and Jo told them to go on out while she got a tray ready to bring.

When the three of them were settled, Carrie asked, "Since guests do sit with you on the porch, and the truck people are used to that, how about the possibility of someone official—say a deputy sheriff—coming here to observe? Sounds as if they could drive a plain vehicle, wear plain clothing, and sit here without it looking suspicious."

"I think that would work fine," Jo said, "but of course I'd have to tell Ben about it then."

"I understand. Can he be trusted to keep this quiet for a while? No talking to anyone?"

"If he knows the possible consequences to you, or even to Shirley and Roger if he blabs, you bet he can," Jo said, and I think . . . oh, look! There's the woman and one of the men I've seen before. Just came out of the small door."

Carrie said, "Shirley, you keep talking and looking at Jo, any kind of conversation you can think of. Jo and I can glance toward the buildings. We can't stare, but I want to see those two in case I might recognize anything about either of them. I sure wish we could hear their voices."

"Way too far for that," Shirley said, "and they can't hear me, either, so I'll tell Jo about the time Henry planned a camping trip to the Buffalo National River as a surprise for you, and . . ."

Chapter Twenty-Seven

THE OBJECT OF A SEARCH

W hen he walked into the house Henry smelled . . . cinnamon rolls? He found Olinda and Edie in the kitchen reading the newspaper.

"What smells so good?"

Olinda said, "I've never made a pie from scratch, and Edie hasn't for years, so, since we had plenty of time, we decided to make one. Your *Grass Valley Bistro Cookbook* doesn't include anything as ordinary as a simple piecrust recipe, but I found instructions online. You didn't have all the stuff called for here in the house, but you had the basics. We substituted the rest, like using margarine instead of shortening and salt. We took the two apples you had in the refrigerator and a can of peaches for our two-crust apple-peach pie." She looked at her watch. "Done in about thirty minutes if our calculations are right."

"Sounds and smells good. I look forward to it."

Edie said, "Things go okay with the police chief? You were gone quite a while."

"Oh. Well, I waited for him to be free. Nice guy. Concerned about Carrie, of course. I guess there's no news or you'd have called."

"No news," Olinda told him. "Sorry. Now it looks like we'll all be here at least another day. That means I need to go out to a grocery store, if you'll loan me your car. I hate to leave you and Edie here alone, but it can't be helped. You know enough to stay inside with the doors locked."

"Edie and I will be okay. No hanky-panky." He attempted a chuckle, and it came out sounding more like the attempt to conceal a burp.

Olinda seemed not to notice. "Well, I was thinking of the safety issue, but, okay, we'll get a list together after lunch. I'll report to the sheriff about where I'm going and why. Overall, it should take me about an hour. Meanwhile, what about lunch?"

We have canned soup, and your pie. There's also lunch meat for sandwiches."

"Out of bread," she said.

"Oh. Well, we can cut the lunch meat into squares and have it on crackers with our soup."

"How about making that tomato soup you made the day I came?" Edie asked.

When they cut the pie, Olinda looked at it in dismay. "It's soupy," she said, and the bottom crust didn't really cook. What's wrong?"

Edie stared into the pie pan. "Probably should cool more, but I also forgot about mixing flour or tapioca into the fruit to thicken the juice."

"Never mind," Henry said. "I'll wash our soup bowls, we can spoon the filling into them, and break pieces of the top crust over the fruit and juice. Anyone for vanilla ice cream?"

As soon as Olinda left for the grocery store, Henry stopped cleaning the soup kettle and said, "We need to talk. Come in the living room. We can finish this later."

Looking wary, she joined him, saying nothing.

As soon as they were seated, he said, "Edie, it's time for the truth. You must have some idea about why our guestroom and your belongings were searched during the time Carrie and her abductors were in this house."

She picked at a piece of dried dough on her jeans and remained silent.

"I am not playing games with you. What do you—or did you—have that someone wants so badly they took my wife captive, used her keys to gain access to this house, and searched your belongings? That must have been the reason they abducted her, and I'm sure that's the reason those two men came here asking for you in the first place. You tell me why right now."

He knew his voice was rising, but didn't bother to control it, or the anger he was intentionally, but very easily, displaying. "What do they want? How did they know where you were, or that you were coming here?"

Edie looked up at him. There was no emotion visible on her face as she said, "I don't know."

He stood. "I'm ready to turn you over to the sheriff and tell them you're connected to drug trafficking in this part of Arkansas. You'll have to prove your innocence, and that may take some time, since I can give a lot of circumstantial evidence against you. My word against yours. Who do you think they'll believe?"

She raised both her hands, palms slanted out. "I'm not lying. I don't blame you for thinking I am, but I really have no idea what they were looking for or how they knew I was coming here. You know as well as I that leaks as far back as DC are possible. My mother knew I was coming, and I didn't tell her to keep my planned visit to Oklahoma and Arkansas a secret. She has lots of friends, and there's a woman checking in on her every day while I'm gone, though, as far as Mother is concerned, this is a vacation and an effort to connect with a long-lost cousin. She knows nothing about my confidential work for the DEA, and I didn't tell her I was going to try and learn what happened to Daddy."

Henry snorted in disgust and turned toward the phone.

"Do you want me to make up something just to appease you? If I knew anything, I'd . . . oh, wait. Maybe I do have an idea. Maybe I can guess."

He turned back toward her, but remained standing. "All right, guess."

"I don't know anything about the drug traffickers Daddy worked with, except, of course, for Milton Sales, who was undercover with him as you know. The only thing I am sure of is that those men were evil. But Milton told me something more.

"He said Daddy was collecting damning evidence against the men he worked with as a form of insurance if they ever turned against him. He was writing things down, and planned to put his information in a safe-deposit box or some other secure place." She stopped talking, and looked at the floor.

"And?" Henry prodded.

"Well, Milton says he has no idea what the evidence could have been. He wasn't far enough into the organization yet to hear many details. I guess he was still sort of on probation with both the DAC Bureau and the gang selling drugs to truckers. He wasn't even sure Daddy trusted him, since he never let him see what was on any of the papers."

"Edie, how long have you known about those papers?"

"Milton mentioned them in our conversation on the bridge at War Eagle."

"And, just now, when you continued to insist you had no clue why your belongings had been searched, it didn't occur to you that those papers might have been a reason? I find that hard to believe."

"Okay, don't believe me, but I honestly thought the matter of the papers was a dead issue. I didn't connect what Milton told me with present-day events. Even while Milton was telling me about them I assumed they were destroyed when Daddy was killed. It never occurred to me they might still be in existence, or that they could be important to someone today."

"Did Milton say any more about the papers that you 'just might remember' now?"

"He did tell me they were in an old black leather portfolio. Milton doesn't think Daddy had time to put them someplace safe before he was killed, since their existence in a safe place was supposed to be a kind of insurance against that very thing. He said the bad guys must have found them and destroyed them when . . . when they killed Daddy."

"And you say, until now, you had no idea they existed?"

"Mother and I found a safe-deposit box key in Daddy's things, but all that was in the box were passports, family papers, the deed to our house, my birth certificate, some other records. All very innocent."

Henry stood there in silence, thinking over what she'd been saying, and trying to decide if he believed she could be so naïve. Finally he said, "There may be copies of those papers somewhere. It seems obvious that at least two or three people believe they exist, either as originals or copies."

"After all these years? And, why would they matter now anyway? Probably people mentioned in the papers are dead. The mortality rate in that business is high, and anyway, people Daddy's age would all be gone by now. Some probably died in prison."

"Milton Sales is certainly still alive and active."

"He was only in his early twenties back then."

"Edie, *use your head.* He wouldn't have been the only one in that age group. And some of the older folks would have had families like your Dad did. Their children could be interested in destroying papers proving their parents were involved in crimes. It's also likely some of the children are carrying on the family business tradition, and therefore wouldn't balk at criminal activity to retrieve damning papers about their relatives."

"Well, I guess that's possible. But it's a lot of trouble to go to for old papers that, so far as we know, either don't exist, or, if they do, don't contain information anyone cares about today. Maybe Milton is all wrong about the papers."

"Maybe he's lying?"

"But what would his point be?" She returned to picking at the spot of dough.

He changed the subject. "You said passports. Whose?"

"Mother's and mine."

"Not your father's?"

"No, but if he was planning to go to Mexico, he'd have taken it with him."

"Back then you could travel legally in and out of Mexico or Canada without a passport."

"Oh, yes, that's true."

"Why passports for all of you?"

"We took a vacation to France when I was in my teens."

"If he had his passport with him when he left home that last time, perhaps he planned to go further afield than Mexico."

"Oh, I . . . well, I . . . uh, why?"

He sat across from her again and didn't answer, leaving her to think about the possibilities by herself. Could her father have abandoned family and country for a life abroad? Was he the sort of man who might do that? Only Edie and her mother would know. Or guess. And, what about Milton Sales? Did he know more than he was willing to tell Edie?

After a silence, he said, "And now are you telling me all you know—the complete truth as you see it?"

"Yes, Henry, I am."

He sighed, blowing out a whoosh of air. "After such a long time, I admit I'm as curious as you are about the interest in those papers."

They were both silent for a few clock ticks, then Edie asked, "Henry, do you trust Milton?"

"Right now, Edie, I don't trust anyone but myself, Carrie, and the Booths."

"Not me?"

"No."

For a minute she looked as if he'd slapped her. Then she nodded slowly.

"Okay," he said. "We'd better go finish cleaning up in the kitchen. You keep thinking about the papers. If they exist, where could they be hidden? And if they don't exist, how can we convince the people looking for them that they don't?"

"And, by doing that, get Carrie out of harm's way?"

"Yes, exactly. And you, as well."

Chapter Twenty-Eight

HENRY AT HOME

B y five o'clock Henry didn't know how much longer he could stand the required secrecy about Carrie's escape or, for that matter, stand more time with Olinda and Edie.

They weren't offensive, just the opposite, but he couldn't be comfortable in his own home. No sloppy dress—or undress—no rude comments or rude noises that Carrie would understand and tolerate. He had to act like a gentleman all the time. Worse, he had to keep up a façade of concern over Carrie's safety.

Now he was sitting on the edge of the bathtub in his and Carrie's bathroom, knowing he'd probably spent more time here than would seem reasonable. Still he sat, enjoying this private space.

Carrie didn't wear perfume, but the room retained scents he associated with her—shampoo, hand and face creams, a Carrie smell. He took a deep breath. Though he knew she was safe now, she still wasn't here, and the smells were comforting.

He wondered if Edie and Olinda felt uncomfortable too. All three of them were virtual prisoners in this house, and it might not be any easier for them than it was for him. He also wondered if Edie had come up with any new ideas about the missing papers. With Olinda always hanging around, they couldn't discuss it.

Oh, well. He stood. *Time to go back on duty.*

He'd talked briefly with Roger, and learned, in a sort of awkward, limited code, that the trip to the Marshall's had been productive. They'd be telling Cousin Norm about it tonight.

Other than the phone call, and an attempt to do a bit of vacuuming, with Edie and Olinda hovering to dust and wipe, Henry had spent most of his time reading. That seemed the safest neutral occupation, since the women were reluctant to bother him with conversation when he had his face in a book. He'd just finished Tony Hillerman's novel, *Hunting Badger*, and was eager to begin the next in the series. For him this was light reading. He no longer chose the thrillers that were once his reading preference. There had been enough of the thriller stuff in real-life Kansas City, though he could now read tough novels without putting himself inside whatever awful action was depicted. His own haunting memories were over and done with. Mostly.

Well, anyway, he was enjoying his visit to the New Mexico-Arizona Four Corners area and learning about Navajo life as depicted by Hillerman. The man obviously knew what he was writing about. Or, at least Henry supposed he did. Sure seemed like it, though he'd never been to that part of the United States so couldn't really judge.

Maybe he and Carrie should take a trip out that way next spring. He'd always wanted to see the Grand Canyon, and wondered now if she had ever been there.

He left his sanctuary in the bathroom, walked to the living room and looked around for more reading. Ah, he could try some of *The Message* Bible by Eugene Peterson that Carrie kept on the coffee table. Bible reading would look appropriate for someone in his supposed situation, and any reading passed the time. Besides, it cut off Olinda and Edie's attempts to comfort and distract him from his pretend anxiety by engaging in rambling conversation.

A while ago Carrie had recommended beginning Bible reading with something in Psalms, and he quickly decided Peterson had an instructive sense of humor. The First Psalm began: "How well God must like you—you don't hang out at Sin Saloon, you don't slink along Dead-End Road, you don't go to Smart-Mouth College." Curious, he left his chair to get Carrie's *King James* Bible for comparison. He'd just started the First Psalm, reading, "Blessed is the man that walketh not in the counsel of the ungodly," when Edie came into the room and stood, waiting for him to acknowledge her presence.

"You and Olinda doing okay?" he said, closing the Bible.

"We've been playing cards, but are getting hungry, and wonder what we should think about for supper. We have plenty of groceries in the house now."

"Let me look through our cookbook. Something there may appeal to all of us."

He got Chef John's book, and the two women sat at the kitchen table with him while he paged through, stopping to read some of the recipes aloud.

"How about this? 'Macaroni-Beef Casserole.' I think we have everything it calls for."

"Read it to us," Edie said.

He did, got approval, and started assembling ingredients while Olinda began peeling and chopping an onion.

Edie put out the large kettle to boil water for cooking macaroni.

"I don't mind doing this by myself," he said, wishing they'd take the hint and get out from underfoot.

"Gives us something to do," Edie said. "We're as bored as you are, and anxious about Carrie, of course." She looked into his face for a long moment before continuing, "though not nearly so anxious as you must be. Let us help."

"What's on TV tonight?" Olinda asked as she dumped the first batch of onions out of the chopper, then stopped to wipe her eyes.

"You two are welcome to the television," he said. "I think I'll read in bed."

He ended up watching a program about whales on AETN with them, then headed for the bedroom to continue his Bible reading. Before ten thirty he was asleep.

The gunshots awakened him at midnight.

Chapter Twenty-Nine

FIRE

T *wo shots! What the devil?*

Henry sat up, saw firelight through the bedroom window.

Conditioned by long experience, he was wide awake and moving in an instant. He grabbed the gun he'd been keeping in the bedside table and slipped into jeans and loafers.

As he opened the bedroom door he heard Olinda shouting, "Edie, someone's set fires on this side too. I'm going after them. Call 911. Put shoes on and get out here to help. Get Henry. Don't pour water on the fires. They used gasoline. Find some dirt and a shovel."

The front door slammed shut and the shouting stopped. There were more gunshots.

He could hear Edie on the phone so he went to get the two fire extinguishers they kept in the house, ran to the front door, then stopped, dead still, his hand on the knob.

Wait. Wait a minute.

He moved his hand to the door lock. Turned it.

Then he ran through the house, looking out all the windows. The only place flames were evident was outside the bedrooms where he, Olinda, and Edie had been sleeping.

Now he was torn by indecision. What if the fire was a ploy to get everyone out of the house—out in the open, and vulnerable? What if some person outside wanted in the house?

He ran back to his bedroom, fire extinguisher in hand, cranked the window open, shoved the screen out, and sprayed foam into the fire below him. It sputtered, didn't go completely out, but appeared to be dying. He looked along the wall of the house and didn't see any other fire, though the smell of gasoline was strong.

Hurrying to the guestroom window, he opened it and used the second extinguisher to spray more foam. He was returning to check on the fire outside the master bedroom when Edie joined him.

"Where can I find a shovel? Olinda said to shovel dirt on the fire." Her voice was high, almost a screech.

"I heard her. Stay inside. It's possible the fires were set to get us out of the house. I only saw fire outside our bedrooms and I think they're under control now. I'll keep patrolling inside. Stay with me. I locked the front door."

"Locked? But Olinda's outside. She was shooting at someone."

"As soon as I'm sure the fires are out I'll stand here by the door. I'll let her in the minute she comes back." He said no more, but wondered if Olinda was innocent in all this. Tonight's events might prove that, one way or another.

"Oh, I hope she's okay. Henry, we should go check, no matter what."

"Calm down Edie. Olinda is obviously armed, and she's trained to handle dangerous situations. I'm not going to put you in harm's way outside, and I will not leave you alone in this house."

She eyed the gun tucked in his waistband, said nothing more, and leaned against the wall, covering her face with her hands.

He said, "What woke you up?"

She moved her hands, looked at him. There were no tears.

"Olinda did. She shot out our window, then ran for the front door, shouting at me. I heard more shots after that."

"How was she dressed?"

"She sleeps in . . . oh. She had her official windbreaker on over, well, I suppose over the t-shirt she sleeps in."

Edie was following him now as he hurried from window to window around the house, checking for any evidence of fire. Several minutes passed with no sounds but their footsteps, then he asked, "What else did Olinda have on?"

"I didn't notice. Shoes of some kind I suppose. Jeans? Her running shoes? Oh, Henry, I don't know, but she may be in danger, and you locked her out."

"I said I'd let her in the minute she returns, and there doesn't seem to be any more evidence of fire now. We stay inside. The doors stay locked."

She chewed the inside of her lip, staring at him.

Then they both heard a heavy rumbling sound. Help had arrived.

Henry looked out the window, saw a volunteer fire department truck pulling up at the edge of their drive. Flashing lights announced a patrol car turning into the lane. He went to open the door, steeling himself against about-to-explode chaos.

An hour and a half later everyone but Investigator Holbrook Burke and a female deputy named Anderson had left the house, though two deputies stood guard outside. Burke sat in Carrie's favorite chair next to Henry's. Edie and a drooping Olinda sat on the couch across from the two men. Deputy Anderson stood behind the couch. The entire room reeked of gasoline.

The investigator said, "Deputy Rosten, I suggest you change your shoes and socks before you tell us more about your actions tonight. Ms Embler, if you will, get something for the deputy to put on her feet and then carry those shoes and socks to the porch. In the meantime, Major King, bring me up-to-date on why you chose to not leave the house, even though, for a time, it seemed to be on fire."

"No fire threatened the inside of the house at any time. I think many people believe, if a home is made of logs, it will burn easily, but I knew that wasn't the case. The type of dense tree trunks used in this log home are almost impossible to set on fire in the manner the arsonist chose. I felt we were safe, at least for the present. The fact fires had been set only under the bedroom windows also made me suspicious. If the intent was to start a real house fire, wouldn't the gasoline have been spread over a larger area, even into the woods, and the fires started as far from the bedrooms as possible so they could get going before we discovered them?"

Burke nodded. "I see what you mean."

"I also knew that there were people interested in finding papers they assume Edith Embler has in her possession. She's just told you about that. You already know the room where she's staying here has been searched by the intruders who abducted my wife. I don't know what the arsonists were thinking, of course, but maybe they assumed someone would grab those papers when leaving the house, or that they could capture Edie outside and make her tell them where the papers were. That's all guessing, of course."

Edie returned, set a pair of white cotton socks and house slippers in front of Olinda, then went to the kitchen to get an empty trash sack. When Olinda had removed her shoes and socks, Edie dropped them in the sack and put the sack on the front porch.

Burke continued, "Weren't you afraid someone might shoot at you through a window?"

Before Henry could reply, Edie said, "Of course he wasn't. I was following him the entire time and we walked with only nightlights to guide us. How could you check on fires outside if there were bright lights inside? Besides, if whoever started the fires only wants papers I'm supposed to have, what good would shooting either Henry or me do? I'm a real coward, Detective Burke, and, believe me, I wouldn't have been anywhere near a window if I thought there might be danger."

Henry suppressed a smile at this outburst, and was startled when Edie looked his way and winked.

Burke crossed one ankle over a knee, leaned back in the chair, and said, "I see."

Henry pulled out his cell phone, punched up the photo he'd taken in the Hobbs Men's Room, and handed it to Burke. "Do you recognize either of these men? They're the ones who abducted my wife." He paused, remembered he wasn't supposed to know who the men were yet, and quickly corrected. "I mean I think they might be the ones who abducted Carrie."

After studying the picture, the investigator handed the phone back and said, "Don't think I recognize them, but it might help if you came to my office and looked through our photo files. How did you get this picture?"

"The men showed up in the restroom at Hobbs when I was there. Probably followed me to the park. They tried to hassle me, but I never learned exactly why, because a bunch of big kids came in the room just then, and I was able to walk away. When I showed this photo to Carrie, she said these are the men who came to our home several days earlier, looking for Edie Embler. They said they were from the FBI."

Burke nodded. "Maybe we have photos of them. We will for sure if they've done time." He turned to Olinda. "We're ready for your report, Deputy Rosten. How did you become aware of the fires?"

Olinda scooted back on the couch and sat up straighter before she spoke. She couldn't hide obvious exhaustion, sitting stiff-spined or not.

Henry knew the feeling. She was coming down after a high-intensity adrenaline rush.

"I had trouble getting to sleep, and finally decided to go to the kitchen and get a drink of water. I stood looking out the kitchen window and thought I saw shadows on the other side of the garage. I didn't react, because at first I believed it must be my imagination, the wind moving underbrush or something.

"Then I saw what looked like fire at the other end of the house. I couldn't tell what was happening, the garage hid my view, but I hurried back to our room to get shoes, a jacket, and my gun. By then I could see flames under our bedroom window, and two figures moving away outside, so I opened the window as quickly as I could and called at them to stop. They didn't. I shot toward them, but they kept moving. I shut the window and shouted at Edie to call 911 and wake Henry. Then I went out the front door. In the faint moonlight I saw the two dark shapes again. I shot at them, and heard a sort of grunt, so maybe a bullet connected. I also heard a metallic clang. As you know, one of the intruders dropped the gasoline can.

"When I moved along the side of the garage to check if anyone had been hit and was down, gasoline was spilling out of the can, and I stepped in it. I assume the two guys were interrupted while dumping out gasoline and lost the lid to the can. We'll probably find it near the house after daylight.

"While I was standing by the gas can I saw two people running up the lane and I ran after them, shooting twice more. Before I could get to the road I heard a car start and head south. They were past the curve by the time I got up there, so I came back to the house and walked around it, seeing that the fires they set were already out. I stood in the driveway until you and the first of the two volunteer fire departments came."

The investigator asked, "You said you heard an exclamation immediately after you shot the second time?"

"Yes."

"Okay, thank you for the report, deputy."

He turned to Henry. "We'll do a lot more looking when it's daylight outside, and also check to see if someone might have dripped blood from a wound. In the meantime, the two deputies on guard outside will remain. I'll take Deputy Rosten back to the sheriff's office with me. After she completes a written report, she can go home."

Olinda started what Henry supposed would be a protest, but one look from Burke stopped her, and he continued, "Deputy Anderson will stay here in the living room the rest of the night. We'll make more complete plans for everyone's safety tomorrow. I hope you, Major King, and Ms. Embler can spend the remainder of the night in peace. I also hope we'll soon have good news about your wife."

Henry said, "I assume you'll be able to find out if any area hospital or clinic reports treating a gunshot wound?"

"The alert has already gone out," Burke said.

Chapter Thirty

WHAT EDIE KNEW

A fter walking Burke and Olinda to the door, Henry and Edie returned to the living room. He didn't feel ready to sleep and supposed she didn't either. Deputy Anderson was invited to sit in the chair Burke had vacated, and for a few minutes, conversation re-hashed the events just past.

Then Edie broke into the dragging discussion and said, "Deputy Anderson, Henry and I have several family matters to discuss. My cousin Carrie has a small study and office down the hall, one of the rooms you saw when you toured the house. Since there is no need for us to burden you with discussions that would probably bore you, please excuse us. We'll be in the office, but will check in with you before we turn in."

Henry said, "Edie, maybe now isn't . . . ."

"Who was it said, 'If not now, when?'" She stood, "Deputy, is there anything we can get you before we leave? That couch looks comfortable for sleeping. I can bring you a pillow and blanket."

The deputy said, "Thanks for your kindness, but I'm fine."

Edie continued, "Okay. There's fresh coffee in the kitchen. Mugs in the cabinet above the coffeepot. Package of cookies alongside. Make yourself at home."

As soon as the office door was shut, Henry said, "What is it?"

Edie didn't answer until he had settled himself in Carrie's desk chair and she was seated in the visitor chair across the desk from him. "What?" he repeated, and realized he sounded impatient. *Well, tough. It's two in the morning, we've had a gosh-awful night. I have a right to feel cross.*

"My turn to talk about a bunch of hanging details," she said. "First, the supposed missing papers. I've thought about them until my brain hurts, and I simply can't identify any way they ever came into my possession—or my mother's, for that matter. I never knew they existed until Milton mentioned them. I'm not convinced they exist today, but, if you're right, and someone's eagerness to find them is what got Carrie abducted and is putting the rest of us in danger, then we should work to uncover the truth and expose whatever that truth is as widely as possible.

"Seems to me the search of my things should have put an end to the problem since searchers couldn't have found what wasn't there, but last night's fire ends that hope."

"I'm following you," Henry said, with grudging respect.

"Therefore, we need to pull out all the stops, and I think we need to bring Milton directly into this. Maybe, if he thinks more carefully, he'll have new insight into what happened to the papers he says he actually saw all those years ago. Do you agree? Do you think you can you trust him now? Can you trust me? Henry, you've got to trust someone besides Carrie, yourself, and your long-time friends."

He said nothing, and wondered if lack of sleep and tension were muddling his usual ability to reason clearly.

Edie continued. "You might not agree but, as far as I'm concerned, if there are papers, the bad guys are welcome to them and good riddance. I wish I could hand them what they want. Get them off our tails."

"You may be right."

"Okay, we agree. Now, here's point two. I'm glad Olinda is out of the way. I sense that she isn't fully trusted, even by the sheriff's department. Some may suspect she's involved with the bad guys. I don't know how all that fits together, and I don't believe she was ever a danger to us personally, but I've decided it is possible she set those fires herself. I can't verify when she dressed and left our room. I was sound asleep until she shot out our window."

"Why didn't you speak up when Investigator Burke was here?"

"You'll recall I never spoke up *for* her, but I didn't feel certain enough to make any accusations against her either. Okay, I admit I've come to like her, and it seems to me now that those were rather puny fires."

"Under different circumstances, they could have been disastrous."

"Okay, okay. But with her out of the way, we'll be freer to pursue our own interests. I assume Deputy Anderson was thoroughly vetted before being assigned here."

He nodded. "I assume so too, but who knows what tomorrow, or today, rather, will bring."

"Yes, exactly.

"Next I have a confession to make. I've grown very fond of Carrie and you, though sometimes, Henry, you do come across as kind of bossy."

He opened his mouth to defend himself, but she held up her hand and continued. "I understand that's probably due to your law officer training, but—whatever—I admire and respect both you and Carrie more than you'll ever know. Not only that, I admit I'm jealous of your closeness and obvious affection for each other. I've had an opportunity to observe that over these past few days. It's a rare gift, as I know from one failed marriage of my own and my observation of other marriages. And, I might add, it was so obvious that the lovers' scene at Hobbs on Sunday was play-acting, maybe even distasteful to you. I apologize if I got into it a bit too strongly."

She paused, looked down at the floor for a moment, then said, "It's been a very long time since any man held me, even as an act of comfort."

Henry nodded, wondering where this was going. "I am more aware every day of how lucky Carrie and I are. How blessed, she would say."

"Good. And that brings me to point three. I believe Carrie is now free, though in hiding for some reason I haven't figured out yet. I think she's been safe since at least night before last."

He stared at her.

"Henry, you are a lousy actor. It's possible Olinda didn't pop to it since she doesn't know how close you two are, but your supposed anxiety over the safety of your wife is as unconvincing as a five-year-old's assertion he did not rob the cookie jar. If you don't want to, you needn't tell me how and where, but am I not right? Isn't she now safe somewhere?"

Slowly, he nodded. "As safe as she, and probably you, can be until all this mess is straightened out, and the ones responsible are caught and put away."

"Yes. And possibly she has knowledge, which I imagine she shared with you while you were gone from here yesterday morning, that will help us in our quest. Can't the three of us—four if you'll agree to bring Milton in—combine what we know? That might give us ideas about a way to solve the issue of those papers, and may even offer some insight into drug distribution methods in Northwest Arkansas.

"Remember, Milton and I still have jobs to do when it comes to uncovering drug distribution. He's cleared the managers of the craft fairs at War Eagle, but the Harleys could easily have been distributing without their knowledge. There were those pull toys, and maybe special under-the-counter bird houses or feeders for the buyer saying the right words? And who knows about all the other fairs? Milton's been talking with fair organizers and, so far, they proclaim shock at the possibility of this happening under their watch, and, of course, also proclaim their own personal innocence. Whether that's entirely true or not, at least they know the DEA and all area law-enforcement agencies will be watching them."

Henry sat in silence for a long minute, then made his decision. "All right. We'll see how to work this out in the morning, or rather, later this morning. Thank you for your honesty, Edie."

He stood. "Now, I'm going to bed."

Henry, unaccustomed to sleeping late, was startled when he opened his eyes to bright daylight and a clock that said 9:30. Running a hand over his bristly face, he decided the first order was a shave, no matter what was going on in the rest of the house.

A second thought had him picking up the phone. When Shirley answered at the Booth's he said, "Your cousin and Carrie's cousin need to meet today. Here is okay. Lots of events to discuss. Suggest you bring Roger if he can shake loose, and it's okay to bring your house guest."

"Are you sure?"

"Yes, you'll see."

"Okay, if you say so. We got things to discuss too. What time? That's supposing Roger can corral his cousin."

"1:00 okay?"

"I'll let you know if it's not."

Thirty minutes later Henry found Edie eating cereal in the kitchen. "Where's Deputy Anderson?" he asked.

"Shift change, I guess. Someone picked her up about an hour ago, and two new deputies are now on duty outside."

"Okay, good. I made a phone call as soon as I woke up," he said. We'll probably all meet here this afternoon. Can you get in touch with Milton when I know a time?"

"Yes, I can. Did you tell Carrie about the fire?"

"Oh."

"Best to tell her or get word to her. It will be an awful shock if she comes down the lane and sees that blackened wall."

"You're right. When they call back about a meeting time, I'll ask them to pass on the information. But won't she worry and want to come here right away to see it for herself?"

"Yes, but just say things are okay now, and the small amount of damage can be easily fixed. Since two deputies are still on guard outside, I felt okay about going out to look at the burned places this morning. The logs are blackened, but not deeply charred. I called one of the log home people in the phone book just now. I didn't know if they were the folks Carrie used, so I didn't give a name. I learned they sand blast the burned area, usually with ground walnut hulls, or even real sand, and refinish the place. It's fairly simple. You can tell her that."

"Oh. Well, thanks, thanks for checking. That's good news, Edie." *Women are amazing creatures. Carrie would probably have wanted information right away too. Probably would have been tomorrow, or even later, before I called anyone about repairs.*

Henry was frying a couple of eggs when the phone rang, and Shirley said, without prelude, "Cousin is okay with this if we can make it 12:00. He has an afternoon meeting. My houseguest and I will bring sandwiches and cookies to tide us over. Still got carrots and turnips in the garden. I'll get us some of those, too. Fix 'em fresh. What do they call it, crude-de-tays?"

"I don't know," Henry said, "I don't speak gourmet. Does your cousin know how to get here?"

"Thought it would be best if he came to our place first and drove up the ridge with us. He said to tell you he's making sure all deputies who come to your house are trustworthy. Well, as sure as he can be, I suppose."

"Uh, Shirley, we had a little incident up here last night. You might want to warn your houseguest." He explained about the fires.

"My gracious sakes, what next? Glad y'all are okay. I'll explain that things look worse than they are. Right?"

"Right."

"Let's see," Edie said, leaning against a kitchen cabinet and counting on her fingers, "Roger, Shirley, the sheriff, Carrie, you, me, Milton." Seven. Do you have what they used to call TV trays? Maybe the dining table is too formal."

"We have four little folding tables, and the rest of us could use the coffee table," Henry said, "but since our reason for getting everyone together is planning, maybe we should sit around the dining table . . . think of it as a conference table?"

"Okay, good point. I'll fill water glasses and make more coffee. We can put plates out and let everyone serve themselves in the kitchen, then take their food to the table."

"I'll get the plastic place mats. The dining table is nice wood, and Carrie would have a fit if I didn't put mats out."

Edie laughed and Henry thought, *Yes, the mood has definitely lightened. But, are we being too optimistic?*

I wonder what Carrie looks like with red hair. I've got to remember not to act shocked.

Chapter Thirty-One

PLANNING SESSION

A s she packed her bag of clothing, Carrie tried to force the anticipation of being home with Henry to cheer her up, but it wasn't working.

We aren't any closer to ending this criminal activity than we were a week ago. Things are all mixed up.

They tried to burn our home.

They think they've killed me.

I'd say they're winning—well, except for the rather important fact I'm not dead.

Maybe that place across from the Marshall's has nothing to do with these people.

Maybe I only imagined similarities to what I heard and felt when we were . . . wherever we were when they stopped to change from the van to a car.

I thought for sure I'd see Arnie from the Marshall's porch, but I didn't. I didn't recognize the man and woman who came out of that building.

I've been no help. I can't identify anyone. I can't help at all.

She stopped, and heard her mother's voice, saying, "The world does not depend on you to solve all its problems, Missy."

When she brought home stray cats and dogs, gave her lunch to someone at school, decided to eat no meat since animals wouldn't be killed to feed her hunger, or stepped in the middle of a playground fight, Mama took the animals to a shelter, made rules about lunch, put fried chicken on her plate, and shook her head over bruises, then said, inevitably: "It's good to be kind, but, Carrie Culpeper, you take things too far. *Don't try to solve the whole world's problems by yourself.*"

Carrie stood next to the bed, one hand motionless on jeans she was ready to put in the sack. *Don't try to solve all the problems by yourself.*

So, what can I do? I feel so helpless, so useless, so confused.

There had to be something. If only her thoughts would clear.

Shirley called from down the hall. "Coming, Carrie? Norm's here. We're ready to take you home so our team can get to work."

Teamwork. That was it.

Carrie stuffed her jeans in the sack, grabbed her make-up case, and prepared to smile. "Coming. I'm coming."

"See, it's not so bad," Henry said as he, Carrie, and the sheriff studied the blackened logs outside the bedroom windows.

"No, though the first impression isn't pretty," Carrie said. "It was good of Edie to check about the repair process, but I guess fixing this will have to wait until our other problems are resolved, if they ever are."

Henry put an arm around her, and the sheriff said, "Oh, I think we'll get there."

After a moment of silence, Henry asked, "Did you find the gasoline can lid?"

"Yes, a deputy picked it up under your bedroom window."

"How about any sign of blood?"

"Nope, but that doesn't mean Olinda didn't hit someone, though I'm beginning to doubt she did."

Before Carrie could ask him about that doubt, he said, "Okay, Let's go inside and start our planning session."

When they were all seated, and everyone had given reports on their activities, Sheriff Cook said, "Interesting that the two men thought those hollow animals had cocaine inside, and brought Ms. McCrite . . . Carrie . . . here to retrieve them. Question now is, who substituted the baking soda?"

"John Harley?" Edie asked. "He's the one who gave the toys to Carrie and said they belonged to Milton. I think he was trying to implicate Milton in drug dealing, and was unwilling to give up so much coke to accomplish that. Hence, the baking soda. But, did he know about Milton's connection to the Drug Task Force? Maybe not. I think telling Carrie the toys were Milton's was an effort to steer any suspicion—present or future—away from himself."

"Your idea about the substitution sounds logical," Henry said. 'Those animals held a lot of powder. Too much money, I'd think, to throw away on making Milton look guilty. Closer analysis will eventually tell if there was any trace of cocaine there, but it may be they always had only baking soda inside. Of course, whoever put it there knew simple testing would show what it was, but thought the look of drug dealing was enough to cast the shadow of doubt over Milton.

"It's also possible someone unknown to us thus far was cheating someone else. That someone, and not John Harley, filled the toys with baking soda. But it seems to me a dealer wouldn't want to take the chance a regular customer might get baking soda instead of what was paid for. That could sure blow up in the dealer's face. So, I'm guessing the animals handed to Carrie were meant for deception from the beginning, and, if not to make Milton look guilty, it could be we're talking rival dealers."

Carrie was watching the sheriff. He looked intensely interested, but was choosing to let them talk out their thoughts and suspicions. It was almost like they'd forgotten he was here.

Henry went on, "Another question is, could Harley have decided independently to trap Milton? Did anyone else know what he was doing? Sounds like Arnie and friend didn't know about the substitution. They thought Carrie had the animals and they were full of cocaine."

Milton said, "In all the years I've worked craft fairs I never saw anything like the wooden pull toys you describe. Of course, until recently, I never suspected John Harley of any wrongdoing, either. But, if the pull toys were part of a drug distribution system, I'd say they weren't being displayed by Harley, or anyone else at the War Eagle Craft Fair. My own interest in wooden toys means I'd notice something like what you describe, and I never have. I'm even wondering if they were made here in the United States. The War Eagle Fair folks judge merchandise being sold very carefully. The rules say that what the crafters bring in must be 'products of their own skill and creativity.'"

Sheriff Cook finally broke in. "What about that? Carrie and Henry, Roger and Shirley, all of you handled them. Any thoughts?"

"Well, they certainly didn't have the smoothness and fine detail of what Milton makes," Carrie said, "but as to being handmade? Handmade in China would be handmade. Peel off or sand off a label, and I suppose they'd pass. They did have a varnish or lacquer finish, though. Could it be tested to see if it's something unique to China?"

"Ha! Probably wouldn't matter," Roger said. "Stuff at the paint store here could come from China."

"Can I change the subject?" Carrie asked. "Did the search of Milton's trailer have anything to do with the papers the two men searched for here? What do all of you think?

"Looking for them in Milton's RV?" the sheriff said. "Interesting point, and certainly worth considering."

I guess I am being of some help after all, Carrie thought. She glanced up at Henry, and he pursed his lips in an imaginary kiss. She looked around to see if anyone was watching her, then returned the gesture.

The sheriff spoke to Milton. "Are you able to tell us more about those papers? Has anything else come to mind?"

"Not any more than I've already told. Edie's father just said he was collecting information about the drug traffickers we worked for in case he needed leverage over them some day. He showed me a handful of papers, but didn't ever let me hold or read them."

"Okay," the sheriff said, "Try this. Picture going back to that time, re-creating all you saw, heard, and felt back then. That sometimes works to call up hidden memories."

He looked at his watch. "I have to leave in a few minutes. Any more ideas?"

Carrie decided that was the opening she needed. "I know one way the business on Marshall road could be observed by deputies without causing any suspicion. Family members and friends often sit on the Marshall's porch with Jo during the day. A deputy could dress in civilian clothing, take the part of a visitor, and observe activities across the road just like Shirley, Roger, and I did.

"Good idea," Norman Cook said, after thinking a minute. "But it seems to me that Milton should be the watcher, to begin with at least. I realize he'd have to create a disguise since, if this business is a cover for drug activity, some of the people there might recognize him, just as we hope he'll recognize them. Don't forget, the two men who abducted Carrie probably also saw Milton and Edie at War Eagle Mill.

"Milton, what do you think? You've worked next to John Harley's craft booth for several years, and would be the most likely of anyone here to have seen those involved with Harley in the drug business. If, after a day or two of observing, you don't identify anyone, it is possible, as Carrie suggested at the beginning, that this was not the place where Arnold Frost and the other man changed vehicles. Are you okay with doing that?"

Milton nodded. "I have a wig, but I'd need help with a more complete disguise."

Carrie asked, "I guess we're assuming Arnie, Second Man, and the Harleys are linked in the same operation?"

"Probably," the sheriff said.

Shirley asked, "What about the suspicious death of Mr. Harley?"

"He'd been drugged, and he didn't make the cuts on his wrists," the sheriff said.

"Then somebody sure didn't get along with him," Shirley mumbled.

Carrie said. "They sure didn't, and if somebody is at odds with another somebody, doesn't that work to our advantage? If one person or group is arrested, they might want to implicate others, and . . . " She stopped. *Could Harley's killer have been Second Man?*

After a moment, she went on. "Would you arrest Arnold Frost if one of us recognizes him at the place on Marshall Road?"

"With your testimony pending, yes, we could, but we'd like to have concrete evidence against some of the others as well. We might lose an opportunity for that if we arrest Frost by himself. And, by the way, though John and Elizabeth Harley went by their real names, we have no evidence that Arnold Frost has, and, of course, none of us has a name for the second man."

Carrie picked at her napkin for a minute before she went on, "You're assuming Liz Harley is dead?

The sheriff hesitated, then answered, "Possibly."

Edie said, "I think I should go to the Marshall's with Milton. I realize I'd need a complete disguise too, but I've seen Arnold Frost and his companion, though only briefly. Milton hasn't seen them at all, so far as any of us knows."

"You're right. I can't say I have," Milton said.

"I've seen them very clearly," Carrie said, earning a frown from both Henry and Edie. *Ah, Edie wants to be the one going with Milton.*

She thought *teamwork,* and continued, "Of course there's no need for both Edie and me to be there unless we make a party of it."

"That's it! Why not a party?" Shirley said. "We could take balloons, gift-wrapped boxes, refreshments. That would be a good cover for a bunch of people."

"Hmmm," the sheriff said. "It's not a bad idea. But don't forget, if this is the place, four of you are known to at least some of those involved. I can see disguising Milton and Edie enough to pass for a while, but a whole group?"

"Well now," Shirley said, "I'm pretty good at making up disguises. Henry, being such a big man, will be toughest with what I have on hand, but I think I can manage. He could also watch from Jo and Ben's bedroom window since it looks out on the place. The rest of us, and any of your deputies, could come and go on the porch. You know, move around, laughing and talking. They have picnic tables and a place for croquet in back of the house, but of course you can't see the place we want to watch from there. Ben might be willing to set up his cooker for hot dogs in the front yard, especially if I bribe Jo with fresh eggs and butter."

The sheriff said, "It would be best to try Milton and Edie there first, and see if they recognize anyone. All of this is a gamble, but since, according to what you say, there's activity at the business seven days a week, those two might recognize someone. If they do, we can move on from there, maybe to a party set-up."

"Should we begin our surveillance this afternoon?" Milton asked

"If you're game," the sheriff said.

"Yes," both Edie and Milton said, and Milton continued, "I'm eager to get started."

Shirley stood. "I'll call Jo, see if it's okay with her. If it is, I'll take Milton and Edie to our place, see what I can do to change their looks. Hey, Norm, you need a disguise person in your department? I'd like to put in for the job."

He grinned at her, but didn't answer.

When Shirley, Roger, Milton and Edie had left, Carrie said, "Sheriff Cook, what about Olinda? Is she involved on the wrong side of this somehow?"

"She admits nothing except that she was solicited a couple of months ago to pass on information from our Drug Task Force."

Henry asked, "I assume she says she refused the deal. Would a reason for suspicion be that she never told anyone about it until now?"

"Correct."

Carrie asked, "Why would they have chosen to solicit her? What made someone think she was open to what they wanted?"

"Very good question," the sheriff said. "We're looking into her private life as well as her work for us."

"Could she have set the fires here?"

"She won't talk about that, either."

Carrie thought a minute, then continued. "Do you think she passed on any information at all? Let's say, information about Milton, or even Edie?"

"Of course we can't be sure, but I doubt it. Milton has been at the office only rarely, and she probably wouldn't have seen him. As to Edie, we didn't know about her confidential work for the DEA before this week, so Deputy Rosten couldn't have learned about it at our office."

"She's been, uh, neutralized now, though?" Carrie asked.

"Yes, no access to information, and she knows we're watching her."

Carrie felt the stirring of an idea. "But mightn't she have helpful information for us? For example, she was with Deputy Rainwater at Milton's trailer. Could she know or have guessed more about that? Oh, I wish I could talk with her." She stopped, then plunged on. "Of course I know your capable people have done so already. But you did say there were things she wouldn't talk about."

"It's always possible that an independent person, especially another woman, might stir some useful information in a heart-to-heart talk, though yes, officers have questioned her. If you'd like to try talking with her yourself, maybe we could set something up in a neutral location. There is a small amount of danger, however, because she still doesn't know you're alive. I don't think we want her to know that yet, just in case she is passing on information to the group that supposedly killed you."

"But she won't be able to have further contact with those people, right?"

"I don't see how she could manage contact now since she's being monitored by us. Time will tell. But let's assume there is still some danger."

"What about Edie talking with her?" Henry asked. "Those two did become fairly close while they were together."

What? Ask Edie to talk with Olinda? No! I'm good at this kind of thing. I suggested it.

"I . . ."

Henry looked at her. "What is it?"

Teamwork. You can't solve all the problems by yourself, Missy.

"I, uh, Edie would be good for that."

The sheriff looked at his watch again. "We'll think about it—see what seems best. Now I need to get to another meeting."

"Anything to do with this?" Carrie asked, then realized the question was probably not appropriate.

"Budget," the sheriff said, making a face.

As the door shut behind him, Carrie smiled to herself. A least neither the sheriff nor Henry had suggested she was being too nosy. Her mother probably would have.

Chapter Thirty-Two

WHO WANTS CARRIE DEAD?

C arrie was eager to hear about all that had happened besides her kidnapping, so as soon as she and Henry finished clearing away the lunch leavings, she said, "Let's take a few minutes to just be together and talk."

They dropped into their favorite chairs in the living room, and she sighed with pleasure. "It's good to be home again."

Henry nodded. "And to have the two of us alone, however brief the interlude might be. The last few days have been horrible for you, Cara, and neither of us has had any privacy to talk about it. I've wanted to say how sorry I am to have let this happen to you."

"Enough! You certainly didn't let it happen, and I know it's been rough on you, too. That's past now. We both came through it without any scars."

"Well, yes, but . . ."

She interrupted him. "You've heard my story, and I've heard some of what else has been going on, but I want to know what happened at the mill after you discovered I was gone, and what went on here after that? The stuff you couldn't talk about in company."

He told her, beginning with when he discovered the man on the bank of the War Eagle River had no interest in fishing, and then turned to see the van driving away. "I still think allowing you to be abducted was mostly my fault. I should have been more alert.

"Quit that," she said. "You couldn't have foreseen what occurred. But, I wonder, do you think the two men were prepared for what happened there? Had they planned it? They couldn't know you and I would separate, or even that we were going to the mill, though, as I said in our discussion, they had parked up the road that morning and planned to follow us when we left.

But, how did they know we'd be leaving?"

Henry swallowed an oath. "Milton and Edie talked on the phone that morning. Those guys must have been able to listen in on their conversation. Edie used our phone, and I assume Milton was on his cell phone. They probably got in through that, or it's possible they'd tapped into our land line by then."

"Oh. Oh, yes. But if they've heard our phone conversations, wouldn't they now know I'm alive and free?"

"If they intended to kidnap you, they'd have to have known our plans. But, since you showed up at Roger and Shirley's we've all been pretty careful about what we said on the phone, and you haven't been on the phone at all. The sheriff warned us about the possibility of listeners." Henry was silent for a few moments before he continued. "I'm trying to remember all I said when talking to Shirley and Roger. I don't think I gave anything away, and I was always careful not to mention your name."

Carrie sighed. "Bother. There's a lot to be concerned about, isn't there."

"If they did get the information about our plans to eat breakfast at the mill from Edie and Milton's conversation, then that explains how they were ready with that fake fishing gear and a plan."

"So it's possible the original plan was to kidnap me?"

"Logically, yes. I hate to say it, but you'd be easier than I would, and they couldn't be sure Edie would have a key to our house. They could just ask you where those animals were hidden once they had you here. Less problem than tearing the whole place apart, assuming they could make you tell where what they thought was valuable merchandise had been hidden."

"They did tear the guest room apart looking for those papers."

"Yes, but it seems to me from what you said that getting ahold of the wooden animals was their first priority, and they expected you to tell them where those were hidden as soon as you got here."

"True, and as it turned out, I wish I'd told them all that I knew about those stupid animals right away and not played dumb. Just look at what happened to your little police car." She sighed.

"I'm sure Milton will make us another one if he doesn't have one in his stock."

After a short silence, she said. "Here's my second question. Why did they think it would be safe to bring me here? Wouldn't it be possible you'd come home, probably with Edie, maybe with others, including deputies?"

"I'm sure they guessed—correctly it turns out—that we'd be involved at

War Eagle Mill for some time, and a search would center there. I admit when Edie first suggested we come home, I resisted. Coming home didn't seem logical."

"I think I would have reacted the same way." She hesitated for a moment as a flashback to her time with Arnie and Second Man popped up in her memory. She quickly shoved that aside with a prayer of gratitude, and said, "Well, now that we've covered that, tell me more about events here."

He did. She felt both touched and sorry over how much he had suffered from guilt and fear until he knew she was alive and safe, and how difficult keeping up the charade after that was.

"In fact, I was so bad at acting that Edie figured it out from the beginning." He told her what Edie had said.

"Henry, that's lovely. I'm glad to have her in our lives. Are you?"

"Yes, especially if you are. But I don't think I'd enjoy having her live next door. She comes on a bit strong. Washington, DC is a safe distance, and we can visit back and forth. There's a lot to see and do in the capitol."

"Yes, indeed."

After a pause she said. "Do you think Olinda figured it out too?"

"Maybe. Suspected, at least. She did give me a lot of funny, searching looks after I got the phone call from Shirley."

"Oh, well. So, what do we do next?"

"Depends on what Edie and Milton see from Jo Marshall's front porch. What happens there this afternoon may motivate future action." He stood. "For now, we just wait for their report and, while I'm waiting, I think I'll e-mail Chef John Bohnert to tell him how successful his recipes have been for us, and how much we're enjoying his cookbook."

"Thank him for me, too. And, while you write him, I'm going to start a load of laundry. How good it is to be thinking about laundry." She laughed. "I can't believe I said that!"

The phone rang at 3:45, just as Carrie was beginning to wonder when Edie, or Edie and Milton, would return, and how many people she and Henry needed to prepare supper for.

Edie sounded breathless. "Carrie, the most amazing thing. Guess who the woman at that place is."

"I don't need to guess, you're going to tell me."

"Liz Harley. Milton says there's no doubt."

"Liz Harley! But that means . . . "

"Exactly. I bet she murdered her own husband. We're going to call the sheriff as soon as I hang up."

"Edie, no! Henry and I think the drug dealers have access to conversations on Milton's cell phone, and probably yours, too. You'd better wait. I assume you're coming back here soon? We can discuss this then."

"Um, okay, but let me talk with Milton. We're still at the Marshall's and I'm on their phone. I think it's probably safe. Just a minute."

When Edie came back she said, "Milton is going to drop me there, then go on to the sheriff's office and report in person.

"Oh, wait. He's saying something else."

Carrie heard, "Yes, Milton. Okay, good idea," then Edie said into the phone, "He says, since he'll be in town, he can bring Chinese for all four of us. Is that okay?"

"That would be great, thank him."

"We both think Shirley's idea of a party at the Marshall's is a good plan. We need to get ready for that. Do Shirley and Roger like Chinese food? And, who has the milking duty down there this evening?"

"Haven't a clue. I'll find out, and we can tell Milton whether it's to be four or six when he drops you off."

As she hung up and went to look for Henry, Carrie's thoughts were whirling. *Since Liz Harley is at the place on Marshall Road, that means I was right about the location.*

Could she really be responsible for the death of her own husband?

Carrie shuddered.

Liz Harley. Then she's the one who ordered me killed.

Chapter Thirty-Three

PARTY PREP

S hirley and Roger, so far as they knew, had never eaten Chinese food.

"Well," Carrie told Shirley, "some of it's kind of like beef stew or chicken and vegetables in a seasoned sauce, served with rice or noodles instead of potatoes. How does that sound?

"Oh, I don't mind trying it out, and Roger will go along. We'll call it an adventure. As for the milking, Junior and Oscar, the new helper he hired, are on tonight. I'll be glad to talk more about a party, and I'm sure Jo and Ben will be pleased they're part of all this excitement."

"Okay. And I have left-over Macaroni Beef Casserole that Henry and the girls made. We can warm that up in case Chinese isn't to your taste."

Carrie had stared at Edie when Milton dropped her off. Ignoring Edie's face, which probably wouldn't be seen in detail over the distance between the Marshall porch and the metal buildings, she could have been looking at a teen-aged boy. No make-up, jeans, a baggy sweatshirt, stocking cap pulled down over the ears, huge shoes with some kind of sports logo. Even the ubiquitous smart phone in one hand.

Later, when Milton came in with sacks of food, she gawked again, because she was looking at the boy's laborer father, hair greying at the temples, partly covered by an oil-stained John Deere gimmee cap. This stranger had a scraggly black and grey mustache and wore a sweat shirt with sleeves cut off at the biceps, displaying arms almost solidly blue-black with tattoos. Milton had work boots on his feet with thick soles and what looked like two inch heels. He seemed at least two inches taller.

And, now that they were all seated around the dining table, Shirley and Roger were the ones gawking. They both stared at Milton and Edie, who had begun, very successfully, to eat their meals with chopsticks. Milton brought chopsticks for each of them, but, after looking at Carrie and Henry, who were using forks, Roger and Shirley left the bamboo sticks in their white paper covers and picked up forks too.

As the meal ended, Carrie decided it had been a success. Containers brought by Milton were largely empty, and no one had touched the Macaroni and Beef Casserole.

"Now," she said, when the empty containers were rinsed and put in a trash bag, "We won't wait any longer. Time to tell us more about what happened at the Marshall's."

As soon as everyone was seated on sofa and chairs, Milton said, "As Edie told Carrie, the woman we saw at the business on Marshall Road is Liz Harley. Not only that, I recognized two of the men who came in and out of the large building. I don't know the names of either of them, but, during the last two or three years, I've seen both talking with John at his fair booth. I assumed they were friends who lived in this area."

"No sign of Arnie Frost?" Carrie asked Edie.

"No, I didn't see him."

Henry asked, "What did the sheriff say?"

"Wanted to think, do a bit of planning and surveying of deputies in the Drug Task Force," Milton said, "but, Shirley, he's ready to go with your idea of a party. He'll phone you in the morning, and either invite you to a party, which means it's definitely on, or, if there have been complications, say the party is cancelled. After that, most all phone communication will be between the sheriff's office and the Marshalls, since we assume their phone line is clear.

"As you noticed, he's still concerned about everyone's safety. He sent the two new deputies who're on guard outside, and asked that I spend the night here if there is some way to accommodate me. He also wanted me to tell Roger and Shirley to stay in their house and lock up after dark."

"Whoee," Shirley said, "with those rules, how is anyone supposed to milk cows in the morning?"

"Get Junior to come in and work with you, if he isn't already scheduled," Henry said. "Leave your farm lights on all night. Junior's truck lights will add to those, and he can survey the place when he drives in."

"We'll do it," Roger said. Don't want anything to mess up this deal."

Shirley said, "Speaking of that, since Roger and I are regulars at the Marshalls I don't reckon we need disguises, but looking around at you all, I feel almost nekkid without one."

"You are indeed a master of disguise art," Carrie said.

Ignoring the compliment, Shirley asked Henry, "What do you think of Carrie's red hair?"

"It's okay, now that I'm used to it, but I'll be glad to see the grey curls again when all this is over."

Edie said, "We talked to Jo and Ben Marshall at length before we left their house. Maybe unfortunately, both of them think of this as an adventure, not a potentially dangerous law-enforcement operation. The sheriff reminded us that we don't know yet how many of our phones the drug dealers have access to, so no one here is to call them. He'll talk to them this evening about possible liability issues, but I'd bet they will still welcome the entire—to them exciting—operation."

Neither Carrie nor Henry dared look at either of the Booths.

"We'll be ready, whatever is decided," Milton said. "The sheriff suggested that Henry, Carrie, Edie, and the Booths stay locked in at home during the party, but I told him I already knew that wouldn't fly."

"You're darn tootin,'" Shirley said.

Milton nodded and went on. "So, we'll all be at the party, though you guys are to stay on the porch and keep out of harm's way. Henry will either be out of sight or, using some degree of disguise, mingle on the porch with the deputies.

"If the people we're concerned with come outside during daylight, proving they're at the location, and then go back inside, the sheriff might make a move then. If not, as the day darkens, deputies will spread out around the metal buildings, keeping at a distance, since there is undoubtedly some kind of detection system guarding against intruders."

"Is there parking for us behind the Marshall's house?" Henry asked.

"Yes, between the picnic table area and the workshop and kitchen garden," Milton said, "but we think crowding the road with party guest's cars is a good idea. That will make it harder for anyone across the road to jump in a car and drive away quickly.

"We're all hoping this operation can be completed without firing weapons, but there is the possibility we'll need to.

"Oh, Shirley, the sheriff asked if you could send a few of your gift-wrapped boxes back to the office with the deputies who're keeping watch outside tonight. Then, tomorrow afternoon, those parking on Marshall Road can walk toward the house carrying packages. He's also going to have food prepared for some of them to carry. Potato salad, beans, that sort of stuff, and maybe some kind of dessert."

"Whoee," Shirley said, so we really are going to have us a party."

"You bet," Milton told her, "and there'll be a tub of pop. No beer. The tub, along with ice and cartons of pop will be delivered there tomorrow morning."

Shirley said, "Roger and I will blow up the balloons left over from the birthday party we had for Carolyn's youngest a while back. I've already got some boxes wrapped. Carrie, you got any empty boxes and gift paper here?"

"Yes. Edie and I'll wrap several this evening and be sure the deputies have them to take back to the department in the morning."

"All right," Shirley said. "Looks like we're ready. Roger and I will say goodnight now 'cause we're up early. Thanks for the good food, Milton. I think Roger and I might get Chinese ourselves some time, as long as we can eat with forks and not sticks."

Everyone laughed, and watched from the door as a deputy walked Shirley and Roger to their truck.

"I'll sleep on the couch," Milton said. "I'm afraid to take a shower though, for fear my tattoos will wash off. Have you got an old sheet I can throw over your upholstery in case anything rubs off?"

"We do, and I can loan you a razor." Henry said.

"Not necessary. I always carry shaving gear and a few other necessities in my truck in case of the unexpected."

"Then let me show you around the house now. You can share the guest bath with Edie."

"I guess he could sleep in the bed Olinda was using," Edie said. "I wouldn't mind."

"Couch will be fine," Milton said. "Don't know you well enough yet to spend the night in your bedroom, woman."

"We'll bring out blankets and a pillow for you," Henry said. "I slept on the couch not long after Carrie and I met. I felt she needed a guard when a murderer was stalking her. I found it quite comfortable."

"Any bad guys show up then?" Milton asked.

"No, it stayed quiet."

"Let's hope tonight is quiet, too," Edie said. "Tomorrow is going to be quite a memorable day for all of us." She looked at her cousin. "I suppose you're already praying about success and safety, or something like that."

"Yes," Carrie said, "and so much more."

Chapter Thirty-Four

MISSING PAPERS?

"This feels like a real party," Edie said as she and Carrie looked in vain for a place to put their loaded plates down. "Everyone is either having a good time or they're all good actors."

"Taking advantage of the moment, I guess."

"I'm glad they can. I've been afraid from the first that this isn't going to be as easy as it sounds. I just hope no one gets hurt."

"Amen," Carrie said as a tall man carrying a plate of food and a Pepsi careened into her after an even taller man bumped into him. Both men apologized, and went to join friends perched on the porch railing.

"Hey, I have an idea," Edie said. "The Marshalls have picnic tables out back. Let's go there. We won't have competition for seating since people here have to keep watch across the street."

Carrie shook her head. "I don't know if . . . "

"We can check every so often to see what's going on in front. I'll tell Milton and Henry where we're going. Maybe they'll want to come too."

Both men were involved in what looked like a heavy conversation with Sheriff Cook, so Edie interrupted only long enough to say, "We're going to sit at a picnic table out back." She got a brief nod from Milton, and Carrie followed her through the central hall and out the back door.

"See, it's nice out here. Quiet, and we have the whole place to ourselves."

Carrie said, "Uh-huh," put down her plate and can of Dr.Pepper, and, after she was settled on a bench, asked a question she'd been puzzling over. "Why did you stay away from the kitchen table at Shirley's after the deputy came to look at the animals with powder in them? Shirley and I both wondered. It was kind of obvious to us, though none of the guys seemed to notice."

"That's easy. I didn't want to be part of the discussion because of my involvement with the DEA. Better to stay out of it than get into an awkward conversation."

"Ah, I understand. Okay if I tell Shirley?

"Of course."

"Then I have another, bigger question. What are your plans after today? Will your work here be finished, and can you go back home? I'm sure your mother would like that."

"Yes, I plan to go home before long. Milton has said he wants to come back with me, meet Mom—you know, that stuff. My leaving will have something to do with his schedule, and how long it takes to clear things up here."

"Maybe he can give your mother some interesting information about your father that isn't too harsh?"

"I think that's his plan." Edie bit off one end of her hot dog, chewed, and looked at Carrie with an expression that said she was waiting for the next question.

"And then what?"

"Carrie, you are so transparent. Yes, Milton and I have become good friends. Yes, it may develop into something more."

"I'm glad. You two seem attracted to each other, and you certainly have a lot of interests in common."

"That's true, though living so far apart is a problem. I can't move Mom from the only home she's known for over fifty years, and Milton loves this area and his craft work here. We'll see. I admit it would sure be nice to have someone, but I'm leery of being swayed by observations of your closeness to Henry. My previous attempt at marriage makes me extra cautious. You and Henry have the ideal marriage. How many can expect that?"

"We are blessed, but so are many others. And you know, Edie, I think maturity helps. We're softened in our wants and expectations by this time in our lives. Not so demanding, maybe? They say we become more rigid as the years pass, but I don't believe that's necessarily true. In fact, it can be just the opposite."

"Perhaps your faith in God has something to do with it."

"I'm sure it does."

They ate in silence for a few minutes, then Edie said, "I don't want you to worry about me becoming a permanent house guest. If Milton needs to be here for a while I plan to get a furnished apartment. If it's only going to be a week or two, I'll move to a motel. I've imposed on you long enough."

"Oh Edie, of course you can stay with us."

"Hush. You and Henry are used to quiet and privacy. Goodness knows you've had enough company and riotous activity since I came. So, don't give me arguments. Remember how I said when I came that I didn't like pious protests? I don't want to hear one now."

She reached over to take Carrie's hand. "It isn't that I don't enjoy being with you two. But, were I you, I'd long for peace and quiet with my husband after all this turmoil. If I find my own place, all of us will have that."

Carrie squeezed Edie's hand and, after a moment, said, "It is nice out here, with the forest on either side of us, and the view out back going past Jo's gardens to pastures in the distance. Her cutting garden still has mums, and aren't those zinnias? I always thought of them as hot weather flowers."

"Yes, I've been looking at the garden too. I have a small garden at our home in DC, but it was mostly gone by the time I left. The only edible thing I grow is tomatoes. The rest is planted in flowers."

"Henry is the gardener in our family," Carrie said, loving the term *our family*.

Once more they were silent—until the voice of a woman coming from the stand of trees behind them caused two startled exclamations.

"Ah, I was right to check out the party area before I went to the office, and look what I found. The jackpot. Oh, I admit you two were hard to identify at first. Those are excellent disguises, but am I not addressing Edith Embler and, oh my goodness, isn't it Carrie McCrite—who, it seems, has been resurrected from the dead?

"No, don't turn around. I'm holding a gun with a silencer. I'll prove it to you the instant either of you starts to get up or turn around. The party goers out front are making so much noise they wouldn't hear a thing if I shot you both right now."

She stayed in the trees, but her words had brought them both to rigid attention. "Now, Ms. Embler," she said, "I want you to tell me where I'll find the copy of those papers your father prepared before he died. I wondered if Milton Sales had them, but no luck there. Arnie and Sid failed at the McCrite house on Blackberry Road, and I couldn't chase them out of that house with fire. John missed making a promising connection with you when you were at the fair, which was just one of John's many mess-ups, though trying to pin those hollow toys on Milton Sales and giving them to McCrite was his biggest mistake.

"Now it looks like Sid failed to remove a witness as well. No wonder he disappeared last Monday.

Sid, Carrie thought. *And he's gone.*

The woman continued, "So, Ms. Embler, I'm not going to fail this time. You might as well tell me about those papers now. Where are they? I can't assume you carry them with you, but I won't let you out of my sight until I have them in my hands. We can leave here after I deal with the McCrite problem."

Edie's voice began with a quiver, but got stronger and stronger as she said, "If I'd ever had papers related to my father's death, I would be very glad to turn them over to you, but I never heard about any such papers until I came here. I assure you I have never seen them and know nothing about what they said. "Liz—it is Liz, isn't it?—why do you want them after all these years? Why do you think they still exist?"

The voice, sounding closer now, said, "Why would you come here if they didn't?"

Edie's answer was an explosive, "*What?* Is that it? Well, you are mistaken. I came here to visit my cousin Carrie, and to see if I could find out what happened to my father all those years ago. I wanted my mother to know, at last, why he disappeared and, if possible, be able to take her to visit his grave. I had been told that a man in this area who worked at craft fairs knew about my dad's last hours and could help me gain closure for my mother."

Carrie spoke up quickly, before Edie could say more or mention Milton Sales's name, "That's right. Edie wanted to find a man named John Harley because her source said he knew about the death of her father. She heard he'd be at the fair."

The laugh was humorless. "Well now, I do hate to tell you this, but John Harley had no connection at all to Art Embler and didn't know anything about his business dealings. It was my parents who were connected to him."

Carrie saw Edie start to turn, and quickly put a hand on her knee. Without moving any farther, Edie said, "At least tell me why the papers matter so much to you."

The silence went on for so long that Carrie hoped the woman had left, but then she said, "You really don't know, do you?" She laughed again. "Gee, I hate to kill any imaginary dream you may have about your daddy, but he was a bigger crook than most. Worked both sides of the road, betraying men left and right. Had ties to distribution at this fair all those years ago. He also had two wives."

Edie's whole body jerked and, once more, she started to turn toward Liz Harley, but Carrie quickly put an arm around her as both comfort and restraint.

"I don't believe that."

Liz Harley laughed again. "Oh, too bad. Believe what you want, but he had a wife in McAllen. That woman was my grandmother. In Texas, their name was Emerson, and your father had a son born in Texas, my father."

Liz stopped talking and, under Carrie's protecting arm, Edie began shaking. "I . . . I don't . . . " she began, then was silent.

Carrie was doing some quick calculating. "So, you and Edie are related? You are Edie's niece? Can you prove that?"

"You want birth certificates? I could provide them if I wanted to, but why? Maybe my dear Aunt Edith would rather not see concrete proof."

Carrie said, "And you want those papers because they, somehow, prove who you are? I'm sure you're aware any supposed second marriage would be bigamy."

"I need the papers because they prove my grandfather and my father were working two sides of the road. Grandpa Emerson laid out the names of double-dealers on paper, documenting many of their activities. He wrote mostly about the men he worked for, but my father was just beginning his career then, and there are a few details about his business associates as well. Grandpa made a record of as much of it as he could, thinking it would serve as insurance for him and Dad. Then he leaked information about the documents, letting it be known the names of many dealers were included, along with proof of their activities. He also let it be known the papers were secure unless or until something happened to him or his son.

"Seems our family likes living dangerously. Grandpa was killed in spite of the papers, and my father died in a gun battle ten years ago. Who knows if the papers could have saved them, but they never came to light.

"Now I want those papers before they fall into the wrong hands. I want to protect my mother and myself from reprisal. If the wrong people read them now, I don't doubt they'll kill both of us."

"How do you know what they said?" Carrie asked. Edie was still shaking and seemed incapable of speech. Carrie began rubbing a hand up and down her cousin's back.

"Because I saw the originals. My father had them after Grandpa died, and said he would keep them safe. He said Grandpa had sent copies to his Embler wife. I don't know what happened to them after that.

"See, Aunt Edith, your experience has not been so different from mine. I'm certain you understand now why I must find and destroy Grandpa Emerson's papers. They could harm you as much as me, and if you don't have them, who does?"

Edie still said nothing. After a quick shudder when Liz said "Aunt Edith," her face and body went stone still—unmoving and hard. For at least a mini-second, watching her cousin, Carrie wished she had the means to permanently silence Liz Harley.

Chapter Thirty-Five

WHO CAN SAVE CARRIE THIS TIME?

L iz stopped talking, but Carrie could occasionally hear a rustle in the leaves at the edge of the forest, so, other than continuing to rub Edie's back, she didn't move. There was still that gun.

Finally, deciding to take a soft path, she said, "It seems to me, if copies of the original papers you describe ever existed, they're long gone, and you're free from reprisals.

"When I told Edie about the men searching for papers in the room where she's staying, she said her dad did have a safe deposit box, and she and her mother opened it after his death. It held family papers, passports, her birth certificate, but nothing at all like you describe. There were no papers unrelated to personal family matters."

Carrie waited for a response from Liz, but none came, so she continued.

"Edie and her mother live together. They've been in the family home for something like fifty years, and have never seen papers related to Mr. Embler's business. If anyone who might harm you had knowledge of dangerous papers, wouldn't they have taken advantage of that long before now?

"You can leave here safely. Neither Edie nor I will bother you. I haven't seen you, therefore I can't identify you, and neither can Edie. We're no threat to you."

The silence went on so long, with only soft rustling in the leaves, that Carrie decided Liz Harley had pondered her options and decided to walk away. She was about to stand up and turn toward where Liz had been when two gunshots and shouting from across the road stopped her.

NO! Not yet, not now. She's leaving us.

Liz Harley's sudden oath was too close by for comfort and, in an instant, she had grabbed Carrie's arm and pushed the gun barrel against her cheek. She began moving back into the stand of trees, pulling Carrie with her. "I don't know what's going on," she said, "but I know you're coming with me. Aunt Edith, stay where you are, or this friend of yours will die in an instant and you'll be the one leaving here with me. Don't think I won't kill her. I've learned killing people is surprisingly easy."

"Wait!" Edie said. "Take me instead. If you do, I'll tell you where to find the papers."

Liz's backward motion stopped. Her left arm snaked all the way around Carrie, holding the two of them together so tightly that Carrie's every breath struggled against the confining arm and her words came out in gasps. "No, Edie. No!"

"Carrie, I really do think I know where they could be, if they exist. But she will have no chance to find out if she takes you. She has to take me instead."

Edie stepped over the bench and came toward them as she said, "Liz, don't give up this last chance to find what you're looking for."

Carrie sagged against the front of Liz Harley's body, hoping to throw her off balance.

It didn't work, the woman didn't budge an inch, but at least her movement toward the trees had stopped.

Jo Marshall was right. Liz Harley has a well-padded chest.

Stupid, useless thought. There has to be something productive you can do or say, Carrie. THINK!

It was quiet everywhere. No more sounds from out front or across the road. No party noises. No nothing.

What's going on? Shouldn't we hear people shouting, or at least talking? A car door slamming? Where is Henry? Where is everyone—Shirley and Roger, Milton? Are they all involved in whatever is taking place out front? Why hasn't someone come looking for us? There were two shots. What, WHAT is going on?

Liz hadn't moved.

She must be thinking over Edie's offer. But Edie convinced us all there are no papers. Isn't that the truth? If it is true, Edie's doing this for me. Oh, please.

Carrie began, "Edie . . . " then couldn't think what else to say.

Liz's indecision continued to convey itself through her inaction. She still held Carrie tightly, and now they both seemed frozen in time and space.

It lasted long enough. There was another rustle in the forest floor leaves. The gun moved away from Carrie's face when a voice behind them said, "Put the gun down, Lizzie. The party's over"

Chapter Thirty-Six

STRANGER IN THE WOODS

"Don't—call—me—Lizzie!"

The gun was pushed against Carrie's head again, and she fought an urge to scream, wail, cry over this repeated danger. *How long can I manage to endure, to stand strong?*

"Why not, Lizzie? It's Lindie and Lizzie. Momma liked that."

"I don't care if she . . . what are you doing here?"

"Checking up on you, baby sister. Seems you've backed yourself into a corner."

That voice. Pitched lower, tougher sounding, but . . .

Liz, still facing away from the newcomer, said, "I have not! You're the one in trouble. House arrest, or something like that? Seems like always clever Lindie got away though, which is handy for both of us."

As Liz continued talking, Carrie thought, *She knows who this woman is, and I think I know. Sisters?* She felt a wisp of hope.

"Could you see what's going on at my distribution center? Did you hear the shots?"

Liz was now breathing so heavily that Carrie's body moved forward and back with each gasp.

"The party out front was a cover for drug busters. They watched until they knew your people were inside the buildings, surrounded the place, and that was it. Arnie had just come back, and was in the mood to resist. He shot a deputy, then of course someone shot Arnie. They've called ambulances."

Carrie had never heard such a string of foul language in her life. It finally stopped, and Liz said, "Dead?"

"Neither of them, at this point."

Silence. More heavy breathing, then Liz turned partly toward the woman in the woods. Carrie didn't feel ready to face the woman, and kept her head turned away. Edie, who had started walking toward them when the newcomer appeared, was now taking slow steps back. Liz didn't seem to notice, and the stranger didn't comment.

"We just got a shipment," Liz said.

"Uh-huh, so no problem with them finding evidence. They're all inside your place now, probably having a good ol' time. I didn't dare try to see in, but of course they've already found your drugs. I don't know what they'll end up doing with the cases of hollow dolls and toys, or the special books on CD meant to go to your truck stop customers. Maybe the sheriff will have a big garage sale. The money ends up in law enforcement accounts, of course." The voice laughed, low, melodious.

Liz gasped, "You—shut—up." After taking a couple of moments to control her breathing, she spoke again. "How did they know to look over there?"

"It may have something to do with the folks who own this place."

"But how did *they* know?" It was almost a whine.

"You can ask the sheriff later. Hmm, what else did you have for them to find? What about John's birdhouses? Are they still there, or are they gone, now that John is gone?"

"John was a stupid fool. He broke the propane connections in Sales's RV after I'd searched the place and left. No good reason but spite. He gave those wood animals he told me had coke in them to McCrite, and said they belonged to Sales. What did he think that would accomplish? You know what happened. It got the attention of the sheriff, and the drug army was brought in. So, why did John act like such a fool in the first place? Jealousy. He was jealous of Milton Sales's craft fair business. Milton always did beat John in dollar amount."

The woman's arm tightened painfully around Carrie's chest, and she murmured an involuntary "Oooo."

"Shut up. You may become more trouble than you're worth, even as a hostage."

The voice in the woods continued. "John was jealous of Milton Sales?

Oh, I think it was much more than that, Lizzie. You know what I do think? I think John was tired of the drug business. By the way, it won't take them long to break into your customer lists. A lot of people are going to be angry at you."

"Those lists are coded."

"No matter. The sheriff's department has really, really good computer whizzes. Oh my, didn't you know that, baby sister?"

More awful language. Between swearing, Liz made enough sense for Carrie to figure out that she had evidently thought her location here was invincible. While the two women talked, she glanced back at her cousin, who was now inching slowly toward the house. Liz still wasn't noticing. She was turned half-way toward her sister, and wrapped up in conversation about events across the road.

"Where are Chet, Bobby, and Johnson? Did they get away?"

"No. They're probably hogtied, wrist and ankle, and lying on the men's room floor. My bet is that, once they get Bobby alone, he'll make a deal and tell all he knows."

"That son of a. . . . . Well, at least I can get away."

"How, Lizzie?"

"In your car. Did you park it on the road? It's getting dark now, and I've got a hostage if we need her. We can stay in the woods until full dark. I assume no one knows I'm anywhere near."

"They know."

"Well, maybe generally, but not that I'm right here. Let's go."

"No."

Liz's body jerked like Edie's had when Liz called her Aunt Edith. "Don't kid around with me Lindie."

Some family members can be such a problem, Carrie thought and, in spite of her fear, a giggle tried to bubble out. She started gasping her breath in and out to stop it, and Liz said, "Stop that," tightening her arm again.

"I'm not kidding. I'm through with you and your business dealings."

"Don't be stupid. You're under suspicion, under guard, and in big trouble, even if you never were directly involved here. Tarred by association, right? I don't know how you got away from them, but, however it was, you can leave with me. We'll change our names and start over somewhere else. I have connections, and I always have kept my escape options open."

"I am on leave from my job, but no one is guarding me. I came to look for you and tell you I'm finished with even a remote connection to your business dealings. My career here is wrecked, but maybe I can still salvage some part of a sane, worthwhile life."

Liz said, "You can't get by blaming me for your career problems, and don't forget, I can put you in jail. You knew I set those fires and didn't report it. There's more I could tell them. The decisions you made are all on your plate."

"Yes, I know that, and I'll just have to deal with it. Sadly, I put too much importance on family ties. I've learned better."

"Come on, Lindie, let's get out of here before someone from across the road decides to have a look around."

"Not a worry for us now, sister dear."

Carrie wondered if Liz detected the growing menace in her sister's voice as she continued. "You've forgotten one thing, Lizzie. You've forgotten those papers."

Liz's body jerked again. "You know about them? I thought you said you didn't." Her gun hand dropped away from Carrie's head as she turned fully toward the woods.

Olinda Rosten said, "Well, I lied about that, partly because I was protecting Gran. The papers were supposed to be insurance for Grampa and Dad, so, after they were gone, why not the same for Gran and me? But she decided they were too volatile to hang on to. Dad told me where the originals were, and gave the copies to me. He told me to keep them safe. I did. Grandma and I burned all of them. You didn't know because you and Mom had left us by then."

"You . . . "

"Burned them. The copies were never mailed, though that's what we were supposed to do. They were to go to the people Grampa called his 'First Family.' He called them that once too often. Gran said why should we help them out or let them know anything?"

Both women were silent. Carrie heard a car start across the road, and a siren in the distance. Edie had disappeared into the house. Liz must have forgotten all about her, and Olinda, who would have seen her clearly, had chosen to say nothing. It sounded like everyone from the party was now in the big metal buildings across the road, and any danger had been neutralized. Edie would be running over there to get help.

For a minute she wondered why Henry and Milton hadn't been more concerned about her safety and Edie's, but then reason took over. Coming out here had been Edie's idea, and she had agreed. They assumed the back yard was safe, and everyone else would have too.

A horrible thought struck her. If Edie was bringing help, that meant Carrie and Olinda needed to cancel the menace of Liz's gun. If the two of them didn't manage that, not only they, but anyone coming here to find them, would be in danger.

"I told you to put the gun down, Liz."

"Not possible. I'm getting out of here. Whether you come along or not, my hostage and I are leaving. Where's your car? I need the key."

"I'm not giving you my car key."

"Then I'll take it from you."

"How do you propose doing that? Are you going to shoot me?"

"Could, I guess, if you don't shoot me first."

"I don't have a weapon, Lizzie."

"No gun?"

"No gun. It's locked up in a safe at the office."

"Well, then." Liz Harley began laughing as she turned the gun barrel toward her sister.

Chapter Thirty-Seven

THE REST OF THE PARTY

O linda had begun staring at Carrie's face, and then shifting her gaze back and forth to Liz's feet. Finally Carrie thought she understood, gave a tiny nod, and got another in return. Carrie immediately bumped her rear end against Liz as hard as she could while Olinda dived for Liz's ankles, attempting to throw her backwards. Instead, bent at the waist by Carrie's bump, Liz fell forward with Carrie under her. They crashed to the brick patio, and the gun fired.

There was an instant of horrible silence while Carrie tried to catch her breath. Then Liz sat up, laughing wildly, and Olinda rolled away from her, trailing blood.

"Ah ha! Gotcha, Lindie. That'll teach you to go against me. Now, I'll have that key."

Liz stood, pushed a foot against her sister, then bent over to search her pockets. With an exclamation of triumph she grabbed a key ring and ran into the woods.

Still gasping, Carrie pulled herself toward Olinda and stretched out an arm until she could reach the pulse in her neck. Strong. She was bleeding, but alive, and when Carrie touched her, she whispered, "I have a new car. Liz has never seen it." She started a laugh, coughed, and was silent.

Carrie put a protective arm over the deputy and scooted close to her back. She needed to keep Lindie warm.

Why, oh why doesn't someone come? As soon as this dizziness is gone, I'll have to go find help.

Had she imagined hearing a yell of fury coming through the woods and a bustle of people suddenly swirling around the patio? Someone was touching her. A hand stroked her hair, then her forehead.

Carrie opened her eyes and blinked into bright patio lights when Henry said, "No, oh, no! Where are you hurt, Cara? That blood! I left you alone— left you alone again. God forgive me."

"Quit that! I'm not hurt," she said, though the place where her cheek had connected with patio bricks now stung enough to have erased all dizziness. "This is Olinda's blood. Take care of her. Henry, she was so brave . . . ought to get a medal. Did you know she's Liz Harley's *sister?*"

"Well, doesn't that beat all?" Shirley's voice said. "Sounds like you and Olinda have quite a story to tell, and don't you worry, she'll help tell it before long. It's her shoulder that's shot, not her mouth. Rest of us have a story too. This has been some party."

"Liz has a gun. She ran away."

"Deputy Rainwater got her as she was looking at cars along the road," Henry said, "but not because he knew who she was. He went outside to . . . uh, for personal reasons, saw a woman looking closely at each parked car along the road, and thought she might be planning to break into one or more of them, or even steal one. He came up behind her, grabbed her, and was able to take her gun. Maybe you heard the resulting howl of rage. I think we all did, including the cows in the Marshall's farthest pasture. Poor Rainwater got a few bruises and scratches, but he did manage to drag her, kicking and swearing, into the building where deputies are working. Milton identified her the minute they came inside."

"Ah," said Carrie.

In the background Jo Marshall's voice announced, "I have coffee, brownies, and oatmeal bars ready for those who'd like a pick-me-up."

Chapter Thirty-Eight

WAS IT WORTH IT?

"Was it worth it?"

No one responded to Edie's question. At the stove, Henry dropped the last hamburger patty on its bun, and Carrie added a stack of French fries to the plate. The two of them carried their plates to the dining table as Edie repeated, "Was it worth it?"

"Well now," Shirley said, "Depends on what you mean by worth, doesn't it?"

Once more, Shirley's cut to the center of an issue, Carrie thought. *Should we discuss this from a law enforcement angle, or on a more personal level? Probably it's both.*

"I set off a chain reaction the day I appeared at this house," Edie said. "There was a huge, mostly negative impact on all your lives. Now I can't decide how guilty I should feel. Was it worth it?"

"On a personal level," Carrie said, "I gained a cousin and several new friends. I certainly had adventures, though, had I been able, I would have gladly omitted a couple of them."

Edie shook her head. "And I'll regret those the rest of my life. Okay, Henry, what do you think? Was it worth it?"

Carrie interrupted, afraid of what Henry would say. "Wait, I'm not through yet. There's the law enforcement angle."

"Right," Roger said. "That was worth it. Cousin Norm is mighty pleased."

"Yes," Carrie said. "At least one major Ozarks drug operation is obliterated, its organizer and employees headed for prison. Their opportunity for distributing drugs through outlets like craft fairs and truck stops is closed down. That should be extremely satisfying for the County Sheriff's Office overall, as well as for Edie and Milton, and," she turned to the woman beside her, "you too, Olinda, if you don't mind my saying so. Is that any compensation? Your sister is going to prison and you lost what I assume is a pretty good job."

"My sister brought her problems on herself," Olinda said. "I'm coming to terms with that. As for my job, well, who knows?" She started to move her shoulders in a shrug, thought better of it, and said, "We can get by on my husband's salary while I sort out my life. I do love law enforcement. Maybe I can go back to it after a probationary period."

Carrie nodded. "Then," she said, "there is the question of redemption."

"Redemption?" Edie and Henry asked in unison.

"I know what she means," Shirley said. "Some folks got shaken out of bad patterns of action that might have led to worse things. 'Scuse me, Olinda, but you did. Carrie's Second Man sure did. The man they call Bobby told Norm's deputies all he knew about Liz's operation, even if it was mostly to lighten up on his own punishment. And," she looked around the table, "some-a the rest of us may have better thoughts about a few things, too. We all learned a lot."

Olinda, who was staring into space, said, "Yes. I needed to stop and think about family connections and right and wrong. My sister and I never were close, but that didn't stop me from feeling protective toward her. After the two parts of our family split, and until she married John, she lived with Mom. Since Mom wanted to separate herself from the family business, I thought Liz would want the same thing. Obviously, I was wrong. Neither Mom nor I had any positive influence on her. I guess you could say I've given up on that now."

She looked around the table as if testing the level of understanding offered there. "I have always felt I should do something to help make up for the sins of my father and grandfather. When I think of the lives that were probably ruined by drugs they sent out to vulnerable people, I . . . " She turned toward Carrie as tears began leaking down her cheeks. "And now, Lizzie."

Carrie handed her a paper napkin, then said, "You'll probably never know what positive impact you had on her. But, no matter. You are your own person, an individual who has guided her life by a different code than those family members. You broke the pattern, and that showed great courage. Now I see you as standing free, no matter what the sheriff's department says at this moment. I'd bet no one here finds you tainted by past family connections."

She looked at Edie and Milton, Shirley and Roger, and Henry in turn, saying, as if willing them to respond positively, "Right?"

There was affirmation all around the table, and Shirley said, "You will never be judged here for what others did. They alone bear the burden for their sins."

Edie spoke up. "Olinda, don't forget you and I share the same background. What applies to you applies to me, but I won't accept that it damages me. Neither should you."

Olinda blew her nose, looked at Edie, blew her nose again, opened her mouth, "But, I . . . " then shook her head and was silent.

"Okay," Carrie said, "sounds like we agree on redemption. Edie, as to worth, we know now that you had several good reasons for coming here. It wasn't your fault we got tangled with drug dealing at the craft fair."

"It *is* my fault. You wouldn't have known about any of that if it hadn't been for me."

Henry cleared his throat. "Hmmm, I agree with Edie as to fault, but Carrie does seem to have a way of discovering people breaking a law or two."

"I do not," Carrie said. "I just notice people in trouble."

Henry shrugged, then laughed. "Okay. So, Edie, Milton, what about you? Was it worth it for you? I think I know the answer to that already. Of course it was."

"Yes," Milton said. "Edie and I found each other, and we both accomplished what we came here to achieve—the closing down of a major drug pipeline into the Ozarks."

"One negative though, and a sad one for me," Edie said. "I found out my father really was a drug dealer using his work for the Bureau of Drug Abuse Control as a cover, and that Carrie's father had justification for keeping his family away from mine." She held up a hand as Carrie started to protest. "Remember, no pious protests, Cousin Carrie.

"Of course, that means Milton lied to me when he said my father was only an undercover agent for Drug Abuse Control. You knew better, didn't you, dear man?"

Milton stuttered, said, "Well, uh, maybe there were circumstances we don't know about."

"No, no pious protests from you, either. I appreciate what you did, and I may even incorporate some of your story into what I eventually tell Mother."

Olinda said, "I want my husband to meet all of you. For years he's been telling me the same thing you are, that I shouldn't bear the burden for what my family did. But he has no idea how much I knew about Lizzie's business. Nobody does but Lizzie herself."

"Well, as to if all these goings-on were worth it, have we figured that out now?" Shirley asked. "Things and people got shook up a bit, but what came out was good overall. That right?"

There were nods from everyone but Henry. Shirley, studying him thoughtfully, said, "O'course, Henry, more than maybe anyone here—even you, Carrie—had a rough time of it. For too long he had to wonder if Carrie was okay, or even alive. Y'all understand that? It's the not knowing, living on hope only."

"I understand," Edie said, "because Olinda and I saw it. We were with him the whole time. In fact, it was so awful for him that, the minute he knew Carrie was safe, there was a dramatic change. Even though he couldn't tell us she was okay I guessed it, and I suspect Olinda did too."

Olinda said, "Yes, I knew. I never said anything, but I knew."

Henry looked around the table. "If we're confessing, well yes, it was rough. I don't think I'll ever get over how I felt when Carrie was abducted. Probably the worst time of my life. I wasn't with her, and if I had been, I could have prevented it."

Everyone stayed silent, even Carrie, who was wishing she and Henry were alone to talk this out.

"Well," Shirley said, "I guess the main good thing is that both you and she got through it. Henry, none of us can be with the ones we love every single minute. We have to trust. It's a hard lesson when things go wrong. Parents learn the lesson early. You came to it later than most. And, truth be told, all that happened—and I mean all of it—was like stuff shoved in a funnel. Maybe things were uncomfortably tight at times, but what came out at the bottom was the taking of that place on Marshall Road and, like Carrie says, redemption in some way for all of us here."

"Hmmm," Henry said, looking at his wife. "You're right, results do matter, and it's interesting to me that we're all willing to be open about what we have just been through. Maybe we're like soldiers who have suffered through a battle together. Maybe it's teamwork, which is how we often think of it in law enforcement."

After an awkward moment, Milton said, "Here's a good outcome, if it's okay to lighten up a bit. Edie has promised she'll be here next fall to work with me in my booth at the War Eagle Fair."

"Uh-huh," Shirley said. "Well now, that brings us to the next important business matter. I've started on sewing for next year's fair. I guess Edie is out as my helper, though Milton better be glad for how well she's trained. Roger will help me, o'course. What about the two of you, Carrie and Henry? Are you willing to help again?"

"I'll help," three voices said, Olinda's the loudest.

The End

ABOUT THE AUTHOR

For more than twenty-five years, Radine Trees Nehring's magazine features, essays, newspaper articles, and radio broadcasts have been sharing colorful stories about the people, places, events, and natural world near her Arkansas home. She's also the author of a book of essays set in the Ozarks. "DEAR EARTH: A Love Letter from Spring Hollow" was published in 1995, and this novel is the seventh in her "Something to Die For" mystery series.

RECIPES

With thanks to John Bohnert of Grass Valley, California,
who is well-known for his outstanding recipes

In this novel, John plays the part of Chef John Bohnert, Henry's valued
Internet friend, author of
THE GRASS VALLEY BISTRO COOKBOOK

John Bohnert's
TUNA SALAD SANDWICH

1 can tuna,12 oz, drained
2 Tbsp mayonnaise
½ tsp celery seed
½ Tbsp onion powder

lettuce
tomato slices
whole-wheat bread

Drain tuna and place in mixing bowl. Add mayo, celery seed, onion power
and mix well with a spoon.

Toast bread. Add tuna spread to toast and top with lettuce and tomato.
Serve with potato chips.

John Bohnert's
CROCKPOT BEEF STEW

1 ½ lbs. beef stew meat, cubed
¼ cup flour
2 cups frozen pearl onions, thawed
1 can diced tomatoes (14.5 oz.)
2 cups mini carrots, cut in half
1 cup celery, chopped
6 baby red potatoes, cut in fourths
1 Tbsp Italian seasoning
2 bay leaves
1 Tbsp Worcestershire sauce
4 cloves minced garlic
1 ½ cups dry red wine
1 Tbsp garlic powder
salt and pepper to taste

Place beef in a bag with flour and garlic powder, shake until meat is well coated. Brown beef in a large skillet and drain off any fat.

Cut baby carrots in half, cut potatoes into fourths. Put vegetables In bottom of slow cooker.

Add beef and remaining ingredients.

Pour wine over all.

Place bay leaves on top.

Cover and cook on low for six hours.

Remove bay leaves and discard before serving.

John Bohnert's
MACARONI-BEEF CASSEROLE

2 Tbsp olive oil
1 lb lean ground beef
1 cup chopped onion
1 can Cream of Mushroom soup (10.75 oz. can)
1 cup elbow macaroni
1 cup grated Parmesan cheese
1 cup frozen corn, thawed
2 cans diced tomatoes (14.5 oz. can)
 1 ½ tsp dried oregano
½ tsp salt
½ tsp garlic powder
½ tsp dried thyme
½ tsp dried rosemary
½ tsp dried basil

Preheat oven to 350.
Cook macaroni according to package directions. Drain. Put macaroni in a large mixing bowl.

Brown ground beef and onions in olive oil in skillet. Drain off any fat. Add meat and onions to mixing bowl. Add remaining ingredients, stir well.

Place all ingredients in a greased 3 quart casserole dish
Cover and bake at 350 for 45 minutes.

(Note from the chef: I use Campbell's Healthy Request Cream of Mushroom Soup which is 98% fat free and has 45% less sodium than their regular soup.)

Henry King's
SORT-OF RECIPE FOR TOMATO SOUP

Henry insisted initially that there is no recipe, he just "dumps stuff in." However, after urging, he came up with these suggestions:

Begin with 1 can of Campbell's Healthy Request Tomato Soup. Dump in pot. Add 1 can water. Stir.

Add 1 can diced tomatoes with green chilies. (Ro-tel or house brand.) Carrie buys only the mild. If you like more fire, use whatever degree of heat suits. Stir.

Look in refrigerator. If there are any small bits of left-over veggies that sound good, add them. Left-over picante sauce or salsa? Why not? Other small amounts of left-overs can be added if it looks like they will fit, left-over Macaroni-Beef casserole, for example. Stir.

If there are no promising left-overs and there isn't enough for the planned meal, a can of seasoned tomato bits will take up the slack. Stir that in.

Cooked rice also a possible addition, a half to one cup, depending on the number you plan to feed.

If you have them, add several fresh basil leaves, torn into small pieces. Lovely fragrance! (Carrie has a pot of basil on the kitchen window.) No fresh? Well, dried will have to do. Four to five fresh. Henry doesn't know amount for dried. Experiment.

If soup looks too thick, add water. Heat and stir for a few minutes to blend flavors. Serve in bowls with crackers spread with Chef John's tuna salad.

"And," Henry adds, "don't be afraid to be creative. You really can't spoil this soup. Have fun!"